Dark Veil

Mason Sabre

Mason Sabre

Dedications

To those who know me truly and still don't

disappear.

Thank you to the following people for making sure that everything was as correct as humanly possible:

Cynthia Michal
Vicky Michalopoulou
Andrea Whittle
Angela Peters
Teresa Meerschaert

Thank you to my street team for all the hard work you put in for me, without you, this would not be possible. (Names listed at the end).

Dark Veil
Mason Sabre

This book is a work of fiction. All characters in this novel are fictitious. Any resemblance to actual events or locales or persons, living or dead, is entirely coincidental.

Author: Mason Sabre

Cover Art by Kellie Dennis at Book Cover by Design

www.bookcoverbydesign.co.uk

ISBN-13:978-1530863952

ISBN-10:1530863953

www.masonsabre.com

masonsabre2@gmail.com

https://www.facebook.com/msabre3

Mason Sabre

Other Titles

Watch Over You

The Rise of the Phoenix

Cade

Hidden

Dark Veil

Mason Sabre

Mason Sabre

Chapter One

Gemma Davies held the small plastic stick in her hand and stared at it as if it were something that had been born of evil intent, but maybe that was exactly what it was. Something evil—something to fear. The two blue lines mocked her. They were the worst image that she could have ever seen, and her heart sank with despondency, disbelief flooding her. They were the end of her life. Shit, she might as well go and write her own damn name on the execution order before Trevor got the chance to do it himself. Breathless, she gripped the edges of the cold, white porcelain sink to keep herself from collapsing to the floor. Her mind all but floated away as the world started to tip sideways.

Slowly, she raised her gaze and glared at her reflection in the mirror. "How could I have been so stupid?"

Pregnant.

The word burnt through her mind and sent shivers of cold down her spine. Her mind refused to accept what it was she was seeing as she wrapped her fingers around the tester stick and crushed it as she tried to force the result away.

Mason Sabre

It was wrong.

Wrong.

It had to be.

The flimsy plastic in her hand gave way with a crack and splintered. She winced as the plastic splinters bit into her flesh.

These things give false-positives all the time, she reassured herself. She was just one of the unlucky ones. That was all. With a newfound sense of urgency, she flung the broken tester stick into the discarded carrier bag and then fumbled with the box for the second test. She had bought a double test. This would come out as negative—she knew it. She could feel it in her gut as she tore it from its wrapper.

Three minutes—three goddamn minutes of excruciating waiting. The first test hadn't taken this long, so why had time suddenly decided that it was going to stand still? She breathed in and exhaled slowly to calm herself, but that proved impossible. Every sense she had was on alert. With a twist of her wrist, she gave her watch a shake and then tapped the glass.

Fifty seconds.

She got up nervously to look at the test, gulped and changed her mind, flipping it back over before she could see it. She sat down on the edge of the bath and bit down on her lip.

Forty seconds.

The test stared at her from the back of the sink. It sat there like judge and jury over the rest of her life, getting ready to stand up and issue her with a death sentence.

Twenty seconds.

Her hands grew clammy and she wiped them down the legs of her jeans and glared at the test.

Ten seconds.

Gemma tapped her foot against the floor and wrung her hands together. Her chest tightened, making it hard to breathe.

"Everything okay in there?" Stephen's deep voice echoed through the door, making her squeal and jump. "You've been in there almost an hour."

"What are you? The bathroom police? I didn't realise there was a time restriction." She rubbed her face and scowled. She shouldn't snap at her brother. "I'm fine."

He tried the door handle, making it rattle, and she froze. He could snap it and force the door open if he chose to. The rattling was just shit and Stephen trying to scare her, and she knew it. She watched wide-eyed as the handle twisted again and the wood strained under Stephen's hold. In her mind, she could hear the echo of the crack it would make if he forced it open. "Gemma, let me in."

"I'm using the bathroom. I like to do it in private."

He ignored her. "Open the door."

She bit down on her lip and stared at the door, willing him to go away.

"If you don't open this door, I am going to break it down, and then Dad will hear it and come and see what is going on. I get the feeling that you don't want that."

Gemma scowled at the door. How did he do that? All the time. It was like having a damn lie

detector around the house. He seemed to know
everything—literally everything. It was more than
coincidence. He was right so many times.

"Open the door, Gemma."

She loved her brother with all her heart, but
right now, she wished that he would just leave her
alone. Could he not just keep out of her life? Live his
own? Why had he decided that keeping his sister
safe was his job? And by safe, she meant stalked
and prisoner. Now it would seem he had upgraded
to bathroom supervision.

"You have until the count of three," he said
calmly, his voice sure and laced with authority. "One
..."

"For god's sake, Stephen."

Both Stephen and Gemma were shifters—
tigers to be exact. She knew that if he wanted in the
room, he would get in. Opening that lock would be
as easy as the door not being there at all. No lock or
barricade would stop him. That was why he was
protector to the alpha—their father—and the best
damn fighter the Society had.

"Two ..."

She grabbed the test from the back of the sink and shoved it into the back pocket of her jeans before yanking the door open. Stephen stood there with his big arms folded over his chest and a smug expression upon his face.

"Smart girl." His green eyes scanned the room behind her, his expression giving nothing away, as usual. Although Gemma was by no means a short woman, Stephen's incredible height practically dwarfed her. His entire presence was big. It was impossible to block his view, even though she tried.

The test stick in her back pocket pressed against her as a reminder that the three minutes were now up. She had to fight the urge to pull it out and look. She couldn't think so much right then as Stephen blocked her way. She just wanted to pull the stick out and confirm that it said negative. One line—that was all that would be there.

She was sure of it.

"What do you want?" she finally asked.

"I want to know what you're doing in here." He nodded towards the bathroom, but his penetrating green eyes didn't leave hers. "You were almost an hour."

"I was using the bathroom. Can't I have privacy to do that? I didn't know there was a time limit. Do I come in here and ask what you're doing when you spend hours upon hours flexing your muscles and admiring yourself?"

He cocked his head to one side. "No, because you know exactly what I am doing. You don't need to check."

"Don't be a jerk." Of course Stephen was back to looking across every inch of the room. "What are you looking for? It's a bathroom. You know … where people do bathroom things."

He smirked at her, his all-knowing smirk. "Apparently."

Gemma stormed past him and out of the room, hoping that her dramatic exit would make him follow her. She was two feet from the door when her step faltered. Oh god. The bag. The fucking bag. Heart pounding loudly in her chest, she wheeled around and raced back to the bathroom, but it was too late. Stephen was standing there with the test in his hand. His eyes lifted and met

Gemma's, the gold flecks in his eyes flickering with the same intensity that she had seem many times in her father's eyes when she knew she was in trouble.

"It's a false test."

"Really?" he raised an eyebrow at her and then put the two halves of the test together. "How do you know that?"

"Because I took another one," she said more assuredly as she patted her back pocket.

Stephen narrowed his gaze at her before putting the broken test back in the bag. He crushed it in his strong hands, the muscles and veins in his arms standing out in stark relief as he did so, belying the exterior he was presenting. He stalked towards Gemma, leaving her no choice but to back up or get trampled on. He didn't stop until he had walked her all the way back to her room. He kicked the door closed behind him—the rooms weren't totally secure from sound, but they were reinforced enough. "Give me the other test."

She backed up, almost tumbling backwards when her legs hit the bed. "It doesn't matter. It's fine. It's negative."

"If I have to physically take the test from you, I will."

"Stephen …"

He stared at her, unrelenting, waiting. There was no way she was getting out of this and she knew it. He could take it from her and there was not a damn thing she would be able to do about it.

"Give me the other test."

Gemma couldn't make her hand move to pull it out. She told herself to do it, even visualised the movements in her mind, but the message wasn't getting through.

"Now."

She swallowed hard. There was nothing she could do now. With a shaky hand, she reached behind her and gingerly fingered the test to pull it out. Suddenly, she didn't want to look at the test at all. "Stephen, please," she wailed, panic flooding her and burning like cold fire in her veins.

But he simply held out his hand to her, ignoring her pleas. She felt like a naughty child as she choked back a sob. Chest tight, she covered the results window with her fingers and then placed it face down in Stephen's hand. She slid down onto the floor and leaned back against the side of the bed. "It's negative," she breathed, hoping that saying the words out loud would make them true.

She watched him as he studied the white stick in his hand and waited for his shoulders to lose their tension and for a smile to cross his face. But it didn't happen. Instead, he lifted his eyes from the tester and met hers. "It's positive, Gemma."

She stopped breathing and stared at him. "No." She shook her head. "It's wrong. They're both wrong." Stephen held the stick out to her, and there they were, bold as anything. Two lines waving like greeting flags at her. "Oh god," was all she managed as she buried her face in her hands. She felt the bed move behind her as Stephen lowered himself to the floor next to her, his back against the bed, knees up. He put the bagged test on the floor beside him and then put his arm around his sister's shoulders and pulled her close. He held her for what felt like hours, when it was really just minutes.

"Does he know?"

He … *Cade*. Cade MacDonald. Stephen's best friend. Gemma's … she didn't even know what he was—forbidden desire? Secret? He was *everything*, that's what he was. He was her world—her secret world that she wasn't allowed to have, but that she couldn't live without. He was *wolf* and she was *tiger,* and this was all wrong. She shook her head. "I didn't think it would be positive. I thought that it was just one of these things."

"You need to tell him."

She knew that—she did—but she also knew what would happen. He'd want to keep the baby and he'd try to convince her to leave with him. He had already begun to ask, even without any pregnancy to spur them on. Like her, he had grown tired of the lies and the secrecy. He wanted Gemma living with him, waking in his bed, and there was nothing Gemma wanted more herself. But things weren't that simple. "I can't."

Stephen relaxed his hold on her so that he could look at her. She stared up at him, eyes glistening with tears. He was her big brother, the one who protected her from everything. She desperately wished he could protect her from this.

"You have to tell him. You have to give him the chance to get away. You realise this?"

Oh god, she did. She knew that he would have to run, but he wouldn't. That was the problem. He'd fucking stay here and die, and they both knew it.

"Dad will want him executed?" She could hardly get the words out. She was not just anyone. She was Gemma Davies, daughter of the Alpha, the head of the Society and the Leader of the Council.

She was screwed.

They had broken the law and both fathers would want their heads on sticks. The only thing was, which father would get the execution order faster? Because she was sure as shit that Trevor MacDonald would want her head. Not that he had any love for his son. No, what he cared about was his pride and his position. He would use this to get to the top—to get Malcolm from his seat.

"Please tell me you won't say anything to him."

"You have to tell Cade. You know you do."

"I have to get rid of it," she whispered miserably.

"It's his baby, Gemma."

She stared at her brother. "It's his life."

Chapter Two

Gemma's chest constricted fiercely as she sat in the front seat of Stephen's car, where he had parked just opposite Cade's house. She gripped the handle tightly, but didn't push it open. She just couldn't bring herself to do it. Twice she had tried and twice she had removed her hand again as her mind screamed at her to tell her brother to drive them home again.

Why did everything have to be so hard? It was okay for Stephen to say what he thought she should do, but she was the one having to do it. "If I'm not keeping it, why tell him?" she whispered, her eyes still on Cade's place.

"If you abort his baby and don't tell him, will you be able to look him in the eye? Will you be able to hold that secret inside of you forever?" Stephen put a finger under Gemma's chin and turned her head so that she faced him. "You know you won't be able to. You know you have to tell him, or you two are screwed."

"We're screwed anyway." The thoughts played over in her mind. It was like a mental game of ping pong with the argument back and forth with herself. She couldn't find any reasons good enough to tell him—anything more than what Stephen had said, that was. Would she be able to keep it a secret? No, she didn't think so. She couldn't keep anything from Cade, not even small things. It would eat at her until she was completely devoured and then Cade would be gone anyway.

Stephen shifted in his seat, the soft leather rustling as he moved. He drew Gemma closer and rested his lips against her forehead, holding her there. He cupped her face with both hands and Gemma took comfort from his touch. The soft stubble on his chin gently scratched at her skin as he spoke. "I'll wait right here for you. Okay?"

Gemma covered his hands with hers. She wasn't raised to seek that kind of comfort, to need touch, but there was something inexplicable with Cade and Stephen ... It was like she craved it, and only when they were close did she feel calm. Even Stephen, her big brother—tough, fighter—he seemed to seek out the contact, too. It didn't make any sense to her.

"I can tell him tomorrow," she whispered.

Stephen tilted her head back, still cupping her face. "This is tomorrow. It's yesterday's tomorrow.

"I can't break his heart. He's going to hate me."

Stephen rubbed a thumb lightly over Gemma's cheek. "How broken will his heart be if you go ahead without telling him, and he finds out after? How much would he hate you then? This is Cade, remember? He won't ever hate you."

"Everyone has their limits." Maybe this would be Cade's. She had run it through her mind a thousand times and none of them ended up anyplace good. All of them ended with him leaving her—but then maybe that's what she deserved. What woman aborts her own child?

Stephen glanced over Gemma's shoulder and let his hands drop. Gemma noticed he was looking somewhere over her head, and she followed his gaze. Phoenix was coming out from the side of Cade's house. Phoenix … of all people. He was a stark reminder of the father Cade could be—would be. The agony of it lanced through her like an icy spike in her chest, threatening to steal her breath away. Phoenix was sixteen, a *wolf*. Cade had taken him in two years ago when he had found him half dead and beaten in the woods. He was a bitten *wolf*, not a born one, but Cade had taken him in despite all that it had cost him to do so.

"If he fought for Phoenix, he is going to fight for this baby, too," Gemma said as Phoenix approached them, his face beaming at the sight of them. Gemma opened the door and got out of the car.

"Gemma," Phoenix said excitedly. He raced over to her and threw his arms around her. She returned his embrace, holding him tighter than he probably would have liked, but right now she needed it. He smelt like Cade, not solely, but enough. The soft musky smell that lingered all around. It slammed into her senses and brought a sob to her throat. She pressed her face into Phoenix's shoulder for a moment. "Is everything okay?" he asked when she released him.

She nodded and turned from him. She daren't speak, her voice ready to crack.

"Women," Stephen said and winked at him. "You'll learn soon enough. Keep clear of them. They're more dangerous than the *Humans*."

Phoenix laughed. He had a good laugh—it was deepening now as he aged a bit, his voice losing that childish squeak that boys had. He'd not lost his accent, though. It was southern and strong. He'd grown a lot in the two years, too, not just in height. Gemma and Stephen's mother, Emily, had been supplying him with nutrition to bulk him out—that, and him tagging along with Cade and Stephen when they worked out, meant he was developing into a well-built young man, his muscles already firm and showing definition.

"Cade is in his office," Phoenix said. "I'm just heading out to the library."

"Need a ride?" asked Stephen, and both Gemma and Phoenix's eyes snapped to his— both with a hint of fear there. Stephen understood why Gemma looked afraid, but there seemed no reason why Phoenix should be. Something was wrong.

"It's okay. I can cycle there."

Stephen walked around the car until he was standing right in front of the boy. He put a hand on

Phoenix's shoulder and studied him for a moment before speaking again. "I have to wait for Gemma anyway. I'll come with you." He turned and clicked the car lock before either of them could protest.

Gemma silently cursed her brother. She had no choice now but to go in, and he damn well knew it, too. Even if she wanted to leave, she couldn't because Phoenix had seen her. He would tell Cade that she had been there. She straightened her back and took a deep breath. She had to face him—face this.

"I won't be long," Gemma said.

"We'll just be at the library." Stephen gave her a small encouraging smile before turning to look at Phoenix, his eyebrow rising questioningly. Phoenix swallowed and they set off walking—the library wasn't far. Cade lived in the middle of a lane with no houses around him, but at either end, if one walked far enough, there were houses one way and a small town the other. Phoenix cast Gemma a last glance as they walked away, and the breeze caught his floppy blonde hair, lifting it to reveal the scar across his left eyebrow and a little down the side of his face. It never changed, never faded. It shouldn't have been there at all really—not with the speed with which *Others* healed. But they had a theory that if the wound inside didn't heal, then maybe the wound on the outside didn't, either. That was certainly true with Phoenix and Stephen. Phoenix's scar was from the car accident that had claimed his mother's life, and sure as hell that wound was as raw as the day they had all met. Stephen's scars ran down his arm from shoulder to wrist—scars he had covered with an elaborate tattoo—but he wouldn't say why they were there or how he had got them.

When they were finally out of sight, Gemma crossed the lane and forced her legs to carry her to the house. The house was silent when she entered, and she hesitated for a moment before closing the door and putting the chain on it. It wouldn't keep anyone out—not really. If they wanted in, they would get in, but it would at least give warning of someone in the house. With what she was going to tell Cade, she needed to know that no one could sneak in and hear them, no matter how paranoid that made her sound.

Cade's office was upstairs—a converted bedroom. His house was like a warehouse, filled with bags of plaster, tins of paint and stacks of wood. He still hadn't fitted lights in the place, and so there were lamps propped on chairs in every room. He had bought the house as a shell and was still working on it. He was making it into a home—a home that one day would house his child. She pressed a hand to her flat stomach and her heart squeezed.

But not this child.

"Phoenix?" Cade called just as Gemma put her foot on the bottom step.

She swallowed. "It's me." She dragged herself up the stairs to his office, and even though her mind was yelling at her to go home and forget this idea, she pushed herself forward.

Cade was waiting for her at the doorway when she reached the landing. He stood there with a sensual smile on his lips, his eyes travelling languorously down her body. Her stomach twisted and her legs threatened to buckle from the sight of him. Big, gorgeous, sexy.

"I didn't expect to see you today. Not that I am complaining." He pushed himself from the door frame and sauntered over to her.

Mason Sabre

"I didn't expect to see you, either," she said breathlessly, trying to calm her heart as it thumped loudly in her chest. She needed to stay focused on why she was here. She couldn't let Cade's animal magnetism distract her.

He stopped just short of her, and before she had the chance to react in any way, his arms slid around her waist and drew her hard against the solid steel of his chest. His mouth came down on hers and, just like that, she was lost.

He didn't break their kiss as he pulled her into his office, kissing her with such hunger that it called to her *tiger*, pulling it from the depths of her soul. His lips were warm against hers, sweet with a hint of coffee that still lingered there. She moaned into the kiss, welcoming the feel of stubble against her skin—she slowly lost all resolve. She held onto him, dragging him closer as her fingers dug into the hard muscle of his shoulders. Her breathing became ragged as his hands moved up and found the top button to her blouse. He flicked it open and then worked his way down. When his fingers touched her skin, she sucked in a shuddering breath and dug her nails into his back. Oh, god. She knew she had to stop him now or there would be no going back.

Dark Veil

"Cade," she breathed against his mouth. "Cade …"

He wasn't listening, though. He moved from her mouth, trailing kisses along her neck, sucking and biting as he went. Her mind threatened to make an exit at the pleasure that invaded her senses. She clutched at his shirt with tight fists.

"Cade, please. I need to talk to you."

His fingers froze and his head lifted so he could look at her. His eyes searched hers and she tried to blink away the tears that suddenly sprang forward. He frowned and all at once his hands were gently cupping her face. "Gem?"

The tone of his voice, the concern on his face—it was enough. She leaned into him and buried her face in his chest, unable to hold back her tears any longer. Selfishly, she held onto him as she sobbed.

"What's wrong?" He held her tightly, the *wolf* needing to protect his mate.

She pressed her face into his chest and pressed closer, wishing she could just melt into him. His heart thudded in his chest, its rhythm calming her somewhat. She felt like such a liar. She was about to break his heart, but she was using him for her own comfort first. His hard chest rose and fell in tandem with his breathing. His concern was evident, and she clung onto him as if he would vanish with the next breath she took—and maybe he would, with her words at least.

"I'm pregnant," she eventually whispered. The words were spoken quietly, but she knew that he had heard. His body tensed and he froze.

"Really?" He pulled back to look down at her, his face fast transforming into an expression of absolute delight. "I mean, *really*? We're going to have a baby?"

"I can't keep it," she said quickly, trying to push away from him now. "You know we can't."

"Why?" Cade kept a firm grip on her, keeping her from moving away.

"I'm not keeping it." She tried to put determination in her voice, but it was a feeble attempt. There was none, because she didn't really want to get rid of it. This was her and Cade's child. Their baby lay inside her. But she was trying to think rationally—keeping this baby was impossible. She knew what she had to do. She swallowed hard and forced herself to talk. "I'm only telling you because it is the right thing to do. I'm going to call tomorrow to get it fixed."

"Get it fixed?" He let go of her so abruptly that she stumbled back. "Get it *fixed*?" His voice rose as he spoke. "It's not a car or a fucking thing. Get it fixed?"

Gemma stepped back from him and wrapped her arms around herself, jumping at the harshness of his words. He had never sworn at her. Not in temper, at least. Not like this. The word cut through her. "We can't keep it," she said resolutely.

"Why?"

She couldn't look at him. She hated herself in this moment. "They'll kill us. They'll kill the baby." She raised her eyes to his then. "They'll kill *you*."

"We can leave. I have money ..."

"Cade ..."

"No. We can do this. We can." Desperation tinged his voice and tore at her. He grabbed hold of her hands and pulled her over to his desk, but she didn't sit like he wanted her to. "I can sell this house. We can leave. We can be gone by the end of the week. They won't kill the baby out there."

"Become stray?"

"Yes, if we have to."

"We won't survive it. You know it. Do you really think we can get away?" She knew they couldn't. They weren't like others in the Society. They were children of the Alphas, which meant that they were known to all sides, and they would be targets out on their own—prizes waiting to be caught. "Think about it, Cade. It isn't possible. Stray life is for the nobodies. Not us. Not *Others* who would be recognised on the spot. What if we did get away? Don't you think that the *Humans* over there would cash us in? What would my dad give as a reward for your head? Or your dad for mine?"

Others did leave Society, it was true. They could buy their way out—but it was hard. They had nothing and no rights. Most of them ended up dead anyway, and there was no remorse, no funeral. Just a body on a slab that got burnt to save space. Gemma knew that Cade's father would seek an execution warrant the moment he found out—not about the baby, but that they had left together.

"We can make it work."

"We'll have price tags on our heads. I can't risk your life for anything. Don't you realise that?"

"Not even for our child? You put your needs and wants before the life of our baby?" He clenched his jaw and let go of her hands. "Perhaps you should get rid of it then. I never thought that you would be so selfish."

He was angry. She tried to tell herself that, but his words ripped through her and tore her apart.

Eyes hard, he stared right at her. "If you abort our baby, then you won't have me in your life."

Gemma held onto her composure as she stared at him. It was the first time she had ever seen anything close to hostility towards her in Cade's eyes. Knowing she was about to fall to pieces in front of him, she turned abruptly and walked out of his office, leaving him standing there. It wasn't until she had reached the bottom of his stairs that she began to crumble. She stumbled through the hall to the front door of the house and fumbled with the chain. She got the door open and cool air hit her face, making her gasp through her tears.

"Gemma ..." Cade's tortured voice carried through the air. She glanced over her shoulder to see him standing at the foot of the stairs.

"I'm sorry," she sobbed and then ran out of the house and onto the lane. She ran in a desperate attempt to get away. Away from Cade and away from everything. The cold air cooled her hot tears as they rolled down her face.

"Gemma," Cade called. He was right behind her. She felt his hand grab her arm and she came to a stop, half sobbing, half panting from the run. She braced herself for more harsh words, more anger from him, but none came now. Instead, Cade wrapped strong arms around her, bands of steel holding her tight. In that moment, she felt safe. She clung to him as if he were her lifeline.

"Please, Gemma," he whispered against her hair. "Please think about this."

She didn't want to let him go. Not now. Not ever. He was the thing that kept her alive. He was what made sense in her world. She was never safer than when in his arms. He was her world.

"Please don't," he murmured, and then his mouth was on hers again, his kiss desperate and all-consuming. When he released her, they were both breathing hard. "We can renounce everything. We can buy our way out and do it properly."

"We leave our families if we do that. You leave Phoenix."

"He can come, too. I don't care about the rest. Please don't take our child away."

She shook her head and clutched at his shirt. "They won't let us leave. You know that. They'll kill Phoenix for being with us."

Perhaps Cade did know. Perhaps she had finally got through to him. He didn't say anymore—just held her. He held onto her tightly, and although he would probably never admit it, she knew that he was crying, too.

Her heart broke.

Chapter Three

Stephen stretched himself out on one of the softer chairs that were positioned in front of the window. Not that it was any more comfortable than the hard modern chairs that Phoenix was sitting on—it just gave the illusion it was. His tiger would much rather lie on the floor instead of sitting on the rickety chair that threatened to give way under his weight at any moment. The leather on it was so torn that he could feel edges of it sticking into his jeans and irritating the shit out of him. He grumbled and shifted position ... again. Two more minutes and he was going to pick the damn chair up and launch it into the skip outside.

He stared aimlessly out of the window— there wasn't much to see. Public library for *Others*— the *Humans* had outdone themselves with this one. Why give them windows with views, right? The window which Stephen was staring out of held the picturesque scene of a large skip and card compactor. Two men were shoving broken down cardboard boxes into the shoot at the side. One of them had climbed up and was jamming his foot in the shoot to get the boxes in. Stephen wondered what would happen if the man slipped and fell into the shoot. Would the blades in there stop? Would his friend help and pull him out before his legs became some macabre prop right out of a horror movie? It would certainly make his day more interesting if something more exciting happened out there. Sitting in the library waiting for Gemma was not exactly a thrilling way to pass his time.

Stephen let out an exasperated sigh, stretched his legs out and let his head fall back. Every minute felt like an hour and time seemed to drag on. He was ready to just close his eyes and sleep. He stretched his arms over his head, his tall frame looking even longer with the movement. He caught sight of a blonde in the corner as he pulled himself upright once more. She had been staring at him and as their eyes met, she quickly looked away. Stephen tried to hide his smirk. Typical. He could write a book on how this game went. These women were all the same—so predictable. It was like they got given this script to follow. Phase one—stare at a man until she caught his eye. Check. Blondie had done that. Next was phase two. Look away for a second and pretend to do whatever it was that she had been doing before she noticed him. Check.

Phase three was a little different. It required strategic manoeuvring and had to be just right, otherwise the woman would end up looking more like an idiot. But this was their chance—like walking on stage for their one big shot. First, she would glance over her shoulder to make sure that he was still looking. Then came the fixing of the hair and clothes. Everything had to be just so. The next step would be to put something on display. Whatever the asset, every woman had one part they liked about themselves. Tits or ass—which one was she?

Blondie bent down to one of the lower shelves. Stephen's lips turned up at the corners. Ass. He had a perfect view of it. Even he had to admit, it wasn't a bad one. He wasn't really interested, but he supposed that this was better than staring at the men outside with the trash. They obviously weren't going to climb inside and cause any major damage to themselves just to amuse him.

The blonde glanced over to see if he had noticed. He stared straight at her, bold and brazen. She flushed at his intent look and quickly averted her eyes again. He kept them on her as she moved, because this was his phase and he knew how to play the game, too. All too well. She walked around one of the shelves and then to the seating area where they served coffee. She sat down next to another woman—sister maybe—they looked similar. Maybe it could get interesting after all. Both of them glanced his way and he winked at them, causing them to blush and giggle.

Phoenix was sitting at one of the computers working away. He had chosen a seat that was opposite Stephen, which meant that Stephen couldn't see what he was doing. Instead, he sat staring at the back of the large monitor. Maybe it was intentional, maybe it wasn't. But still, it roused Stephen's interest—especially since Phoenix seemed to glance over at him one too many times.

The main desk behind Phoenix was manned by an elderly *Other*. Her hands were twisted with age, her hair grey. She bent over her archives awkwardly as she tried to work, but the fact that she was there told Stephen that Phoenix wasn't just being a typical sixteen-year-old—no smut was being viewed.

Bored, Stephen rose slowly from his seat and wandered over to Phoenix. He didn't miss the lascivious looks the two women threw him as he walked over to the other side of the desk. Phoenix's hand shot out to the mouse and clicked.

Bingo.

The boy was definitely doing something he shouldn't.

"What are you up to?" he asked him coolly as he came to stand behind him. He had a page about horticulture up on the screen. "Plants?"

Phoenix kept a firm grip on the mouse. "Cade said that it was okay if I grew some things in the garden. Your mum said that she would help me."

Stephen leaned in and tapped his finger against the screen where another browser had been minimised. "What is that one?"

"Just more plants and things," he muttered and quickly lifted a finger to click the mouse. But Stephen was faster. He closed his hand down over Phoenix's before he could make the page vanish.

That was a mistake, though. The muscles in his neck tensed and the walls in his mind came crashing down. The wind was knocked out of him and he struggled to breathe.

"Fuck." He gripped the back of Phoenix's chair to keep himself steady as his mind was suddenly blasted by an influx of sensory details. The world swayed around him and pain shot through his chest. Voices echoed in the distance but he couldn't grab onto any of them. They were all loud—so fucking loud. He staggered back, almost taking Phoenix with him. He let go of the chair and clutched his head, swearing viciously.

"Stephen?"

Stephen shook his head to clear it, holding up a hand to keep Phoenix back. Three times this had happened this week. Three damn times, and he had no idea what it was. The shit in his head was getting worse, that was for sure, but why? He didn't have a clue. Didn't even know what had set it all off to begin with. But he needed it to stop. He closed his eyes and breathed into his hands for a moment.

"What were you really looking at?" he eventually rasped.

Phoenix motioned to the screen. "I told you ..."

Stephen blinked hard. It was like trying to lift the morning fog off the hills by will alone. He had to fight his way through it and the only way to do it was to ground himself in reality. "Don't give me that plant shit. I can come over there and clock the history. What were you looking at?"

Phoenix remained silent and stared up at Stephen with that expression only teenagers could perfect—the one that said they knew the answer but weren't about to say it.

"I can stand here all day long."

Phoenix shuffled in his seat then said meekly, "I was looking up my dad." The depth of sadness in his voice made Stephen sorry that he had asked.

"Your dad?"

Phoenix swivelled his seat back so that he was facing the monitor again, his head down. "It's been two years. I thought maybe he'd been looking for me or something."

"And?"

"Nothing."

If he could have taken the boy's pain away, he would have. He couldn't imagine what it would be like to have the man who raised you just suddenly toss you out on the street. Fucking *Humans*, that's what it was. Their brainwashing shit made it so they viewed *Others* like something born of evil, when really it was their hatred that came from the darkness. He pulled a chair up from another work station and sat down. "Maybe he just hasn't stuck an advert out."

Phoenix maximised the browser and then closed it properly and logged off the machine. Stephen kept his distance, not wanting to set off another episode. If this carried on, he was going to have to start wearing gloves before touching anyone, and that would really screw him up.

"He might be looking for you. You don't know that he isn't."

"He might not."

"No. He might not," he agreed. "*Humans* are funny about *Others*. It isn't his fault. He's probably been taught how bad we are."

"But doesn't he miss me?"

Stephen wanted so badly to say yes and get rid of the sadness that the boy's eyes held. He stared at him hopelessly, waiting for the right answer. Did his dad miss him? Probably not. *Humans* were assholes. They'd kill their own just because they crossed to *Other*. Because in their world, the *Human* that had once been his kin was now nothing more than an abomination. Chances were that Phoenix's father hadn't looked for him at all. If anything, he had probably barricaded the fucking doors to keep him from coming back. "Have you talked to Cade about this?"

Phoenix glanced away, embarrassed. "He won't understand."

"He might."

"He will think that I want to leave."

"Do you?"

The look in Phoenix's eyes was enough to tell him he didn't. "No, but ..."

Stephen moved closer but avoided touching him at all. He moved close enough that Phoenix might at least feel some connection there. "But?"

"I just want to see my dad. That's all."

Stephen could understand that. At least he thought he could. What would it be like to leave your family behind at that age? Shit. Stephen was twenty-six and he hadn't even managed to leave the family home yet, and maybe he never would. As the beta, he needed to be close to his alpha. It was his duty.

"There are two women staring at you," Phoenix whispered suddenly, making Stephen blink at the abrupt change of topic. He hesitated, feeling they had left the matter hanging. Maybe it was best he didn't push Phoenix right now, however.

He winked at him and smiled. "Yep."

Phoenix chewed on his bottom lip. He did it all the time, Stephen realised. "How do you do it?"

Stephen's brow puckered. "What?"

"Get the girls all staring at you like that?"

Stephen grinned then. Now this was something he could help with. "Pretend like you don't care."

Phoenix frowned, and Stephen laughed and leaned back in his seat. He surveyed the library—it was busy enough and crappy enough—another decrepit place for *Others*, but it was enough that *Others* used it often. He found what he wanted. "See that girl there? The one with the blue sweater?" He nodded towards the girl in question.

Phoenix followed Stephen's gaze. "The one with her mother?"

"Yep, that one."

"She is with her *mother*." The words were uttered as if they were sanctified. Stephen chuckled. He was so young—but he would learn.

"Yes, she is. Makes it all the more fun. When I was your age, they were the best kind. Cade and I …" Stephen stopped short, realising who he was talking to. This was Cade's ward and he was about to spill about their fun and frolics? That was a *no no*. "Watch her until she notices. She is the prey and you're the hunter. You're *wolf*. Remember that. And she is just a little lamb."

"And then?"

"Look away. Look busy and uninterested. But make sure that she sees your eyes first. Show her the intent in them." Stephen grabbed the arm rest of Phoenix's chair and spun him around. "Like this."

It took the girl less than twenty seconds to notice that Phoenix was watching her.

"Now look away. Turn yourself back to me, but watch her until the last moment."

Phoenix shuffled his chair back. "Now what?"

"Now I make myself busy and you wait." Every time Phoenix tried to lift his eyes to look at the girl, Stephen shook his head. "You need patience. She's seen you. Don't you worry about that." Stephen slid to the computer next to him and switched it on. He had no intention of using it. He didn't even have a log in for it, but that wasn't the point. The point was to seem busy and to give Phoenix the space. It didn't take too long for the girl to reach the books closest to them. Judging by her pretty little dress, dainty shoes and delicate fingers, Stephen doubted she was really interested in the sport section. Phoenix couldn't resist as he quickly glanced her way and then back again. He smiled to himself as he did.

The door to the library swung open and the bell above the door chimed as Gemma walked in. Her face was blotchy. She had been crying. "Shit," Stephen said to Phoenix. "Time to go."

Chapter Four

Perhaps the biggest paradox that existed for Cade in that very moment was the one between himself and his mind. His heart ached with such agony that he was sure he would die from it. Yet, even as it hurt so badly, he was sure that he wasn't real at all—it was like existing in some thick fog that he couldn't see through. All the sounds that existed within the world were nothing more than hushed voices off in the distance somewhere. He tried to move, tried to do something with himself. It had been hours of this, but every part of his being was numb. But his heart—its heavy thumping in his chest reminded him that he was very much alive and very much in pain. It beat with such ferocity that it was the only thing that let him know he was still alive.

A baby. *Their* baby. The very thought of it was something beyond belief. Never in his wildest dreams had he even though it were possible. What a cruel hand fate had dealt them this time. Even his *wolf* had taken it upon himself to lay low, brooding in the confines of his mind as everything sank in. The *wolf* should have been raging, should have been fighting to protect his mate, to keep every other male at bay, because now he had claimed her fully as his own. But the *wolf* was quiet.

As Cade stood there staring into nothingness, the muffled sounds of voices began to come to life. Phoenix's voice slowly penetrated the dense fog that was surrounding him.

"Cade …" He said his name in such a way that Cade realised he'd probably been saying it a while. But even then, he couldn't bring his mouth to move and form words in response. "Cade, your father is on the phone."

He felt Phoenix's gentle touch on his arm and turned to him. "Tell him I'll call him back."

"He says it is urgent. He's not going to go away."

No, of course he wouldn't. That was Trevor—what Trevor wanted, Trevor got. The thought just ignited some fury deep within Cade. It was people like his father who always caused the shit, yet they were the ones who came up smelling like fucking roses. Pretty much everything worked out for Trevor—well, almost everything. Phoenix was the one thing that hadn't. Oh, defeat must have tasted bitter in his foul mouth, but Cade wasn't stupid enough to let his guard down fully on that one. Maybe the battle was over, but the war between Trevor and his hatred of the half-breed was just simmering under the surface.

Cade greeted his father in the usual manner. Their relationship had never been a strong one. Trevor saw Cade like his mother—weak—but Cade saw his father as greedy and power hungry. He would never forgive his father for setting Phoenix up and leaving him to die. If it wasn't for the oaths that kept him in place, Cade would have no qualms about telling his father that he would drop the MacDonald name.

"Council meeting tonight. We need all of the family in attendance," his father barked at him down the phone.

"You made it quite clear some time ago that I am not your family. I think you have the wrong number." The two years since Cade had been taken to the cage as punishment for breaking Society law by taking in Phoenix now seemed like a lifetime ago. Trevor had been furious that he had taken a half-breed in, and had informed him then that he and Cade were family in name only. What right did he have now to make these demands? He could piss off for all Cade cared. It had been months since they had actually exchanged a word—any kind of word. Even then, he had only seen and spoken to him because it was a pack run, and Cade had to show his face to make sure that his father didn't look like an idiot who couldn't even control his own family. Wouldn't want to show Trevor's little band of followers that one of his sons had got away. Fuck no. The man had an image to keep.

"Tonight you are, and you will come to this meeting."

"Or?"

"There is no *or*, Cade. Tonight, at seven. I will see you there. And do yourself a favour and leave the little half-breed at home … this is family business. It does not concern him." With that, Trevor hung up the phone. Cade stared at the receiver, wishing that there was a way he could ram his fist into it, reach inside and wrap his fingers tightly around his father's throat. It was long overdue. He slammed the receiver down instead. He didn't need this shit and he certainly didn't need his father's stupid games.

Phoenix was standing near him, waiting and listening, of course. Cade said nothing about his father's remark, but he was sure that Phoenix had heard it. He might have started out as a *Human*, but his hearing was now like an *Other*. "I'm going to go out for a run," he said. "I'll catch dinner. I have to go out this evening."

Phoenix nodded but said nothing. Cade wanted to tell him that this meeting was nothing to worry about—that it wasn't about him—but he couldn't. The truth was that he didn't know what it was about, but knowing his father, it would be something that was going to make his mood sink even more than it already had.

You can come run with me if you like," he said, trying to offer maybe a little reassurance to the boy that nothing had changed between them, no matter what his father wanted.

It was dark when Cade shifted back from *wolf* to man. It had calmed him at least, and he had hunted rabbit. Nothing special in that—rabbit was so common in this area. Phoenix had come, too, and they had each ripped into their kill as they had sat together in the grass after the hunt, still in their *wolf* forms, with the crisp air around them. Then they had sat and cleaned themselves, Cade leaning over to Phoenix to clean him like a protective wolf would do to its young. He wondered if this is what it would be like with his actual chid. Would his child be *wolf* or *tiger*? Would he get to run with it this way, and then share these moments of parental intimacy? And although Phoenix was not his son, they were bonded, and acting this way didn't feel wrong to him.

He left Phoenix to the television and his studies, and then he drove to Malcolm's house. When he pulled into the drive, he sat in his car, hesitating, every part of him wanting to leave—not just this house, but everything. Gemma would be in there. As much as he was burning inside to see her, he needed his mind clear, because if he saw her, he would beg. He would plead with her not to kill their child.

He'd asked her for some time to think about things. He hoped that time would help her see things differently, to change her mind about having an abortion. He couldn't believe that she would even consider killing their child. He gripped the steering wheel and fought the rage that surged inside, fought not to burst into the house and find Gemma. His *wolf* urged him to go get his mate, force her to leave with him, to keep her and their baby safe. Frustration ate away at him, at his inability to force Gemma to do anything. He wished he could just let the animal inside take charge. Things would be so clear-cut then. Logic and Society would not play any role, and all that would matter was that his mate and child were protected.

He would call her tomorrow maybe, but he needed time and so did she. It was so hard for him, though. It went against everything that he was. It went against his *wolf,* who needed to protect his mate. If she was there, his resolve would break down and it wouldn't matter what his dad wanted just now—he'd be focused on Gemma. He would take her and leave. He'd take Phoenix, too. But then Stephen … Everything was so fucking complicated. He slammed his hand against the steering wheel of the car and got out before he drove himself crazy with it all. He banged the car door closed too and made his way down the drive.

There were many cars leading up to the house. It seemed that Cade was the late one. When he went into the house, they were all gathered in the usual room, the silent room, but the door was open, so whatever it was didn't need to be kept quiet. Every member of the Society was there, as well as the Council. This was big—fucking big. He entered without knocking, his eyes instantly scanning the room for Gemma. But she wasn't there—neither was Gemma's kid sister, Evie. Stephen was there, however. He caught Cade's eye and gave him a curt nod the moment Cade entered the room. Cade didn't go to him, though. His eyes fell on his mother, Katherine, instead. She went to stand up to greet her son, but Trevor grasped her hand and stopped her—just another show of his power and dominance. He was forcing her to lose her son, too, whether she wanted it or not. Trevor had spoken so it was tough shit what his wife may want.

He couldn't stop Cade, though. He strode over to them, his eyes defiant on his father as he approached, Trevor's expression hardening with each forbidden step. Cade stopped when he reached his mother and stooped to embrace her, leaving her no choice but to do the same. He would take the blame for it—he didn't care. Maybe she wasn't allowed to hold her son, but sure as hell Trevor couldn't stop Cade from doing it.

"I've missed you," he whispered softly against her ear before placing a delicate kiss on her cheek. She raised her hand and gently stroked the back of his head, her eyes shining with unshed tears that made his heart clench painfully in his chest. He wished she could send Trevor to hell and leave the fucking asshole—but Cade knew his mother would never leave her husband.

"You too," she whispered back. "Have you been looking after yourself?"

Cade nodded and smiled before kissing the top of his mother's head and letting her go. She was the one who didn't look like she was eating properly. Her eyes were dark, her hair duller than normal. Had she always seemed so small? Cade didn't remember, but she looked different and not in a good way. It was his mother he probably missed the most—her and maybe Danny.

Danny was young—Phoenix's age. He was too naïve to make his own decisions just now so anything he thought, Cade could forgive him for, but the boy needed to open his eyes. He needed to see what Aaron and Trevor were really like. Oh, Trevor must have been so pleased with Aaron, to see that he had managed to breed himself a carbon copy. What a shame for Aaron, though—already his life was marked for one of misery and greed as he blindly followed in their father's footsteps because he had been taught that it was the right thing to do.

"I think everyone is here," Malcolm said, as Cade found himself an empty chair and sat down. This wasn't such a private meeting it would seem. There were four people at the table that he didn't recognise, and the tables had been extended so that everyone had a place to sit. Cade surveyed them all wondering what surprise it was that Trevor had up his sleeve. There had to be something.

Malcolm nodded to Aaron. "We're ready."

A woman sat beside Aaron—attractive, rich—the kind you could tell had been born into money, lacked brains as all spoilt little rich girls did. Daddy would have provided her with whatever her heart had desired. She smiled up at Aaron as he stood and Cade felt his stomach twist. Oh god … no.

"Malcolm …" Aaron began by addressing the head of the Society and Council before his own father. A piece of respect that Cade was sure pissed Trevor off every single time. "Mother, father." He cleared his throat and smoothed down the non-existent creases from the front of his jacket. "I asked Malcom to call this meeting tonight because I come here seeking the Society and the Council's permission. I wish to put forward an official potential." Cade's blood froze. The woman next to Aaron took her cue and stood. "This is Isobel Dean. I request that the Council and Society approve a permanent mating between us and a joining of our families and packs." He reached down to the file that was in front of him and pulled out some papers, which he handed to Malcolm and Trevor. "We have done all of the appropriate tests. Isobel is able to bear my young and she is deemed fit and healthy. We will be a good match."

Malcolm said nothing at first but took the papers and started to inspect them. If Malcom was anything, it was that he was fair and kept the rules the same for everyone, no matter who they were to him. He looked up when he was done with a perfunctory smile. "It seems that you have done all of our work for us."

"Yes. To save you the bother. I have copies for everyone here. May I pass them around?"

Malcolm nodded his permission. It was customary for the Society, and then the Council, to agree on the mating. It seemed that Aaron had both of them there, but of course, everything had to be checked first. What would be the point in a mating, especially if one of them was beta, when the potential mate couldn't or wouldn't produce offspring? Or maybe there was something in their blood that would bring risk to the family line. Aaron handed the copies to everyone at the table, but the only thing that really mattered was that Malcolm had read his, and he was happy with the request. If he wasn't, he wouldn't have allowed Aaron to carry on. In turn, the heads around the table muttered and nodded their agreement, too. Cade felt the world around him slipping farther away with each nod. It seemed that fate wasn't done with him today. No, she was here to make sure that he was well and truly screwed.

"I have no objections," Malcolm said as he took a pen from the holder in front of him and signed the bottom of the document. He held out the pen to Trevor, whose eyes were alight with his excitement. After everyone had put down their signature, the pile of agreements mounted up in the middle of the table.

Aaron could mate with Isobel.

Cade glared at his father. There was no doubt the son of a bitch had known. This was why Cade had been summoned. His heart sunk as he suddenly realised that, apart from Isobel and her parents, the fourth person sitting at the table that he didn't recognise had to be one of the Castle women—and judging by her age, Cade guessed it was the mother. He had been set up and he'd walked right into it like a world class fool.

Two years ago, he had made a pact with his father in order to protect Phoenix. He had agreed that when his older brother, the heir, mated and then produced his first born, he would in turn mate with one of the Castle girls. It would be a legal contract that strengthened the ranks. The Castle family were powerful people, but with the death of Mr Castle, they had fallen on hard times and couldn't afford their Society fees. They were too valuable to let go, though. They had many contacts that would be useful assets to Trevor and the Society. They just needed a way to stay and that was to have one of the daughters marry someone in a good position—and that someone was Cade.

He glanced over at Stephen who sat in his chair with a clenched jaw and a murderous look on his face as he stared at Trevor. Cade knew that his friend was well aware of what all this meant. Stephen also knew that Cade was backed in a corner and that there was little he could do to avoid the fate Trevor had decided for him.

Aaron sat back down with a more than pleased smile upon his face. That was it. The next full moon and pack run, he would officially mate with this woman.

"With this new development, we have another contract to adhere to it would seem." Malcolm nodded to Trevor, who then stood to address the congregation.

"It had been agreed that when my first heir mated, my second would mate with a member of the Castle family," Trevor proclaimed.

"That was not the agreement," Cade cut in. "My brother has to have his first child before that happens."

"And how long do you think that is going to take?" Trevor asked, tilting his head and eyebrows rising in question. Cade could hear the underlying smugness in his father's voice—everyone knew that Aaron would set about trying to acquire an heir as soon as was possible. Turning his attention back to his audience, Trevor addressed them once more. "After the official mating, I propose that Cadence MacDonald is to meet with the three," he paused and smiled at the widow, "lovely daughters and make his selection." He stared Cade straight in the eyes now. "We had these made out for you, to help you decide." He slid some papers across the table— three sheets with details of each of the women on them. Cade took the papers without glancing at them.

"This is with Ms Castle's permission, of course." The woman nodded in consensus, tying a noose around Cade's neck, so much that he was sure he would suffocate very soon. There was nothing he could say—to argue would be to hand Phoenix over to his father, which would be like signing his death warrant. Cade wasn't about to do that.

His mind raced with thoughts and ways of escape. He had to get the three of them, four if he counted the baby, out of there. There was no other way. If they ended up stray, then they would cope ... somehow.

When the meeting closed and everyone started to mingle, Cade strode over to Stephen and grabbed his arm. He didn't give him time to speak as he pulled him outside. Stephen went without question.

"Where is Gemma?" Cade demanded when they were outside of the house and far enough away that no one would hear them.

"She went to Shelley's. Said she couldn't see you tonight."

"Is she okay?"

Stephen shrugged. "Is she going to be okay again?"

"This is all fucking bullshit. You know that, right?"

Stephen nodded and then started to walk along the driveway and to the lane that led to the main road, letting Cade follow suit. When they were far enough away, Stephen stopped and turned towards him. "She doesn't know about this tonight. She needs to, but she doesn't yet. I lied to her … told her that there was a meeting and maybe she should go out. It would be hell if anyone sensed she is upset. I'm on your side, you know that, right?"

Cade swore and started to pace. "I have no idea what I am supposed to do here."

"I don't, either. But now you've signed to mate some woman, so you've got to talk to Gemma. You've got to make your decisions. I'll back you whatever it is." He paused before adding quietly, "If you need to leave, you leave. Okay?"

Cade's eyes flew to his. He knew Stephen would have known his friend might consider that option, but Cade hadn't been sure how Stephen would take it. "What about you?"

"I'm going to be king of my father's castle. No way am I giving that up. Do you know how many requests from the ladies I get a day?"

Stephen was lying, Cade knew it, and Stephen knew that Cade knew it, but he didn't call him out on it. Stephen didn't care for the women—

they bored him mostly. It would take a better woman than any on offer to make him want to stay. But he also knew that what he was doing was telling him to run and not worry. For that he was grateful because they had to do something, and they had to do it fast.

"Together, remember? Whatever happens."

Chapter Five

Gemma had been nursing her mug of coffee for almost half an hour as she sat at the kitchen table in her best friend, Shelley's, house. She sat and stared into the now too cool drink and wondered, isn't coffee bad for expectant mothers? This was how it had gone these last couple of days, driving herself crazy with these thoughts and questions, which were always followed by one thought—*the* one thought. What did it matter if she wasn't keeping the baby anyway? She could go out clubbing for the night and down shots while dancing half-naked on the bar if she wanted to. It would be impossible to do harm to a child that she wasn't intending to keep anyway … right?

Shelley leaned forward with her elbows resting on the table. "Are you going to tell me what's wrong or do I need to beat it out of you?"

Gemma scowled at her friend. Shelley, beautiful, perfect Shelley. Her hair was many shades redder than Gemma's, and it cascaded down her back in waves of tight curls. Her eyes were an emerald-green that reminded Gemma of the most beautiful tropical seas in the world. Compared to

Gemma, Shelley's colours were darker, deeper, but both woman held an allure that was uniquely theirs. They had been the two ginger kids of the Council—except Gemma wasn't ginger, she was auburn. That was what her mother always said anyway.

"Nothing is wrong. I told you."

"Mmhmmm. You've been sitting there for ages staring into your mug. You didn't flinch even when Tom came down to give you some shit, so I know something is wrong. Spill it."

Gemma frowned. "Tom was here?"

Shelley shook her head in gentle reproof and gave a gentle sigh. She reached over and cupped Gemma's hands in her own, the mug still between them. "What's wrong, Gem?" she asked lowering her voice.

Gemma wanted to tell her friend about the baby so badly. The words were right there on her tongue. This was Shelley for god's sake. Shelley … the person she had grown up with, who knew everything from the smallest of irrelevant things to her biggest, most momentous moments. She was Gemma's go to person, and had been since that very first day. Of course, back then, Shelley had still been a respectable member of the Unseelie Court, until she had met and fallen in love with Tom. Not that there was anything wrong with that in itself, except that Tom was *Human* and Shelley was *Fae*. She had given up everything to be with him—even her family. That hadn't changed Gemma's relationship with her best friend, however, and she was still the person Gemma turned to—as she was for Shelley.

Yet, she struggled to get the words out now. They caught in her throat and got stuck there, leaving a bitter taste that no amount of coffee would swill away.

"Did you make the right choice?" she finally said.

Shelley blinked in surprise at the question. "In what?"

"Tom." Gemma pulled her hands free and brought the mug to her lips. She screwed up her face and forced herself to gulp down the cold liquid before continuing. "Picking him over everything else. Was it worth it?"

Without a moment's hesitation, her friend replied, "Without a doubt."

Mason Sabre

"You don't have any regrets?"

"None." Shelley eyed Gemma suspiciously. "Are you and Cade thinking about leaving? Making it together?"

Gemma gulped down more cold coffee and looked away.

"Gem?"

"Tom really came down? I was *that* out of it?"

"For ages. I was debating on heading to bed at one point ... you were boring the shit out of me. Now quit changing the subject and answer my question. Are you and Cade planning to leave Society?" Shelley knew about Cade. She knew nearly everything that went on in Gemma's life— well, almost everything—except this one thing just now that was so god damn hard to say. When Shelley had announced her pregnancy the year before, they had celebrated together and had got excited over it like little girls. But as Gemma sat opposite Shelley with the tables turned, she couldn't find the right words to tell her friend. Maybe that was the problem. While in Shelley's case there had been joy and celebrating, it wouldn't be so with Gemma now. No celebrations. No girly nights with the bump.

It wasn't meant to be this way

"Gem?"

Gemma set her mug down and took in a shaky breath. "I'm pregnant."

For a moment, Shelley simply stared at Gemma, making her feel uncomfortable and ill at ease. She could see the thoughts running through Shelley's mind, almost hear her brain working. "It's Cade's, right?"

Gemma slumped back in her seat. "Jesus, Shell …"

Shelley raised her hands in defence. "Just making sure. Maybe you went all 'do-as-you're-told' and met a tiger." She paused, eyes still trained on Gemma. "Does Cade know?"

"Yep, he knows."

"And … he's not happy?" she prompted.

Gemma scoffed. "He's over the god damn moon."

"And you?"

Gemma sighed and put her hands to her face. This was all stupid. All of it. She couldn't keep the baby, yet everyone was acting like it was an option. "It's like I take my life and put it in a snow globe, then I shake it to see where all the shit lands just for kicks."

"You could just say you aren't happy," Shelley teased her gently, but Gemma couldn't muster even a hint of a smile in return.

"Does Stephen know?" she asked softly.

"He knows. You know what he is like. He would know even if I didn't tell him."

"Still doing his creepy-ass know-everything shit?"

Gemma nodded and sighed.

"He's sexy as hell with it, though," Shelley winked.

"Shelley ..."

"What? I'm not blind. Have you seen him?"

"Every damn day," Gemma scowled. "You're married."

"Doesn't' make me blind. I can still look."

"Not at my brother."

Shelley laughed. "Cade or no Cade, if I had a brother like yours, you'd constantly be around here drooling like a puppy."

"He's my brother," Gemma protested again. She wasn't mad at her friend's joking. She was used to it mostly. Being Stephen's younger sister sure was a pain in the ass some days. Over the years, so many girls and women had tried to be her friend just so that they could come over and see the big, sexy tiger—maybe even catch his eye if they were lucky enough. They were idiots, the lot of them. Stephen didn't have eyes for any of them—and if he did, it was only to relieve his natural urges. But beyond that, there was no other interest. Stephen was a born bachelor. It would take a truly special woman to get under his skin, someone who could match his wit and not take any of his shit.

Gemma had had to ban him at one point. Anyone that she was friends with was strictly off limits. She had got so sick of them asking her if he would call or if he asked about them ... because he didn't. Stephen didn't care, he didn't call and he wasn't interested. Why they never got the message, she never knew.

"I came here for some comfort," Gemma scolded her friend.

Shelley chuckled then reached for Gemma's hand again. "You know I'm kidding, Gem. I was just trying to make you smile a bit." She stood then, pulling Gemma up with her. "Come with me. I want to show you something." She didn't let go of Gemma's hand as she led her through the house and up the stairs. They stopped on the landing, just outside the bathroom. The door was closed, but the heat from the running shower permeated through ... along with a sound that was somewhere between a screech and a howl.

"Hear that?" Shelley whispered, an undertone of laughter in her voice.

"You mean Tom's awful rendition of something undistinguishable?"

"Yep," her friend chortled, making Gemma giggle.

"He sings in the shower?"

"Every god damn night." Shelley pulled Gemma towards the small room at the front, the one that overlooked the small driveway. Inside it, there was a nightlight which slowly rotated. Trains danced about the wall with clouds overhead. There was a gentle tune to it as it went, something soothing as the little music box twanged the chords. Shelley walked Gemma over to the cot that stood next to the wall. Harry, Shelley's nine-month-old son, was asleep in there. Gemma smiled. He looked much like his father—all he needed was the small glasses and the funny little smirk, and he'd be set. "See him in there?"

"Yes," Gemma breathed, her heart squeezing at the sight.

"Do you know what I wake up to every morning?"

"His cute smile?" Gemma said with a sigh.

Shelley snorted. "Nope, usually it's his shitty nappy."

Gemma let out a surprised laugh and her eyes shot to her friend. "Between shitty nappies and

Tom's awful singing, I think I am missing the point."
She had expected this to be a lesson in all things
great and wonderful.

"Close your eyes and listen."

Gemma frowned.

"Just do it. Trust me. Close your eyes, and
keep them closed."

Gemma did as she was told and Shelley
moved around so that she was behind her. She felt
the warmth of her there as she snaked an arm
around her waist and rested her hand against her
still-flat stomach. Gemma tensed, but she didn't
open her eyes—instead, she leaned into her friend.

"In there is a life ... a life that you both
created. Can you hear my life here? The singing?
The soft snores? Tom drives me nuts most of the
days, and Harry has me running around until I am so
tired I just want to pass out." She paused, and
Gemma could hear the smile in her voice as she
continued. "But I'd never give it up. Not in a million
years. These two men in my life *are* my life. You
have to decide if Cade and this baby are yours."

Gemma rested her hand over Shelley's and fought down tears. It was easier said than done. She wasn't just choosing to have a baby—she was choosing to leave the life she knew. To leave her parents and the Society, to leave Stephen, and even Shelley. Shelley was an outcast now herself, but Gemma still wouldn't be able to see her as she wouldn't be allowed back here—not in the area, at least. It wasn't just a case of choosing.

"If I choose this life, they'll kill us. You know they will. And the baby? What do you think will happen to the baby? They will kill it, too."

Shelley turned Gemma around gently so that they were facing each other and stared her right in the eyes. "If you abort this baby, what do you think *you* are doing? Aren't you killing it anyway? Doesn't that make you the same as them?"

Gemma's bottom lip trembled. "At least it will be a merciful death."

"Will it? You're taking away a child's choice and chance at life."

The words tore at Gemma. It wasn't so simple as that. Her breathing grew laborious as the pressure in her chest intensified. "What if they kill Cade?"

"He wants the baby, right? You said that. He is happy?"

"Yes, but ..."

"If you abort his baby ..." She stopped short and leaned in to embrace Gemma. "If you abort this baby," she whispered, "there are more ways to die than death."

And that was the truth of it. Shelley was right. What would aborting the baby do to Cade? He'd never forgive her, and if he did, would they stay together? "I don't know what I am supposed to do," she sobbed, hugging her friend back tightly. "If we run, I have to leave everything behind."

Shelley held her while she broke down in her arms. Only when Gemma seemed to calm did she whisper, "You have to choose. That's what it is." She peered down into Gemma's face, lifting a hand to wipe her tears away. "If you didn't want his baby, you wouldn't be crying. You'd not be here, either. If you came here for me to tell you that you're doing the right thing, I won't. I can't make this decision for you, Gemma. *You* have to do it. I will support you whatever you choose, even if I don't agree, okay? I'll be here for everything, but you have to choose because you are the one who has to live with it."

"I have a life here. How can I just give it up?"

"Tell me what life? Do you know what I was facing before I met Tom? Marrying some bloke that my mother picked out for me. I don't even know who he was. I didn't care, either. And for what? To carry on the pure lines? I was going to spend the rest of my life doing my mother's bidding. Do you think that I would have been happy? Is that a life ... is that a way to live? Just because I was born into the position I had, didn't mean that it was what I wanted to keep." She stopped, jaw clenching. "Do you know that my mother is taking my power?"

Gemma raised her eyes to Shelley's, shocked. "Because of Tom?"

"Yep," she nodded. "She thinks that it will make me come running home if I can't do shit." Shelley stepped away from Gemma and held her hand out with her palm up. It glowed blue in the darkened room and then the smallest of flames bubbled in her hand. "I used to be able to throw fire, remember? Now I am lucky if I can make the bloody smoke alarm go off." She sighed and shrugged. "Does it matter, though? Because inside, I have everything I need."

Gemma was prevented from replying by a knock on the door downstairs. They both jumped at the sound and Shelley quickly went to the window to peer down.

"Looks like your decision is outside," she said with a smile.

Gemma raced to Shelley's side, her heart in her mouth. Cade was standing at the front door. "Shit." She turned to go, but Shelley grabbed hold of her hand.

"Look at him and think about what you see and feel just now. If it is not love, if your stomach isn't flipping at the sight of him or screaming in longing, if your arms aren't craving him, go down there and tell him to leave. Let him go because he also has a life, and it isn't fair to make him hang between what he wants and what he has. If there is no hope, let him go."

Gemma stared down at Cade's tall, well-built frame as he stood there, her heart thumping loudly in her chest.

Dark Veil

"Make your decision, Gem."

It was Shelley who left the room first, leaving Gemma standing there staring down at the man who meant the world to her. He hadn't looked up, hadn't seen them in the dark room above. She watched him, the way he stood, the way he held himself ... his strong, muscled form. Every single part of him called to her and every part of her craved him. Light flowed out and he was framed in a soft glow for a moment when Shelley answered the door to let him in.

Tom emerged from the bathroom just as Gemma was sneaking out of Harry's room. He wasn't as built as Cade or Stephen—normal height, slim build. He was just *Human* ... but his eyes and his heart were pure. Purer than most *Others* she knew.

"You okay, Kitty Kat?"

"I am now that you have stopped singing," she teased, but her smile felt as fake as her lie.

Tom grinned at her. "It's what Shelley loves about me. Won her right over."

"She must be tone deaf," Gemma joked, leaving him there chuckling softly and heading towards the muffled voices downstairs.

Cade was standing in the lounge—just standing. He didn't need to be doing anything else to make Gemma's heart race at the mere sight of him. It pounded loudly in her chest, the sound reverberating in her ears. Everything about him was perfect. His blue eyes, broad shoulders—everything about him was so male. But as he stood there silently staring at her, she had the overwhelming urge to go to him and ease the ache that she knew was in his heart.

"I know I shouldn't have come …"

"Is something wrong?" she breathed.

He put his head down and it was enough to make Gemma grow cold, fear filling her. "Cade?"

"Aaron has chosen his mate," he said slowly.

Gemma's heart plummeted.

Chapter Six

Gemma couldn't stop shaking as she sat at the dinner table in Shelley's dining room. Despite the comfortable warmth of the house, her teeth wouldn't stop chattering. She was glad that Shelley and Tom had gone back upstairs to give them some privacy.

Aaron had chosen his mate.

The words tumbled around in Gemma's mind, unable to compute. She could understand it, she knew what it meant, but to actually believe it was another thing entirely. "The Council have agreed? My dad?" she whispered the last part with a touch of hope.

"They set me up ... my father ..." Cade sat next to Gemma, his chair turned so that he was facing her. He reached out to take her hand between his, running his thumb across the back as he sat thinking. She didn't pull away from him, needing his touch as much as he did in that moment. He brought her hand to his mouth and laid a gentle kiss in her palm. She didn't dare to make it more, though. She didn't trust herself. She needed logic right now—*they* needed it. Decisions fuelled with overriding emotions would sure as shit get them in more trouble than they were already in.

Cade lifted his eyes to hers, his gaze penetrating. "The Castle woman was there," he said carefully.

Jealousy surged through her, red-hot and malevolent. So much as she didn't want to know, and didn't want him to say yes, she had to ask, "And her daughters?"

"No. Just the mother. No doubt to witness it all and tie the noose around my neck more tightly." Cade exhaled heavily. "My father knew. He had to. There was no other reason for me to be there except for him to set me up like this. He loved every minute of it, too."

Gemma's stomach clenched with dread. It would be typical of Trevor to do something like this. "He wanted to see your reaction when they told you?"

"I think he wanted to see if I would back out. It would be his chance to snatch Phoenix then and get rid of him. I can't even give him the flicker of a reason."

Gemma swallowed hard. "You didn't back out, did you?" Part of her wished he would say yes, because it fixed everything, but the other part of her knew she couldn't do that to Phoenix. He would be out on his own, and he wouldn't last long. She could never sacrifice his happiness for hers. God, she hated this gridlock they were stuck in.

Cade's expression fell, his jaw clenching. "I can't."

"I know. "She leaned into him, resting her forehead against his, their hands clasped between them. Nothing else in the world existed right then— just them. The Castle woman was nothing more than a bogeyman made up to scare her. It couldn't hurt her if she had Cade. That was what she tried to tell herself anyway. But looking into Cade's deep blue eyes, she could see that he was scared, too. His *wolf* roamed in the back, waiting to emerge. All Cade had to do was say the word.

Pressing her hands firmly to his lips, he inhaled deeply. "If I don't do this, my father will come and take Phoenix. There won't be any second chances. He is just waiting for me to mess up and give him the chance." He breathed hard as he clutched her hands. "I love you so much."

Her insides knotted with longing for him—a longing to be closer to him. When she was with him, she couldn't ever get enough of him. Her *tiger* was hungry for him, just the way his *wolf* was for her. And when he let her hands go and cupped her face, bringing her mouth to his, she didn't fight it. Instead, she opened her mouth to him and held on. She could kiss him forever, taste him this way. Just the feel of his mouth on hers had her wanting to cry out from the frustration of it. "I love you, too," she whispered against his mouth as she broke their kiss. "This baby makes everything so impossible."

And that was the word that did it—baby. Cade let go of Gemma and stood up so abruptly that his chair almost toppled over. She tried to grab for his hand to stop him, but he was too fast.

"Don't you see that we can't keep it?" Her tone was pleading, urging him to see how hopeless and crazy it was to even entertain the idea.

Cade turned and pinned her with a stony stare, the warmth that had been in his eyes just a moment before gone. "Don't use this as justification to get rid of our child."

His words were a stab to the heart. She looked at him, a hurt expression on her face. "Cade ..."

In two strides, he was in front of her again. He sat down on his haunches and grabbed hold of her hands, his eyes boring into hers, desperation glimmering in their depths. "Leave with me, Gem," he begged. "If you truly love me, leave with me. Please don't take my child away."

Her heart squeezed painfully in her chest. There was nothing more she wanted than to be with Cade, to have his child. Why did life have to be so cruel? "It isn't that simple," she whispered, "and you know it."

"Isn't it? We could just pack a bag and go. We could leave right now ..."

"And what about Phoenix? You just said that your father would take him out if he got the chance ... and there would be no second chances. All Trevor needs is to see the opportunity and he will grab it."

"We take him with us." The words were spoken so matter-of-factly, so flatly, that she knew there was no moving him on this. His mind was made up. But this wasn't Cade—this wasn't the logical, reasonable man who never made rash decisions and who always thought things through rationally first. Right now, Cade wasn't thinking at all. "We can leave tonight. No one will know. It will be days before they realise."

"But they will realise eventually, Cade." And they would. Maybe not Trevor—Cade didn't live with him and their contact was sparse—but her father and her mother would know. Not that Gemma was a child, but she lived with them. It would just be a matter of how fast Malcolm or Emily noticed their daughter was missing.

"We can be gone before then. We can go to Exile." Exile was the row of islands around the coast, far enough away that you couldn't just swim there, but close enough that they were used to house prisoners and unwanted *Others*.

"How do we get there, Cade? Swim? We don't even have papers." That was the other problem. Admission into Exile needed papers. There were communities there—or so she had heard. She had never been herself. There were pockets of *Others*, but it wasn't all fun and games. They lived in gated areas that were nothing short of prisons.

Dark Veil

He pushed himself back up to his feet and ran agitated fingers through his short hair. "We can get papers. We can get them and do this properly. We take Phoenix with us." He reached down suddenly and pulled her up from the chair, his movements gentle. Then his arms were around her, holding her with such tenderness that it threatened to break her heart all over again. She fought the onslaught of emotions as he held her, his proximity having its usual dizzying effect on her senses. It was so hard to say no to him, to push him away when all she wanted to do was seek comfort and safety in his arms. The look of desperation on his face inked itself on her heart.

"I can't leave Stephen," she murmured against his hard chest.

"Stephen is a big boy … he will cope."

She shook her head. "He is sick. Haven't you seen it? The way he is? Something is wrong. I can't leave him like that, and neither can you. He's your friend. Can you walk out on him?"

It was true. Something was getting worse with Stephen. He wasn't sleeping—she'd hear him go to bed around two, and then he would be up roaming the house around four-ish again. She had no idea how he hadn't passed out from so little sleep.

"Something is going on with him. I don't want to leave him."

Cade exhaled heavily then let his arms drop from around her. He ran both his hands through his hair and turned back to the window. This whole thing was impossible and they both knew it.

"I don't want to get rid of the baby any more than you do," she whispered.

"Then why do it? We can find ways."

Gemma's heart cried with sorrow and frustration. "You are about to marry another woman. How …?" Her voice broke and trailed off as the weight of everything pressed down heavily on her. She sat back down, and let her head fall to her hands. She could feel Cade there—he had moved back to her—but he didn't touch her this time. When she looked back up at him, he was staring at her, a tormented look in his eyes.

"How can I just have a baby when you are going to be with someone else? She will have your children. It is her place, not mine." Each word tore another piece from inside of Gemma—each like a new sword piercing her flesh. But it was the truth. He wasn't hers, and there was nothing she could do about it.

A light knock on the door brought both their heads around, their attention on Shelley as she slowly eased the door open and popped her head through the gap. "I wasn't listening," she said.

"Yes, you were," Gemma smiled sadly. "But it's okay."

"Okay, I was listening a little." She pushed the door open further and slipped into the room. "I'm not trying to interfere ..."

"But?"

"Do you know how far along you are?"

Gemma shook her head. "I missed this month, that's all."

"So, early then. Chances are just a couple of weeks. It means you have some time." She glanced from Cade and Gemma. "If you abort the baby tomorrow, the day after, or even next week, it's final. It's done. You can't ever bring it back. Take some time and think about the possibilities." She faced Cade. His anger was still etched on his face, palpable in the room. "If you leave tomorrow like you want, what will happen? All you have is the money in the bank. You have no papers, nowhere to go, nothing. You can't uproot Phoenix like that. What if he doesn't want to leave? Have you thought about that? He is quite attached to Stephen, right?"

Gemma nodded at Shelley's words, her eyes seeking Cade's, gauging his reaction. Over the past two years, Phoenix had found different parental qualities in all of them in a way. Though he was way too young to be considered it, Cade played the part of a father—he was for the more serious stuff. He was there to teach him and guide him, to give him his education and to offer him protection. Gemma was more like the big sister to him—protective and loving and teasing. But Stephen ... he had taken on the fun role—they went running and shifted together, and Stephen had taught him how to hunt more efficiently. He taught him the things that Cade had felt could come with time and didn't bother with so much. But that was unacceptable to Stephen, who thought that they were fundamental to his role in the shifter world. Phoenix had got attached to all three of them, and each of them had connected with him in turn.

"You both need to sit and think about this properly. You need to sit and talk about it without the emotions." She walked over to Gemma and knelt down in front of her, placing her hands gently over her own. "You have some time still." Shelley smiled reassuringly at her before glancing over her shoulder at Cade. "How long until you have to choose one of the women?"

Cade's hands balled into fists at his side. "I don't know," he said gruffly. "My father didn't say. I would imagine he'd want this one nailed as soon as possible."

Shelley grimaced. "Business deal, right? I forget what an asshole your father is." She turned back to Gemma. "Give it two weeks. Okay? See what you both want. See what is possible. Maybe you can get the papers and leave. Maybe Phoenix wants to come. Shit, maybe even Stephen wants to come. Maybe the pregnancy …" Shelley's voice trailed off as she got carried away with the maybes.

"Doesn't last?" Gemma finished for her.

Shelley glanced away. "Sorry."

Mason Sabre

The thought echoed in Gemma's mind. That would be the best solution—not that she wanted to lose the baby. Some part of her feared it more than anything. Mix babies were harder to carry to term. "It happens," she eventually said slowly. "At least then we know it wasn't meant to be."

"You're hoping to lose the baby?" Cade's tone was hard, cutting.

Gemma's eyes flew to his. "No, I wish I had never ..." She was going to say hadn't got pregnant in the first place, but it was a lie. To know that she was carrying part of Cade inside her filled her with a warmth she couldn't ever begin to explain.

"You never ...?" Cade urged her to finish, anger written all over his face. She couldn't say what she had thought, though. She knew that if she did, he would walk out. She didn't want that, either. "You wish you never ...?" His jaw clenched as he shoved his fists into the pockets of his jeans as if to keep from ramming them into a wall.

Gemma knew she was walking a fine line. She met his stare, refusing to look away. "I don't know. I wish lots of things."

"Got pregnant?" he persisted.

Gemma squeezed Shelley's hand tightly and Shelley squeezed back. If it wasn't for her friend grounding her, Gemma was sure that she would have passed out and slid to the floor. Her mind was swimming with the agony of everything.

Her expression was anguished as she looked at Cade. "If you die because of this baby, I don't know how I can live with myself."

Cade's stare was unblinking as he said, "If the baby dies to save my life, how do I live with that?"

Unwittingly, tears rolled down her cheeks. Why couldn't he see that she was hurting, too? Why couldn't he see beyond his own pain and what his words were doing? She had always known she would never carry Cade's child, but it had never stopped her dreaming about it. It didn't stop her imagining her belly swollen with their child. It didn't stop her imagining Cade holding his newborn child—the child that she had given to him.

Cade opened his mouth as if to say more but then promptly shut it again. He looked away, as if unable to bear the sight of her tears. After a moment, he straightened his shoulders and cast

Shelley an inscrutable look. "I'm sorry to have bothered you at such a late hour." With that, he turned and walked out.

Both Shelley and Gemma remained silent as they listened to the front door opening and closing, and then moments later, the sound of his engine roaring to life before tearing away.

"He left," Gemma sobbed in disbelief.

"He's hurting," Shelley tried to reassure her, but Gemma's tears just kept rolling down her cheeks. "Hey," she said softly, "he loves you, okay?"

Gemma blinked, trying to get herself under control. "I don't know what to do," she whispered morosely.

Shelley stared at her hard. "I can't lose either of you, okay? I'll support whatever you decide, but please, don't do anything that means you both end up dead. I wouldn't be able to stand it."

Chapter Seven

The murky water lapped against Stephen's shins as he stood on a large rock just at the edge of the river. Although the rock was slippery, it stopped his feet from sinking into the soft earth. His hands were icy cold, his fingers almost numb as they clutched the ragged cloth of a man's shirt that covered the lifeless body of a young girl. Though it was hard to tell how old she was, Stephen would have bet she was younger than twenty. Her face was grey, red lines having wormed their way into her skin and water bloating her inanimate body. Her unseeing eyes stared out into nothingness, taking with them deadly secrets.

Stephen had no idea how long she had been there. Her dirty, wet hair clung to his leg like icy fingers where he held her. He had tried to drag her further out before the tide came up and covered her again, but every time he pulled, her clothes tore. He tried stepping down, so that he could give himself some leverage, but the earth beneath was just too soft and the current too strong. He was so close to the mouth of the river—one wrong step and he'd end up in the water, swept away. The winter was coming, the winds building up; they knew no bounds and didn't discriminate its victims, *Human* or *Other*, it didn't matter. Once the sea had you, it was too late. The estuary wasn't so bad closer to the bridge, the one that led to where Cade lived. Two years ago, he, Cade and Gemma had swum across it with Phoenix—when Cade had just found him and was trying to save his life—but this was very different.

His arm ached from the effort of holding such a dead weight for so long. His head fell back and he swore. Where the fuck was the DSA? It felt like hours had passed since he had called them. He had been out running, letting his tiger roam free and trying to forget all the shit that was going on around him, when he had seen her. He'd come for some peace and solace, and a dead body was the last thing he had needed to find. He had spotted her hand first and had immediately waded in to try and get to her. He had gone to her first as a *tiger*, clamped his teeth down on the sleeve of her shirt to pull her up, but all he had managed to do was pull away some torn and tatty, and rather disgusting-tasting, fabric. He'd taken his chances then and left her to shift back and call it in to the DSA from the call box—but time was not on his side right now, and letting go of the body to go try make another call could well mean coming back to the tide having come in and carried her away.

He leaned down, careful not to slip and lose his balance. His bare feet made it difficult—they were cold and numb and there was a dull ache in his thighs from the effort to withstand the current and stay on the rock. The tide must have exposed her; it was out farther tonight. That was why the ground was so soft, but it was coming in again and would soon claim her once more. If DSA didn't hurry up, he was going to have to let her go.

His eyes raked the land that was considered *Human* land—*Others* weren't meant to run here, but Stephen didn't give a shit. What were they going to do to him? By the time anyone came to clear him off, he'd be gone. Except *this* had happened tonight ...

He heard the sound of the first car pulling up in the distance and after a couple of minutes, the sound of a second. Of course, they couldn't use the main car park—that was for *Humans* only. He strained to listen. It would be just his luck for it to be bloody *Humans* who showed up, maybe for some late night fishing or some shit like that, and wouldn't they be chuffed they had struck lucky and caught themselves a *tiger*.

Stephen relaxed when he heard the familiar voices of Cade, and William Harvey. Harvey was the main DSA operative, the man Cade worked under and trained with. One day, Cade would take over and run the agency, but for now, he was simply his lackey. Harvey was a decent guy, though—didn't pull any shit with Cade or act like an arrogant bastard. Except now …

Stephen might have laughed at the expression on Cade's face when Harvey handed him the gloves and Cade realised it would be him to have to wade out into the sludge and water and, generally, into the foul-smelling gunk, but right now, Stephen's back was aching, his legs had long since gone to sleep, the cold that had now seeped into his bones bordering on excruciating pain.

One of the vehicles they had driven in was that of a multifunctional van they used. Thomas Barnes served as the baker as well as the coroner and person who dealt with any dead shit in general. Stephen knew him from way back, but the young *Other* trailing along behind him was not somebody Stephen recognised—a rookie no doubt. Not that

Stephen gave a shit. They were here to collect the body and that was all that mattered.

"You're going to need some rope or something. This girl is wedged in tighter than a virgin on a ..."

Harvey gave Stephen a stern look and raised his hand, silencing him.

"She's stuck," Stephen grumbled. "I can't feel my fucking arms. One of you needs to come and get her out before the tide comes right up and there's jack all I can do."

"I have rope and a board," shouted Thomas. He placed what looked like a flight case that bands carry their gear around in on a patch of dry ground and opened it. Stephen missed the length of rope as it was thrown to him, landing in the water and bringing about violent swearing from him as he strained to reach it. After he eventually grabbed a hold of it, he tied the rope securely around the girl's waist and threw the other end to Cade, who was standing right at the edge of the river, partly in the mud but not too much so he wouldn't stand firm. "Got a good hold on it? Because I'm letting go, and if she comes free and floats off down there," he nodded towards the rapids a little further up the river, "then you're getting her your god damn self."

"I've got her. Don't worry," Cade called out. He held out his hand to him as Stephen approached, fighting not to be pulled downstream by the strong current. He grabbed Cade's hand and Cade gritted his teeth in his effort not to let Stephen's much larger frame pull them both right back into the sludge instead. The problem was Stephen was the bigger of the two—not that Cade was small or weak by any means—but Stephen tended to tower above everyone else. His broad shoulders and well-defined physique, but his incredible height as well, gave him the appearance not only of always being physically larger than any of them there, but made his mere presence overwhelming, one that demanded people pay attention, and even fear.

Stephen's jeans, which he had hastily dragged on when he'd shifted to go to the callbox earlier, were soaked through, the cold seeping into his skin as if he had ice coating his body.

It took Stephen, Cade, Thomas and the rookie a good few tugs and pulls, and a lot of cursing, but they finally managed to get the girl out. Her legs had been tied to something, and Stephen and Cade both crouched down to get a better look. "Well, she wasn't meant to come back up," Stephen observed, and Cade murmured his agreement.

"Why do you think she was so close to the edge?" Harvey asked Cade. It wasn't that she was actually so close, but more that the shoreline had gone far out this evening. Or that Harvey did know, but he was training Cade's mind to see everything.

"She was probably thrown into the water when the tide was high." He remained crouched down next to Stephen as he examined the girl's appearance. "Doesn't look like she has been in the water long, though." He glanced up at Harvey. "I'll check when the last high tide was. It will probably give us time of death, or at least the date. Maybe there is some kind of missing person's report around that time, too."

Harvey nodded. "Very good."

The girl didn't seem to have any outward causes of death. There were no marks on her, no cuts or wounds—nothing that looked to be fatal. Cade did notice, however, that there was a puckered hole on her arm, in the crook of her elbow. She had been injected with something, and maybe more than once. A junkie, perhaps? Cade stood and dried his hands on the legs of his jeans as best as he could before taking back his forms from Harvey and beginning to fill them in. He turned to Stephen, who was now standing and stretching out his aching arms. "I don't need to call Society, do I? You can sign off on this."

The girl by Stephen's feet was a no one, a nobody—probably a stray. It wouldn't matter if he signed off on it or not. Her death would probably never be solved, not being important enough to bother with. "It isn't Council worthy."

"No, but it is Society, and you're here so what is the point in dragging anyone out?"

Stephen uttered an oath. He should have stayed at home. Surely having to listen to Evie sulk around the house and dealing with Gemma's foul moods would have been better than this. He looked back down at the girl, and the thought that it could well have been one of his sisters suddenly rose unbidden to his mind. Junkie or not, pity flooded him for the young life lost.

Cade was right—someone had to sign off. It was procedure to protect the DSA. The Society signed off on all cases, ensuring that they were done correctly. It was needed in case the perpetrator was *Human*. Best not give them some kind of hook that was easy to get off. Of course, Stephen had no doubt, signed off or not, they would find a way. They always did.

Cade rolled the girl onto her side, looking for anything that could help solve this case sooner. He examined down her back, her arm and neck and the rear part of the head, then rolled her over the other way and froze. "Shit," he murmured, and leaned in to take a closer look. "Another one."

Harvey stepped closer and Stephen crouched back down again, frowning. "Another what?"

Cade pushed the girl's ear so that it folded over. "See this?" There was a tattoo behind her ear with a number on it.

Stephen nodded and Harvey swore.

"Five so far this year. They have all turned up dead and with numbers like this."

Stephen leaned in to get a closer look and ran his finger over the tattoo. "It's a proper one?"

"Yeah. All of them are like this."

Stephen looked from Cade to Harvey. "Why doesn't Society know about this? Or my father?"

"It does," Harvey said. "But so far, these kids ..."

"Kids?"

Cade's expression hardened. "All of them have been kids." He scrutinised the girl's face. "I think this is the oldest one we have found."

Stephen's jaw clenched in anger. "What's the youngest?" Even as he asked, he wasn't sure he actually wanted to hear the answer.

"We guess at about seven, but they're always strays. No one has ever reported them missing. I bet when I check this girl, no one will have reported her missing, either."

"We don't bother the Council with it. Usually it is just signed off and done with," Harvey added with a resigned sigh.

Five children missing and no one noticed? Stephen couldn't fathom it. One, maybe, a runaway.

But they couldn't all be runaways. "How were the others killed?"

"Overdosed."

"All of them?"

It was Thomas who spoke this time. "Yep, all of them."

"Shit."

Chapter Eight

Cade stopped at the end of the driveway that led to the Davies home and climbed out of the car. His eyes were riveted to the house, but he made no move toward it. Stephen's eyes fell to his friend's stiff posture as he stood there with his back straight and his shoulders squared. He didn't need to be a genius to know where his mind was, and he knew there was pretty much nothing he could say right now to ease Cade's mind. What a fucking mess.

He debated asking him what had happened when he had seen Gemma but then decided if he had wanted to tell Stephen, he'd have done so. Stephen decided to let him talk when he was ready. "Are you going to come in, or do we stay out here all night?"

Cade stared off into the darkness. "I don't know if it is a good idea. She doesn't want to talk to me …" He swore and ran a hand through his hair. "But being so close …"

"The wolf's going shit?"

"He's ready to smash down every fucking wall in your house. It's been days, and we've hardly spoken. When we do, we just end up fighting. I can't get past this. I think I have it right in my head, we can leave, then I hear her, and I know what I want."

Stephen leaned against the side of the car and buried his fists in his pockets. How Cade was controlling himself this much, he didn't know. *Other* men went crazy if they were kept away from their unborn child—especially an animal like a *wolf*, one that was pack. "You have to talk to each other sometime."

There was a long silence before Cade looked at him and said quietly, "I asked Gemma to leave with me. I told her we could head to the island."

Stephen went predatory still. "You mean put yourselves in Exile?"

Cade nodded slowly. "It's away from here, and we can take Phoenix with us."

The cautious admission didn't really surprise Stephen—he'd probably have wanted to do the same in Cade's position—but it didn't stop the cold fist that gripped his heart painfully at his words. "You know what is there, right? On the islands? All of our criminals, and *Humans* who don't give a shit?"

"Not all of them are bad. There are communities. And what criminals? Ones deemed by *Humans* to be wrong? But we can head for the enclosed places."

Stephen had heard of those. They were little pockets of *Others* that lived in gated areas. They were controlled and surrounded by *Humans*, of course, but on the islands, it was a *Human*-run world, and they had the power there.

"You need papers to get into there."

"I have money," Cade persisted. "I can get them."

Stephen pushed himself from the car, tension radiating from his every pore. The thought of Cade and Gemma leaving was almost too much to comprehend. The voices in his head echoed, pushing at the edges and threatening to overwhelm him. Only Cade and Gemma ever offered him any silence from it. He didn't want them to leave, but he didn't want them dead, either. Revealing their relationship and the pregnancy to Society would be equal to death. Exile might be a dangerous place,

Dark Veil

but at least they actually stood a chance of making it out there. Cade was a dominant *wolf*, a powerful and formidable opponent should anyone try to fuck with him. Whatever happened, though, Stephen would still be losing the two people—three with Phoenix—who knew him … really knew him. Maybe it was selfish that he wanted them to stay, but he knew he couldn't keep them here just for his own sanity. "Exile isn't a place for children," he said roughly, still clutching on to the last straws of hope.

Cade was aware of this, but he was also aware of his limited options. "We can't stay in the stray lands, though. They all know us."

Stephen swore silently. He knew Cade was right. They'd not be safe there ... like a fucking prize that *Humans* would hunt down for fun, and mercenary strays would hunt for payment. "What did Gemma say?"

Cade uttered a quiet oath. "She refused."

Stephen couldn't help but feel relieved, even though he knew that was the only way Gemma and Cade could ever really be together. Their relationship, as well as the baby, was doomed otherwise. "So what happens next?"

"I've got two days, and then I have to pick one of the Castle women." He pulled out some folded papers from his jacket pocket. His father had given them to him with great pleasure, to help him better make his decision. "It's like a damn catalogue. You'd think I was picking out a sofa or something."

Stephen took the papers Cade handed to him and opened them up. "Ah man, you sure got the shit end of this deal. What is this?" The thought of losing Cade and his sister was just too crushing to deal with, so right now he did what he always did when things got too heavy … he fell back on witticisms. He turned the paper upside down as if the image was too hard to see. The girl in the picture was pale—she looked like something out of a horror movie, where the girl crawls out of the television and kills everyone. Long, black hair draped around her face, her head down, eyes not looking at the camera. "Does she come with a straitjacket?"

"You shit." Cade reached out to retrieve the papers, but Stephen snatched them away.

"Could make for interesting nights," Stephen joked.

Cade stared at him, unamused. "She is the middle sister. She has some … issues."

"I'll say," Stephen snorted as he read what was on the back. "You should pick this one, though. Look." He shoved the paper at Cade, a lopsided grin on his face. "She spends most of her time locked up in establishments. You could pick her and never need to see her."

Cade stared at him. "You're a jerk, you know that?"

Stephen grinned and shrugged. "Maybe, but practical, too." He flicked to the next girl. "This one is nice."

Cade let out a frustrated sigh, but Stephen continued unabashedly.

"Hmmm … Kara …" He flashed Cade the picture of a young, attractive woman. Her long, dark hair was much like her sister's, only not looking like some matted mess. Her face was devoid of any make-up, and the picture looked more like a mug shot, but there was some kind of naivety in her face. "She's twenty-one … has her own place … a vegetarian …" A look of utter disgust and repulsion spread over Stephen's face. "Vegetation? What the

- 113 -

shit is that about? She's a fucking *wolf*." Stephen screwed the paper up and tossed it over his shoulder.

Cade watched as it landed on the driveway and shook his head slowly. If his life didn't feel like it was falling apart, he might have laughed at Stephen's reaction.

"She is a vegetarian. You don't need that shit. Go with the mental one."

"You're not my type," Cade drawled.

"Oh, touché." Stephen held up the last picture." What about this one then? Natalie. She is the oldest ... I swear, their mother must have churned these girls out one after the other ... pop, pop, pop."

"Asshole," Cade muttered as Stephen stuck his finger into his mouth and made a popping sound.

"Oh, come on. Look at her. She's pretty. She eats meat, no mental issues ... nice pair of ..."

Cade gave him a hard look.

"Teeth ... I was going to say teeth." His eyes widened suddenly as if impressed by something else he had just read. He jammed the paper in front of Cade. "Look at this. She wants to work for the DSA. Perfect." Cade exhaled heavily and fixed his gaze on the house—where his mate, and entire reason for living, was calling to him. He went to join Stephen where he was leaning against the car. Stephen stopped his teasing banter and grew quiet.

"If Gemma doesn't come away with me ... if she decides she doesn't want our child ..." Cade's voice trailed off. "Fuck."

It was a mess for sure, one that Stephen was glad he didn't have just now, although if he didn't get his shit together, his father was sure as hell going to pick a mate for him—and their taste in women was very, very different. "What are you going to do?"

"I have no idea. I don't want to mate another woman. But if Gemma carries on being stubborn about this, what choice do I have? This is Phoenix's life we're dealing with."

There was no denying Cade's words—the only way he could avoid mating with one of the

Castle women and being with Gemma instead was if she agreed to run away with him. Stephen exhaled heavily before finally saying, "You're going to have to pick one of them then … unless Gemma changes her mind."

A tick started to work in Cade's jaw. "She wants to abort the baby," He raked his fingers through his hair and expelled a frustrated breath. "She thinks that it will be best if I just go off and mate with this woman."

"And what do you want?"

Grim determination was written in the lines of his face. "Gemma."

Stephen's brow puckered in consternation. If the news of the baby came out, there would be problems—big problems—especially between *wolves* and *tigers*.

"I can't let her have an abortion, Stephen. This is our baby." He swore. "I can't even fathom it."

"I have to hand it to you and my sister," Stephen said, shaking his head. "You make my shit look like child's play." He placed a hand on Cade's shoulder, peace washing over him at the only contact his mind seemed to permit. He hesitated, then said in a sombre tone, "Whatever you decide, I'm here for you. If Exile is the way you want to go, as much as I hate the idea, I'll help you in any way I can."

Cade stared at his friend, gratitude sweeping through him. He knew how much all this was costing him too, how hard it was to make this decision. "I don't even know if Phoenix will come with us ... if he would even want to. He's got pretty attached to you and your mum."

"Yes," he agreed, "but you are more like a father to him—he looks up to you. He's bonded with you more than anyone else." Stephen didn't mention that Phoenix had been looking for his real father. It wasn't something he was willing to tell Cade about even now. It was Phoenix's choice and his right to do what he wanted. Right now, Cade couldn't deal with it ... he had enough to handle already. Stephen would talk to the boy himself—tomorrow maybe.

Cade nodded, though he didn't look convinced. He motioned towards the house with his head. "Shall we get this done? I can't think about this shit anymore."

"Sure." Maybe focusing on the murdered girl and the mystery of the strays was just what Cade needed right now. Stephen's father needed to know about the girl they had just found, as well as the other five before her. They were strays and didn't matter, but they were being killed. Maybe Society and Council needed to take notice for once. What if it got too close to home?

Malcolm Davies, Stephen and Gemma's father, was in his office, as always, sitting at his desk writing away on something. Stephen wondered how it was that he didn't either die from the boredom of it all or go blind from all the reading. One day it would all be his, and he wasn't looking forward to the shackles that chained his father to the desk. He had no desire to be a pen-pushing leader.

Malcolm sat reading the file they had given him and listening carefully as they informed him about the girl and the five strays. It seemed they had all been injected and then dumped—not all of them in water, but all of them had tattoos behind their ears, like some kind of mark. There were high rates of tranquilizers in their systems, too. It suggested they had been given them frequently, and in excessive doses. But this also meant that the culprit was probably *Human*. No *Other* would need to chemically restrain someone. What they were being killed for was another thing that they couldn't figure out.

"Who else knows about these?" Malcolm inquired when they were done bringing him up-to-date.

"Just DSA," Cade said. "They're strays … no one is interested."

He nodded and slowly rose to his feet. "I'd like it to stay that way." Malcolm was as tall as Stephen, but he was slender in his stature compared to his son's well-built frame. He strode across the room, his long legs covering the distance quickly as he headed to the other meeting room— the silent room. This was where he went when he wanted privacy. "Come with me," he instructed them both. "And close the door behind you."

Malcolm moved to the other side of the room where he kept more files and more papers. He searched through one of the drawers until he located an envelope. He opened it and pulled out some pictures, which he slid across the table to Cade and Stephen.

Mason Sabre

"What are these?" Cade asked.

"Another three that you can add to your pile." Stephen felt his stomach turn over. Three more … bloody hell. And his father hadn't said a thing to him. He was meant to be the alpha's second, and yet he had these secrets. He stared hard at his father, his anger evident, but Malcolm showed no reaction.

"Where are these from?" asked Cade.

"Other Societies."

Stephen turned his attention to the photos, deciding he needed to sit and have a heart to heart with Malcolm later on. If he was to take over one day, Malcolm had to fucking talk to him about shit. He picked up one of the photos to get a closer inspection. All the victims were female. Age didn't seem to matter; neither did what species they were, or even their colour. The only thing they had in common was their gender.

Malcom pulled out a folded map and laid it out open on the table. The locations of where the bodies had been found had been marked with red crosses. "See here?" Malcolm pointed to a spot at the top of the map. "Inverness. This is where the first body was found. The Society there didn't bother so much; they were just strays in their eyes. Then the next one moves down a bit, still Scotland, but just before the border." He ran his finger from one point to the next. "Then this one—Cumbria."

Cade grabbed a pencil from the pot in the middle of the table and indicated to the map. "May I?"

Malcolm gave a curt nod. "Of course."

Cade added red crosses to six more locations on the map, then pointed to one. "The one here was found dumped in an alleyway. Same thing ... homeless, tattoo behind the ear." He moved onto the next cross, and then the next, giving details about each incident. Each and every one had been a vagrant, each marked behind the ear. "Then we have this one, tonight."

Malcolm stood looking down at where Cade was pointing on the map, his expression pensive with each new bit of information.

"When did the one in Cumbria happen?" Stephen asked him.

"It was August—late August."

"So that is just before the first one we have," Cade said contemplatively. "The one before tonight's was three weeks ago ..."

"That means this dump was recent," Stephen mused.

"Exactly." Cade frowned. "Did we have a high tide recently?"

"I don't know." Stephen glanced down at the map, his mind looking for links. "Five bodies are a lot for the area. They get killed, and whoever it is moves on."

"Chances are they have moved on again then," added Cade.

Stephen took the pencil from Cade and drew around the Manchester area. "Here," he said and then drew around Liverpool. "And here. One is left, one is right. They're the two major places if we're looking for Society areas."

Malcolm studied the map in a long silence and then nodded slowly in agreement. "I think you're right. So far, these bodies have turned up near Societies. There is a little one in Lancaster, but that's part of this one mostly." He glanced at

Stephen and then Cade. "I need you to both go scope these areas. One each. Cade, you go to Liverpool," he pointed at Stephen, "and you take Manchester. I'll call their alphas and let them know you are coming. This stays under wraps. You speak to the alphas only. I want to know if there are more. If this is something *Human* …"

"We can't let them know we know," Stephen agreed.

"We can't give them a head start. I'll make arrangements for you to stay somewhere."

"And Phoenix?" Cade asked Malcolm. "I can't leave him home alone, and I can't leave him with my father. Trevor would …"

"Take him with you," Malcolm cut him off.

"He's just a kid," Stephen protested. "Maybe we can take Gemma, too? She can look after him."

Cade shot Stephen a look of *What the fuck* … but Stephen ignored him.

"Fine. Gemma goes, too. The four of you leave tomorrow first thing. Get your animals focused. I'll make the arrangements."

Mason Sabre

There was nothing else to discuss. Malcolm left the room, leaving Cade and Stephen staring after him. They said nothing to each other as they emerged from the room and out into the hallway. A sound from the stairs had Cade's head whirling around, his heart thudding fiercely in his chest as his eyes fell on Gemma standing there.

After a minute, Stephen rested his hand on Cade's shoulder. "I'll see you out." This wasn't the place for the shit they needed to talk about.

Once outside, Cade turned to Stephen. "What was that all about?"

Stephen raised his eyebrows questioningly.

"Us all going."

"Well, you are in an impossible situation, and how could you leave without being noticed? Take it as fate offering you a hand. Now you can both leave your homes. They expect us to be gone a while. You've just been handed a head start. Now you have to decide if you want to take it. Just make the right decision."

Stephen left Cade at his car debating his words. He didn't have a clue whether Cade would grab the opportunity or not, but he hoped to hell that his logic would make the right choice and not lead them onto a path that got them killed.

Chapter Nine

Gemma leaned against the window, staring at Cade as he stood outside talking to her brother. He didn't look her way at all, absorbed in whatever it was they were talking about. She pressed her palm against the cool glass and felt the prickle of tears behind her eyes. He didn't even glance back at the house as he walked away. Maybe he had decided he wanted nothing more to do with her. Maybe he really was that upset with her. Her heart was so heavy in her chest that it made it hard to breathe.

Days had gone by and she hadn't seen nor heard from him. It wasn't like him—not at all. It was against the *wolf,* too. She thought his *wolf* would have been clawing at the walls to get here … but apparently not. It left her feeling unsettled inside. She had thought that he would never leave her, that it would never be over between them—it couldn't be—yet, as he took each step farther away from her, her crying heart began to wonder.

She ran a hand over her flat stomach. Their unborn child was growing inside her every day, and she was alone. This wasn't how she had imagined it would be when she had a baby. It was meant to be a magical time, not one that made her scared not only for her life, but for Cade's and the baby's, too.

Gemma cracked the window open slightly so that she could listen to them, but they were too far away to hear anything above a muffled sound. She tried to lean in closer, but she only caught words here and there—nothing that she could make any sense of. Stephen saw Cade to his car and then he stood at the foot of the driveway to watch him drive off. Longing tugged inside Gemma as she watched the glow of the red lights slowly vanish in the dark of the night. Cade was going back to his home and his life, and it seemed she was a part of neither. He had seen her, yet he had left.

She slumped onto her bed and hugged herself for comfort. Her *tiger* pushed inside, asking for release. She hadn't shifted in days—not since she had found out that she was pregnant—but her *tiger* grew more demanding with each passing night. Gemma lay on her side, curling her feet up on the bed and closing her eyes. Nothing mattered. Not even running. Her *tiger* could very well burst through, but she didn't care in that moment. She lay with her hand resting on her stomach. It was still flat and she couldn't feel the life growing inside her yet, but she knew that it was there. Her skin hummed with the new life, a strange calmness to it—some kind of peace within. Maybe all expectant mothers felt this way. She wished she could ask her own mother, or even share these moments with her. Even that had been stolen from her—from both of them. Emily had borne three children. Gemma sighed and let her eyes close, hoping that sleep would take her and give her some peace. She didn't wish to be awake anymore. But just as sleep reached for her, there was a light knock on her bedroom door before it opened, jolting her from her limbo.

"Gem?" Stephen entered without invitation or answer and closed the door behind him. There was no need to turn the light on—they were both *tiger*, their eyesight perfect in the dark.

"He's gone home?" she whispered.

"Yes." He sat down on the edge of the bed and brushed her hair off her face, his gentle touch soothing. It was more than she deserved, but she needed this connection, the warmth that he was offering.

"I've fucked everything up, haven't I?"

Stephen's lips curled into a small smile. "A little bit, but life is boring without the shit we throw into it." He slid further back onto the bed so that Gemma had to move her legs to avoid getting them crushed. He patted the side of the bed next to him and motioned for her to join him. She sat up and shuffled over with her blankets, wrapping them around herself as he placed and arm around her and she nestled against his chest.

He must have been for a run. He smelt of the earth, a scent that she craved, one that called to her inside. She closed her eyes and made herself push past it, but her skin prickled, her *tiger* agitated.

"He's not going anywhere, you know."

"He didn't even say hi."

Stephen pulled her in tighter against him, making her feel safe for a moment—safe from the outside world at least. "He doesn't want to fight." Stephen shifted to get comfortable, but didn't let Gemma go. "Are you really going to let him get mated to one of those woman?"

"What choice do I have?" she said miserably. She had thought through every possibility at least a hundred times. Her mind was tired, none of the damn scenarios seeming to end in any kind of happy ever after. Most of them ended with her or Cade, or both of them, dead, and that wasn't something she was willing to risk. "If I get rid of the baby, then there is no threat. Everything would be how it was."

Stephen slid down a little so that he could face his sister. He stroked her cheek with warm fingers. "If you get rid of the baby, Cade will never forgive you … and maybe neither will you. Can you really do it? Could you let someone kill your child?"

No. No, she couldn't. She knew it, Stephen knew it, and maybe deep down inside, Cade knew it, too. She closed her eyes and rubbed down her arms. The itch bubbled just under the surface of her skin, all the stress of everything making it feel a hundred times worse.

"Are you okay?" asked Stephen, frowning. "And I don't mean all of this shit, I mean physically."

She bit down on her lip and nodded. "What was he here for? Cade, I mean."

Stephen hesitated, concern etching his features. When Gemma waited patiently, he said, "I found a girl today. She was dead ... probably murdered." Gemma's breathing grew shallow, as if she was struggling to breathe. Stephen scowled at her. "Are you sure nothing is wrong?"

"I'm okay," she whispered. "Tell me about the girl."

He paused before reluctantly continuing. "I was running near the Estuary and I spotted her in the water. Some fucker had weighted her down, but the tide must have gone out and I saw her. I had to call it in ... got the DSA down there."

"Cade is working on it?"

"Yeah. He got called out."

Gemma sat up slowly, crossing her legs as she did. Her mind swam with everything, her *tiger* very close to the edge. One wrong move from anyone and she was going to snap. The *tiger* just needed the nod. "Was it someone important?" she asked. Not that she cared so much right then, but it helped to focus her mind.

"Just a stray."

Mason Sabre

Gemma opened her eyes and frowned. "I don't understand. Why did Cade need to come here if it was just a stray?" She rubbed up and down her arms again, the itch seeming to spread upwards. No matter how much she scratched, she couldn't quite get rid of it.

She could feel Stephen watching her, but she couldn't stop scratching. The itch inside just got deeper and more intense. "She was body number five." He eyed her suspiciously. "They all have tattoos on them, so they are linked in some way. We needed to tell Dad that."

"What do you mean?" Gemma started scratching at her legs, her nails digging deep into the flesh of her thighs.

Stephen pushed himself up. "Gem, what's wrong?"

"Nothing." She scratched and then let out a growl of frustration as the itch moved again. It was all over her, like tiny ants under her skin. She leapt from the bed, panting.

Stephen sat up at her sudden movements. "Gem?"

Her eyes were shifting—she could feel it. The world began to change in her vision, the colours blurring into one, like looking out through a kaleidoscope. The sounds around her became nothing more than a muffle. She backed away, almost losing her balance and falling over.

Stephen was off the bed in a heartbeat. Gemma saw him as a fuzzy silhouette as he rushed to her, blinking to try to clear her vision. She vaguely felt hands as they gripped her arms, Stephen's voice coming from far away. Sharp canines dug into her bottom lip as her body started to transform of its own volition.

"No," she whimpered. Pushing her tiger back down, she fought the change. She dug her nails into her palms until the pain started to give her some grasp on reality and helped her focus long enough so that she could take the helm from her tiger. Gemma opened her eyes and found herself crumpled onto the floor with Stephen kneeling down in front of her calling her name.

"Gem, what's going on?" She tried to talk, but her mouth refused to form the words that lay jumbled in her mind. Stephen narrowed his eyes at her. "When did you last shift? The truth."

"I don't know," she managed breathlessly, the effort to keep her *tiger* back a tremendous struggle. The *tiger* wanted out and she wasn't taking no for an answer. "Maybe the shift makes me lose the baby ..."

"Shit, Gem." Stephen pulled her up and tilted her head up so that he could look at her. She stared back at him through eyes that were still *tiger*. "You've been holding back? Since you found out?"

"I don't want to risk it ..."

"And you tell me that you are unsure whether you want this baby. I think it is pretty obvious right now just how much you do. You need to shift, tabby cat," he said affectionately. "You know you do or your *tiger* is going to make you, and then what? You could lose the baby then for sure."

"I can't ..." her voice trailed off in a pathetic whimper.

"You can." He slid his arms under her knees and around her waist, and with no effort at all, picked her up and carried her out of the room. The land at the back of the estate their parents owned was a mass of trees and fields—perfect for running. Stephen carried her away from the house, determination in his every step. Gemma was thankful their parents hadn't heard anything and come out to investigate. When they were far enough away, Stephen set her down carefully. "You need to shift, Gemma."

She leaned against the fence that surrounded the grounds and nodded. "I know, but ..."

"There are no *buts*. You need to do this."

She stared at him with desperation in her eyes. "What if something bad happens?" She was being illogical, she knew that. Women shifted with babies inside them all the time and nothing happened to them. But what if life was waiting to punish her and take away the gift she had been given because she had been debating abortion.

"What's going to happen when your *tiger* is feeling so caged that she bursts out without you being able to stop her? You'll be lucky to survive yourself then." His jaw set into a grim line. "You need to shift."

"Are you sure? Do you promise?" she whispered.

"Do you think that Mum didn't shift when she was pregnant with us? She's never lost a baby, and she is wife of the alpha. She'd have shifted a whole lot, you know that."

"I wish I could ask her." Pain pierced her heart with that thought. She was missing that bonding moment.

Stephen nodded. "I know, but maybe we have to trust nature this time. If you weren't meant to shift while pregnant, your *tiger* would stay back, right?"

"She's been the opposite—like she wants out more than anything."

"See? There can't be any harm to it, because she wouldn't do that. Your body is made for it. I'm right here ... let your *tiger* free."

She hesitated, still scratching and gouging her prickling flesh. "Will you shift with me?" she asked, suddenly feeling panic rising in her chest. He'd shifted earlier so he'd have no need for it now, but she needed him there with her. The prospect of running out in the dark alone filled her with dread. She wanted him there, by her side. Maybe if he was with her, nothing bad could happen to the baby. His presence was powerful and made her feel secure. He'd keep them both safe. "Please, Stephen?"

He ran his knuckles down her cheek, a tender brotherly caress. "Okay. Give me a minute, tabby."

She could have sobbed in relief, even though she knew he'd not have refused her. Stephen would give his life for the people he loved—and that was a very few. He piled his clothes with hers, thick, roped muscle moving fluidly under smooth skin, the tattoo that ran down his arm and back more like intricate shadows that had always been part of him rather than something he had chosen to mark his body with.

"Ready?"

It took Gemma a few minutes before she was able to see her *tiger*, the apprehension in her mind an obstacle that wouldn't let her focus. She breathed in deeply and tried to centre herself. She had to tear down the protective walls she had built around her *tiger* and let her out. Stephen was right there—she was safe.

The shift came slowly at first, seeping in slowly. The bones in her hands began to move and realign, her claws and teeth gradually emerging. The feel of her ascending *tiger* was comforting, a friend she had been missing, and she welcomed her.

Please keep the baby safe, she begged her tiger. *Don't hurt it.* An almighty growl ripped through her in answer, sending shivers along her spine. When she opened her eyes, it was to look out through those of her *tiger*.

She searched for her brother and found him standing a few feet away from her, his *tiger* big and magnificent in the night. Their eyes met and in silent agreement, they both set off in a leisurely run into the woodland.

Stephen had been right. She didn't want to get rid of the baby.

But how could she keep it?

Chapter Ten

The sudden and violent hammering on his front door yanked Cade from his sleep and sent his heart racing. He jolted out of bed, adrenalin surging through his veins. He glanced at the clock on his nightstand ...

Two in the morning.

"Fuck." He snatched the lounge pants from the end of his bed and hastily pulled them on. Bloody hell, it had taken him hours to fall asleep. Couldn't people just leave him in peace? The hammering came again. "I'm coming, I'm coming," he muttered angrily as he ran down the stairs, glancing back at Phoenix's bedroom door and hoping— futilely—that the racket hadn't woken him.

When he opened the door, cool night air rushed in to meet him, along with a very pissed off Stephen, "Jesus man, how long does it take you to answer the bloody door?"

He pushed past Cade into the house without an invite, but Cade wasn't interested in Stephen or his snide remarks just now. His eyes were on

Gemma, who stood quietly in the doorway staring back at him with her big, beautiful green eyes. She still had the power to take his breath away with her mere presence. He wanted so badly to reach out and drag her into his arms, his *wolf* needing for touch, its need to hold and protect and claim its mate consuming.

She stood there clutching her coat around her, even though the night was warm. Cade balled his hands into fists to keep from reaching for her. "Is something wrong?" he rasped, sudden dread filling him. "Something with the …" he swallowed hard, "… baby?"

"The baby is fine," she said softly, her voice a light caress on his frayed nerves. They stood there staring at each other, uneasy and unsure how to act or what to say. "May I?" She motioned to the room behind him, and Cade could have kicked himself for his inconsideration. With a quiet oath aimed at himself, he quickly stood back to let her into the house.

Stephen was in the kitchen, head stuck in the fridge as he searched its contents. "Don't you have anything decent to eat?" he grumbled. "I'm starving."

Cade absently gestured to a plate of rabbit that was on the side, uninterested in Stephen or his hunger. His eyes stayed riveted on Gemma as she walked to the kitchen table and sat at the spot she always liked to pick, her movements feline and graceful. She drew her leg up and wrapped her coat more closely around herself.

Stephen seemed unaware of the tension in the room, or pretended not to notice. He stared at the plate as if Cade had just offered him sludge. "Wow. That's disgusting," he said, screwing up his face. "I still don't know how you eat that shit."

Cade glared at him, wondering how the hell he could be thinking about his stomach when Cade's world was falling to pieces around him.

"Do you know I have shifted twice this evening, and the only thing I actually managed to bite was some tatty rag off a corpse?" Stephen continued to complain bad-temperedly. "I could waste away; you know?"

"I didn't expect dinner guests at fucking two in the morning, or I might have got you something."

Gemma was unusually quiet, no sarcastic or teasing remarks of her own for Stephen. Concern creased Cade's brow and permeated his very essence "Is everything okay?" he asked her softly, paying no mind to Stephen as he continued to gripe about him dying of starvation and no one caring.

Before Gemma had a chance to answer, Phoenix pushed the door open cautiously and peered through the gap. His eyes lit up when he saw Gemma, and he pushed the door open the rest of the way. "Hey," he beamed at her, and she returned his greeting with a warm smile of her own. When he saw Stephen standing there, a huge grin spread across his face, making Cade's heart squeeze painfully in his chest. Could he really take Phoenix away? Uproot him from his life when it was only just getting stable? Take him away from the people he had grown attached to? His gaze fell back to Gemma, discerning the sadness in her eyes despite the smile on her lips.

His jaw set in a determined line. Yes … he had to protect them both.

"Hey, loser," Stephen said affectionately. "Wake you?"

"Nah," Phoenix said casually, trying to look cool and unconcerned.

"Good. Then you can come tell Mr Stick-in-the-mud over here to start keeping *normal* food around the house from now on." Phoenix chuckled and sent Cade an apologetic look, well aware of Stephen's preference for freshly-hunted game and his continuous harrying of Cade over it. Stephen took a bite of an apple he had eventually grabbed from a fruit bowl on the counter and turned his attention back to Cade. "I told Gem about the bodies," he said between bites. "And about us having to go to Manchester and Liverpool."

Cade glanced at Gemma, measuring her reaction, but she rested her chin on her knee and fixed her gaze onto a spot on the floor, not saying a word.

"I told her that maybe it would be a way for us to get you both away. Give you a head start kind of thing ..."

"That's all very well," Cade said before he could stop himself, "but she doesn't want to keep the baby." He couldn't keep the bitterness from his voice, but when he saw the pain that flashed across her face, he immediately regretted his words. There was such fury in him, such pain that she would have even considered hurting their child, that while one part of him sought to protect her from any kind of sorrow, another couldn't stop being angry with her. Why didn't she realise that he was hurting, too? It was all in her hands. It was her body, her choice, and whatever she decided, he would have to live with that. He never imagined that one day he would have to beg for his child's life.

Both Stephen and Phoenix had frozen, standing there quietly as they waited for either Cade or Gemma to say something. Phoenix knew about the baby—Cade had talked to him the same night. He didn't like to keep secrets, and the bond between them would make it hard anyway. He would have to try to lock Phoenix out every single minute, and that was impossible. At least if he told him, he didn't have to worry about keeping his mental shields in place.

Stephen cleared his throat suddenly. "Maybe Phoenix and I should go out and hunt something. There's nothing edible in this god damn place and I'm a grown *tiger* ... can't expect me to survive on bloody apples ..."

While Cade knew it to be a pretext to leave them alone, he was grateful for the privacy they were being given. He didn't look at them as they left the house, his gaze steady on Gemma as they stared at each other.

"I don't ever mean to hurt you," she said meekly. "You mean everything to me. It is the last thing I want."

Cade's features hardened, and his anger rose again full force. "Is this where you tell me that you're booked in to … how did you put it? Get it *fixed*?"

Gemma pushed back her shoulders and kept her stare level with his, refusing to look away. "Stephen made me shift today. I didn't want to because I was afraid, but he made me anyway. My *tiger* was about to rip me apart." Concern flickered in his eyes but Cade said nothing, letting her speak. "I didn't want to shift … because I was afraid," she repeated tremulously.

Her lip quivered and it took every ounce of mental resistance Cade had to stand there and not go to her. She wiped at her eyes and took a deep breath.

"Of?" he prompted, his tone gentler this time.

"I thought that I might lose the baby if I shifted," she said softly. Cade's stomach twisted with hope and fear all at the same time.

"You didn't want to lose the baby?"

She shook her head forlornly. "It's part of me ... it's part of you."

Cade was kneeling in front of her before he could stop himself. He gripped the side of her seat, scared to death of the 'but' that was to come. "What does this mean?" he asked in a hoarse whisper.

"I'm not getting an abortion, Cade," she sobbed. "I can't."

"Gem ..." Cade breathed her name gruffly, relief washing through him.

"It wasn't meant to be this way."

He cupped her face, his eyes searching hers in a desperate attempt to make sure he hadn't heard her wrong. "Maybe it was ... maybe this is how the baby was meant to come into our lives. We'd never have planned one together." He slid his hands down the sides of her legs until she lowered them to the floor, allowing him to slide between them. He rested his face on her thigh and placed a kiss there, his arms slipping around her middle and holding her tight. He finally had what he had been starving for—Gemma and his unborn baby. He squeezed her more tightly when he felt her fingers thread in his hair. "We'll really do this?"

She hesitated. "What if you die?"

Cade pushed himself up so that his face was a breath from hers. He breathed her in—she smelt like apples and soap. "I'm not going anywhere. I promise." He slid a hand up to cup her cheek. "Together ..."

Gemma turned her face into his palm and placed a kiss there. Then his lips were on hers, hungry and demanding. She opened for him, needing the touch of her mate, her *wolf*—hers. When Cade reluctantly broke the kiss, it was to reach for some papers wedged under the plate that he kept his loose change in.

"What's this?" She frowned as she took the papers he handed her.

"I have to pick a mate," he said. "I have a day left and then my father wants an answer. I don't want to answer him because you're not one of them, but if I don't choose by midnight, he is coming for Phoenix."

She froze, and he could sense the distress in her. "Does Phoenix know?"

Cade shook his head. "I figured I would just pick one. It doesn't matter which … they aren't you … they never can be, so what does it matter?"

Gemma stared at the papers in her hands but didn't open them. Cade had retrieved them from the ground where Stephen had tossed them and had tried to flatten them out.

"Stephen chose the top one for me." Despite all the joking and ridiculous teasing on Stephen's part, if Cade had been forced to choose one of them, Natalie was most probably the safest bet like Stephen had suggested.

Hurt flashed across Gemma's face. "Stephen helped you to choose? He helped you to look for another woman?"

"No … shit … it wasn't like that …" he floundered. "Stephen was just being Stephen."

Gemma nodded, but the hurt was still there. She eyed the papers in her hands. "I don't know if I should look. Is she ugly?"

"Fuck ... I don't know, Gem," Cade said uncomfortably. "She's not you."

She took a deep breath and opened the papers slowly. When she saw the woman who was Natalie in the photograph, her eyes brimmed with tears. She brought her hand to cover her mouth and stifle a sob. "Oh god. This is real, isn't it?" Her eyes searched his. "You'd really mate with her?"

Cade stared at her in earnest. "If you don't leave with me, what choice would I have? I'd have to. I can't let them take Phoenix. He is just a kid."

She didn't answer for a minute, letting his words sink in. "When?"

Cade frowned.

"When do you have to mate?"

"I don't know ... maybe when Aaron has his first born. I can't have children till then anyway, so I think that right now it is just a matter of having to pick one of them and make an official announcement. But until Aaron has a child, I'm not obligated to do a damn thing. Couldn't risk the precious throne being stolen by my child."

Gemma gave him a weak smile. "They don't realise you already have."

Cade took the paper from her and threw it back onto the table. He rose to his feet, bringing Gemma up with him and, like he always liked to do, slid his hand along the side of her neck so that his thumb rested against her jaw. He held her there for a minute and simply drank in the sight of her. She was so damn beautiful —and she was his. He pulled her to him and lowered his mouth to hers. Their kiss was gentle this time, one that held a promise of belonging to each other forever.

"We have to leave, don't we?" she asked when he let her go. "We have to try to get away."

"There isn't another way." He slid his hand down to her abdomen—his child was in there. He couldn't feel the swell of it yet, but he could feel it. This child, as well as Gemma and Phoenix, were his sole purpose in life. "You and this life in here mean everything to me. I would leave and walk all the way to Exile if I had to."

Chapter Eleven

Apprehension was not a feeling that Stephen liked to feel. It put him on edge and the voices in his mind grew louder and more jumbled, making him feel like he was going crazy. He tried to focus, to shield the parts of his mind that were threatening to tip into chaos. He couldn't lose it … not now.

He shifted in his seat, but he couldn't get into a position that was comfortable. His *tiger* inside demanded out—demanded it go and protect the young *wolf* that it had somehow become bonded to. He couldn't fathom the connection amongst them all—Stephen was inexplicably linked to Cade and Gemma on a psychic level, and through that link, he had bonded with Phoenix the moment Cade had. He couldn't explain it, but it was there, as was his *tiger's* violent need to protect the boy. The boy was walking into danger, and they both knew it. Yet, it wasn't a danger that Stephen or his *tiger* could do anything to protect him from—it was one that had the power to break his heart and soul. One that was regrettably necessary to give him the closure that he needed.

Agitated, Stephen sat in the car waiting, tension rolling off him in waves. Fuck, this had been a bad idea—such a bad idea. He had taken off his seatbelt and put the car into park so that he could jump out if the need arose, but that was all he could do ... sit, wait and listen as Phoenix made his way from the car to the house he had once lived in. He wound the window down enough so that he could hear more clearly what that asshole of a father would say to his son.

Stephen was sure that Cade would kill him if he found out he had brought Phoenix here. All logic told Stephen that Cade would be right—Phoenix was about to get his heart shattered. His father would reject him, Stephen was certain of that, but the hurt in the boy's eyes had told Stephen that he needed this. It was the only way for Phoenix to let go of his past and accept his new life. There was a big, gaping hole inside him at the moment, and while confronting his father today would not fill the void, it would help him tend to the painful wound at last and gradually let it close.

Stephen rubbed his eyes and face and rolled his shoulders to try to push out some of the stiffness in them. God, he was tired—he had driven miles to get here in good time and his back ached in a way that told him he badly needed to shift and sleep. But they were in *Human* lands ... to shift here would mean he could be shot on sight. They wouldn't ask any questions—just another dead *Other* for them, that would be all that mattered.

He pulled the papers from the glove box for the tenth time and checked them. Cade, Gemma and Phoenix's faces greeted him, but the names matching the pictures were those of Sam, Anne and Nathan Brooke. It had cost him a small fortune for these, but it was worth it—the alternate as Cade and Gemma took their chances in the straylands. Anger surged through him, the unfairness and unethicality that sometimes existed in the world of *Others* infuriating him. Gemma and Cade would be lucky if they made it to the end of day one.

It had been three days since they had left the safety of the Society. Stephen and Phoenix had travelled to Manchester and delivered the information to the Council there. They had shown them what to look for and asked them to check any bodies that were found in the same fashion. So far, it didn't seem they had any. That either meant that the area hadn't been hit, which was highly unlikely, or that they just hadn't got there yet. There was, of course, the other possibility, that the Council there just didn't give a shit.

Cade and Gemma had gone to Liverpool and done the same. Stephen didn't know how that one had gone yet. He hadn't spoken to them since, but the plan was that they crossed the Mersey and then headed towards the ferries that would take them to the Islands.

Stephen's job was to get the papers and then meet them. They would hide out in a cheap bed and breakfast that had been rented for a week under a false name. Stephen could afford a day's delay. It was a long drive there and back, but if it gave the boy closure, it was worth it.

This might be his last chance.

Phoenix had wanted to stop at the cemetery first, and Stephen could tell the boy had needed to pluck up the courage to ask him if he'd mind. In response, Stephen had made a stop at a flower shop and given him money to go buy some flowers. With a shocked but deeply grateful expression on his face, Phoenix had awkwardly stuffed the money into his pocket without looking at Stephen and returned a few minutes later clutching a bouquet of red roses—his mother's favourite, he had murmured.

Once outside the cemetery, Stephen offered to go in with him, but Phoenix had said it was something he would like to do alone. Although he had never lost anyone that close to him, Stephen understood his need to be alone in this moment.

Phoenix had been red-faced when he came back to the car, but Stephen had said nothing about it. If he needed to cry for his mother, then he could cry all he liked. There was no shame in it, nor did it make him weak.

He tried to keep an eye on him now as he approached his old family home, having purposely parked in a position that would give him the advantage of being able to see the front door.

Phoenix walked to the house but didn't enter the small driveway at first. Rather, he stood at the gate and stared at the house that had once been his home—once been his safe place. The garden was overgrown now, the sight of it tearing at Phoenix's chest. His mother's flowers, all dead … just like her. He supposed that no one bothered to care for them now that she was gone. Even the white cladding around the bay window was dull and lifeless, his mother's tender care missing. It had come away in places, and his dad hadn't made any effort to patch it up. Sadness filled him, his mother's absence flaring bright in the dereliction.

He glanced up at the window that was once his room and was surprised to see there were no curtains hanging in there. It was just a window— empty. Maybe all of his possessions had been thrown out, just as he had been.

"Eric?" The sound of the small, careful voice behind him startled him. He turned slowly, heart pounding in his chest as he came face to face with a little boy with eyes much like his mother's. Phoenix could only stare at his brother at first, his mind having gone blank. He was taller than he remembered, but other than that, he looked just the same.

"Grant?" Phoenix's voice came out gruff, the emotion in him threatening to overwhelm him. He hadn't seen his brother in two years, when he had been six and Phoenix had been barely fourteen.

The younger boy's smile grew wide, and he raced to Phoenix, arms flung open. Phoenix kneeled and caught him in a tight embrace, almost toppling over from the force of the collision. Grant clung to his big brother, his scrawny arms wrapped tightly around his neck. Phoenix wasn't the skinny kid that he had been when his father had thrown him out, lean muscle now defining his young body and strength abnormal for any *Human* child. Phoenix was grateful for Stephen's mother's concoction—disgusting as it may taste, it had done miracles to build up his body. His brother seemed weak, however, and not because he was only eight. Despite the strength in his embrace, Phoenix felt that if he squeezed too tight, he could break his little body.

"I thought you were dead," he said tremulously. "Dad said you were …"

Phoenix tensed. "Dad told you that?"

Grant nodded vigorously into his neck. "He said that you ran away, and then he heard you had died because you were too sad about Mum."

Dead? Did his father really believe that? Or was it all just lies he had made up? *You're dead to me.* Those had been his father's parting words to him. Maybe he had kept that up ... maybe he had meant it.

Phoenix disentangled his brother's thin arms from around his neck and gently held him in front of him. "He didn't look for me?"

"He said you'd come home when you were ready. Jenny asked lots of times, but then Dad would shout at her. He said you were gone ..." Grant stopped abruptly, breathless. "Is it really you?"

Phoenix smiled. "Yeah, it's really me. Except they call me ..."

"Eric ..." Stephen called from a few feet away, cutting Phoenix off. He had got out of the car and was walking over to them. Phoenix frowned—it sounded strange to hear Stephen saying his real name.

Seeing Grant's eyes grow wide as he stared at Stephen approaching, Phoenix quickly said, "This is my friend, Stephen." Stephen was a big man—tall, muscled and dangerous-looking. He didn't want his little brother getting scared.

Grant's head tilted all the way back and his eyes grew wide as he looked up at the man towering over him. "Are you *Other*?" he asked without fear.

Stephen smiled and bent down to the young boy. He let his eyes shift ever so slightly so that the green glittered with flecks of gold.

"Wow," the young boy breathed, mesmerised by what he saw. This was *Humans* before they learnt to hate everything.

"Grant, Get away from them." The order was barked from an older man—much older. Phoenix froze. "Move … now." He approached them at a brisk pace and yanked the young boy away. Stephen put his hands up in surrender to show that he meant no harm.

"Dad. It's …"

"It's no one," he cut him off, dragging the poor boy back towards the house.

"But it's Eric. Look, Dad … he isn't dead," he shouted excitedly as he tried to prise his dad's grasp form him.

His father's stony stare fell on Phoenix, his eyes piercing with a hatred that burnt his flesh. "This isn't Eric. This is a monster." he spat hatefully. "Eric is dead."

"Dad …"

"Get back in the house."

"But …"

The man glared down at Grant.

"Grant, it's okay," Phoenix said to him. "Go." He didn't want to get him into any more trouble than he probably already was. "I'll see you again," he said with a smile. Even from where he was standing, Phoenix could smell the putrid stench of alcohol coming from his father. It was a mixture of fresh and stale booze—the kind of smell that men got when they drank so much that they sweated it out of every pore.

His father took a step forward, his face twisted with hatred. "Like hell you will." He pointed towards the door. "Get back in the house now, Grant."

"But Dad …" Grant pouted.

Dark Veil

"Don't push me on this." The man's words came out slurred and Phoenix realised his father was drunk. Grant needed to go inside so they didn't anger their father any more.

Grant's stare jumped from his father to Phoenix, his will to defy his father clearly evident in his eyes. With determination on his boyish face, he didn't go into the house like he had been told, but instead, went to Phoenix and wrapped his arms around him. "I'm glad you're not dead," he whispered.

Phoenix hugged him back tight and pressed his lips onto his brother's head.

"Let go of him," his father growled, and Phoenix wasn't quite sure which son he was talking to. He set hard eyes on Phoenix. "Why are you here?"

Guilt-ridden about all that had transpired in the past, the death of his mother and his role in it, Phoenix's stare wavered, unable to look at his father. "I came to see you …" he croaked.

His father's face contorted with anger. "We don't want you here," he snarled. "We don't want to see you. Now let go of my son."

Mason Sabre

Before Phoenix could take a step back, their father lunged and grabbed for Grant. His brother's arms flailed as he was yanked back and his father backhanded him across the face, knocking him down. Phoenix shot forward, but Stephen grabbed him and stopped him, his face an inscrutable mask. His eyes darted to his brother—Grant's face was red, his eyes wet as he fought to hold in his tears.

"Get in the house now." The small boy stumbled back to the house at his father's command, his head down. When his father turned icy eyes back to him, Phoenix felt the full force of all his hatred. "What did you think? Did you really think that you could just come here? Saunter in after what you did?"

Phoenix's heart sank. "I …"

His dad moved closer and Stephen slapped a hand against the man's chest. "Back off," he growled. Phoenix's father glared down at Stephen's hand as if it were something disgusting that had dared to touch him.

"You …" he pointed at Phoenix accusingly, "you're one of them. You're …" His words faded as he staggered to the side and forgot what he was trying to say. "Get out of here. Fucking *Other* shit bastards." He shoved at Stephen's hand, and Stephen let him knock it away.

Phoenix put his hand up. "Dad ..."

"Don't you call me Dad, you filthy monster." He lifted his hand to hit Phoenix, but Stephen had grabbed him by the throat and pinned him to the side of the house before he could get anywhere near him. Plaster crumbled to the ground from the force with which he shoved him against the wall.

"Don't you fucking dare," Stephen growled. The man stared back at him, his eyes burning with pure hatred.

"He is my son. I can do whatever I damn well please."

"Stephen ... don't ..." Phoenix pleaded hoarsely from behind him.

Stephen stared at the man with menace. "You need to clean your shit up. If I ever fucking find out you've been hitting your child again, I will be back."

"It is none of your business ...."

Stephen's grip tightened around his throat and his father gasped as he struggled to take in breaths. "I am making it my business. Hit the children again and I will make you regret the day you were born."

Phoenix grabbed hold of his wrist. "Please, let him go, Stephen." For a moment, Phoenix thought he wouldn't listen, but then he released him abruptly, giving him one final shove against the wall as he did. His father's hand flew to his throat, coughing and choking as he wheezed for air.

"You don't deserve either of those boys." Stephen pointed a threatening finger at him. "You're nothing but a fucking drunk."

"I'm sorry," Phoenix said to his father. "I just thought … just that … maybe you'd looked for me."

"Why would I look for you," he hissed, rubbing at his throat and keeping one eye on Stephen.

Stephen muttered something unflattering about *Humans* and pulled Phoenix towards the gate. Phoenix glanced back at his brother and stopped, forcing Stephen to stop with him. Grant was standing hiding by the door, watching his brother walk away. "You can come with me if you want to," he called out to him.

Grant glanced over to their father, but his father was too focused on Stephen to be bothered with him. Grant shook his head slowly, the fear in his eyes clear. Phoenix's heart sank, knowing he was leaving his little brother in the hands of their cruel father.

Phoenix stood still at the gate for a few seconds—he saw his father for the first time, *really* saw him. He was nothing more than a pathetic drunk and a bully ... not the father he had known or grown up with. Maybe he was dead to him, too. He wasn't something to fear any more—he was something to pity. Stephen had proved that. Phoenix walked back past him to Grant and wrapped his arms around him one last time before leaving. "The offer is always open," he whispered to him. "I'll always be here for you." He squeezed him tightly before letting him go. He turned to their father, who stood there gritting his teeth at the brotherly embrace. His eyes kept shooting to Stephen, fear flickering in their depths. Phoenix stared at him without fear this time. "If you ever lay another hand on him, I will take him away from you and you will never see us again."

Without waiting for a response, Phoenix turned and walked back to the car, shoulders pulled back. He didn't spare his father another look—he wasn't going to let him see the hurt he had caused.

Stephen followed Phoenix to the car, fury coursing red and hot through his veins. *Humans*. He could never understand them—never understand how they could do things like this. It didn't matter how loving they were to their children; they could change in a matter of a heartbeat.

Funny … it was *Others* who had been christened monsters.

Chapter Twelve

If there was any place in the world that Gemma loved to be, it was lying beside Cade with his arm around her and her leg resting across his. It was the place that felt the most right. She snuggled against him, revelling in the warmth of his hard, naked body beside hers. This was the first time they had managed to be alone since she had told him that she was pregnant. Her lips curved into a smile as she thought about how gentle and protective he had been with her when they had made love during the night. He had made her feel safe—like nothing could harm her or the baby.

According to the digital clock on the bedside table, it was five in the morning— too early to get up yet. They still had a couple of hours before they had to meet Stephen, who would be bringing their papers. Gemma tried not to think about it so much. The more she did, the harder and more impossible it seemed to become. It still wasn't real yet—more like a dream than something they could actually do. *Could they do it? Could they really leave?*

She thought about her mother the most. Surely Emily had dreams of her own about her grandchildren and when they would come. Gemma was sure as hell that they didn't involve secrets and her daughter running away. It wasn't meant to be like this—it was supposed to be a magical time, when a mother passed down the lessons she had learnt to her daughter to prepare her for the pregnancy and the birth. Gemma hated the idea that she would miss all that. A sudden longing for her mother filled her—she would miss her so much. She would miss her dad, too. He might be the Alpha, he might be head of the Council, but inside, he was still her dad. She remembered how he would play with her when she was young; he hadn't always been so serious. Maybe the years as leader had done that to him, or maybe she just had never really recovered from her parent-hating teenage years. It made her face flush sometimes when she thought back to the way she had acted. God knows what had been going through her mind back then, though Stephen had been far worse. Maybe their dad had just got hard to it all.

Cade rolled onto his side and dragged Gemma closer. "Not sleeping?" he murmured, his voice thick with sleep.

"Thinking."

He peered at her through half opened eyes. "Uh, oh. That doesn't sound good." He breathed in deeply and tucked her closer to his side, his strong arms bands of steel around her. The sleepy warmth of his body seeped into hers, his scent so typically masculine and musky, a fine blend of man and *wolf* that she loved so much. Sometimes, she couldn't get enough of it. "It'll all work out, you know? You'll see."

For someone with such a logical mind, Cade was always the one who relied the most on things happening as they were meant to, some hand of fate that would push everything into alignment at the right moment. *Maybe that's just how he deals with fear,* Gemma thought. She could be wrong, but when he couldn't control the situation, that was his go-to thought. Maybe she should do the same— putting his life in the hands of fate seemed to save Cade a lot of worry.

It was such a vast contrast to her brother. Stephen was a fuck-it-and-see-what-happens kind of man. The two men were so different in temperament that it had always amazed Gemma that they had ended up being best friends. If something was a high risk, likely to go very wrong,

Cade would reconsider his options and try to find a more rational approach. Then, he'd take the one that he thought best in the end—even if there was still a certain amount of danger involved. On the other hand, Stephen would grab the bull by the horns, say fuck it, and do it anyway.

But Gemma couldn't be like either of them. Her mind simply turned things over and over again until she was ready to scream from it. There were just so many things that could go wrong. "What if we get caught?"

Cade kissed the top of her hair. "What if we don't? Have you thought about that?"

Legs intertwining with his, she buried her face into the crook of his shoulder and closed her eyes. Maybe she could sleep for another hour. "I don't want anything to go wrong."

"It'll all be okay, you'll see," he reassured her softly. His hand slid up her back and strong fingers tangled in her hair, pulling her head back gently to capture her mouth in a sultry kiss. No matter how much he kissed her, how much he held her, it was never enough. The *wolf* demanded full possession of her, wanting to be mated the same way Aaron was about to be, so that everyone knew that she was his and no one else's. He deepened the kiss and she opened to him willingly, his tongue sweeping in to taste the sweet recesses of her mouth. She moaned softly as he broke away so that he could trail hot kisses along her neck and nip his way down to her full breast. She let out a small gasp when his mouth closed over the turgid peak and sucked her nipple into his mouth, rolling it with his tongue until it hardened enough for him to take between his teeth and bite down gently. He let out a low growl of approval when she arched her back, pushing herself more firmly into his mouth. She let out her own growl as desire overwhelmed her senses and she was burning up for him. His hand slid down along her back, leaving a trace of goose bumps in its wake. "Cold?" he whispered against her skin.

"No," she breathed huskily and tried to pull his head back onto her breast. She felt him smile against her before resting his hand on the curve of her back and pressing her closer. He opened his mouth wider to take in more of the lush fullness of her breast, the hot wetness of his mouth and the flick of his tongue sending lightning through her body. She moved her hand down between them and wrapped her fingers around the rock hardness of him. A groan escaped him and his entire body tensed. With a tight hold, she started to stroke him, slowly at first, and as his attention on her breast became more eager, she sped up.

Another growl tore from his throat, deeper this time. His hands moved down to squeeze the soft flesh of her buttocks. His *wolf* was there, ready, waiting, wanting. The world had shifted when he opened his eyes—new colours, deeper, richer clearer—every sense suddenly alight within him.

He pulled her hand from him abruptly and Gemma tugged her hand back in protest. Any objection died on her lips as he lifted her, both hands on her smooth backside. She gasped at the sheer strength of him as he lifted her up and rolled at the same time, bringing her with him. In the next minute, she was straddling him, breathless as she looked down into his handsome face. Fingers gripping onto the tops of her thighs, he tried to push her down onto him, but her legs tightened around him and a devilish grin spread across her face. Pushing his arms up over his head, she looked down at him and smiled seductively.

"Not so fast." Cade groaned in frustration and craned his neck to capture a taut nipple in his mouth as she leaned over him She gasped and nearly lowered herself down onto him. He thrust up in response, but she quickly pushed up off him once again. "Uh, uh. Not yet."

He growled, not happy with being denied what he was aching for. "I guess you're done with the thinking part?"

"I need a distraction." She leaned down and nipped at his bottom lip before pressing her mouth to his for a searing kiss. A deep growl rumbled against her lips, demanding more. God she loved him so much, it overwhelmed her at times. She wanted to crawl inside him and stay there forever.

His head back fell back as she kissed along his jawline and this time, when he slid his hands down to cup her bottom, she didn't stop him.

"How about this?" he murmured, slipping one hand between them to the slick heat at the apex of her thighs—she was so wet and ready for him. She sucked in a breath as he slid his fingers through her drenched folds, her heart thumping loudly in her chest.

"Cade …"

His mouth was on hers again, cutting her short. "Yes?" Her body tensed when his fingers found and circled that spot that brought her the most pleasure.

"Cade ... stop it." Her words came out weak, breathless, with no conviction. "You're cheating."

"You want me to stop this?" He pressed harder, circled more firmly, then thrust his fingers inside her. She arched her back and cried out. God, she was so ready for him, so wet. Gemma breathed his name over and over again as his fingers continued to tease and flick and stroke. "Doesn't seem to me like you really want me to stop."

"Cade, you need to ..."

She didn't get to finish what she was saying—her body had others ideas. It didn't help that Cade was holding her in place. He felt it coming, felt the build-up in her body. He pressed his mouth to hers as her body shuddered and her pleasure rode her. She threw her head back with a cry and he groaned from the sight of her coming apart in his hands. She nearly gave in and sat herself down just where he wanted her. But as she tried to push herself up again, Cade grabbed hold of her hips and pushed her down so that she took all of him in— deeply, completely. Gemma's eyes grew wide and she gasped.

She was burning up, need spreading through her like wildfire. She slid herself up and down again, the thick fullness of him inside her making her breath catch. She bit her lip at the sheer pleasure of it. "I hate you," she panted and then whimpered as he thrust upwards to match her movements as she rode him. He placed strong hands on her slim hips and pushed her down again so that he was buried deep inside her once more, picking up speed and setting the rhythm. She leaned onto him, hands flat against the solid wall of his chest, her breathing ragged as she moved with him. When he lifted his head to flick his tongue over the sensitive tip of her breast and then take it into his mouth, Gemma thought she would explode. She dug her nails into the smooth skin of his chest, her senses on overload. When he turned his attention onto the next breast, a husky cry escaped her and she begged.

He reared up suddenly so that she straddled his lap and her legs were wrapped around his lean hips. "Oh, god," she whimpered as the new position pushed him back into her slick heat to the hilt. He bit down gently on the fullness of her breast, growling possessively against the lush mound. She groaned and dug her fingers into the hard muscle of his back. The pressure built and grew until she couldn't hold on any longer. Cade thrust deeper, harder, faster—relentless in his devastation of her senses. Gemma's head fell back, her body clenching like a hot fist around him. A scream tore from her, his name ending in a hoarse whisper on her tongue. Cade felt his own climax rise, unable to hold his own need at bay. He let go, his fingers tightening on her buttocks as his own release came with a guttural growl. His arms slid around her trembling form and he held her tightly to him, the aftershocks of her orgasm still rolling through her. When his own body eventually stopped shuddering, he continued to hold her close, burying his face in her neck and breathing her in. They stayed joined together for a moment, panting and damp with perspiration until they both caught their breaths.

Gemma pulled back slightly to look at him, a soft smile playing on her lips. She brushed his damp hair back and stared into his eyes. His face was beaded with perspiration, his cheeks as flushed as hers felt, but his blue eyes were bright. "Do you promise that it will all be okay?" she whispered, still trying to catch her breath.

He gripped her chin gently with his fingers and drew her to him for a hot kiss. "I promise. Together, remember?"

She nodded and gave a small smile, wanting desperately to believe his words. "We need to get ready and go to meet Stephen."

"You shower," he said tenderly. "I'll go find us some breakfast."

She smiled and kissed him before getting up. She didn't bother to dress as she walked to the bathroom, and Cade let his eyes travel appreciatively down her soft curves, wishing he could pull her back to bed and spend the whole day there—just him and Gemma and their baby. His hunger for her seemed insatiable. She disappeared into the other room and a minute later, there was the sound of water running. His mind drifted to Phoenix, wondering how he was doing. In just two years, the kid had come to be such a huge part of his life. But soon, he would grow up and move on— he was almost an adult now. It scared Cade a little if he admitted it. When Phoenix became a man, would he leave and disappear? Walk out of Cade's life as easily as he had walked in? Cade had got used to having him around these last couple of years.

But Phoenix wasn't his …

Gentle knocking brought Cade from his thoughts, and he frowned. His *wolf* snarled, uneasy and wary. Something was off. It was too early for any kind of maid service, and there was no familiar scent from whoever was standing on the other side of the door Senses alert, and his *wolf* warning that something wasn't quite right, Cade slid out of bed quietly and pulled on his jeans from the chair beside the bed, careful not to make any noise. The door handle moved down slowly and his *wolf* growled a warning. He crept to the door and the next thing he knew, a loud echo sounded through the room and he was suddenly falling. In the next moment, he lay crumpled on the floor, clutching at his throbbing shoulder. He stared down at his torn flesh where a silver bullet had just pierced his flesh.

Someone had just shot him through the fucking door.

Two *Humans* and an *Other*—a male he recognised from reception—entered the room, the lock splintered. Confused and weak, Cade tried to call out to Gemma, but his jaw locked tight. The fucking silver had already snaked through his veins and up along his spine, paralysing him as it went. He fought the pain and numbness and grated out her name. One of the *Humans* stepped over him, unconcerned, and headed towards the bathroom. Cade tried to crawl along the floor, but his body wasn't responding. He heard Gemma scream before he saw the man dragging her wet and naked from the bathroom. "D-Don't hurt her," Cade rasped. "Please … sh-she's pregnant."

The *Human* standing with the gun aimed at Cade's head brought his foot forward so it connected with Cade's jaw, sending him rolling back helplessly. He reached for Gemma just before darkness and the silver completely took him.

Chapter Thirteen

Stephen put his head down and charged at the small *wolf* that was just up ahead of him. His paws pounded against the woodland ground as he gained momentum. The *wolf* better move, or he was going to get run right over, and it would hurt—a lot. The *wolf* stayed right where it was, though. In fact, it turned, squared its shoulders and faced the oncoming *tiger* without fear. It lowered itself to the ground, his ears and tail up, showing no intention of submitting to the fully grown *tiger* that was heading his way.

The *tiger* was fast, and as he got closer, the *wolf* dug his hind legs in, getting ready for the incoming impact. He listened to the sound of the *tiger's* paws, taking in the tempo of each step so that he could counterattack at just the right moment.

The *wolf* was ready. He waited until the *tiger* was just a tail's length away and then he leapt up, thrusting himself forward, directly at the *wolf*. The *tiger* twisted, not having expected the *wolf* to react in such a way. He slid and landed awkwardly on the cold ground. The *wolf* was young, but this meant he was small and fast and the *tiger's* fall gave him an advantage. He leapt for him with jaws wide open, canines aiming for the *tiger's* throat. The *tiger* feigned to the side and then leapt—they clashed mid-air. They tumbled back onto the ground and spun away from each other. The *wolf* slashed a paw across the dirt, flinging twigs and dead leaves into the *tiger's* face and blinding him for a moment.

Phoenix ran hard and fast. He pushed himself to get away from Stephen, his paws picking up fallen leaves as he tore through the woodland and leaving a backlash of spray behind him. The *tiger* was coming. He was close behind. A scent in the breeze stopped him in his tracks—earthy and warm— a very afraid rabbit. The *tiger* noticed it, too, because he stopped and crouched low. They stood facing one another, the rabbit somewhere between them. The *tiger* slunk forward with feline grace. In one swift move, he uncovered the rabbit hiding beneath the foliage. He snarled at it, orange and black fur rising to show off long, sharp teeth. The rabbit spun on itself and bolted. Not seeing the *wolf* laying low, it ran right into Phoenix's waiting jaws. Phoenix bit down on the rabbit's neck, giving the animal a quick and merciful death—just like he had been taught.

There was a difference between killing for food and killing for fun. The danger would be if he ever started to enjoy the hunt and the killing in a way that was cruel. Of course, he should enjoy it as part of his shifter—it was who they were—but to take pleasure in the pain of the animal was another thing. The blood gushed into his mouth as the animal's life bled away. When it went limp and its heart ceased to beat, Phoenix flicked his head to the side and tossed the rabbit onto a pile of three other rabbits he had already caught. Stephen's pile was one less, and he bared his teeth at Stephen in a wolf-like smile. It was the first time he had ever beat him.

He was learning fast—Stephen was impressed. Even though tonight was more down to his own tiredness rather than anything else, he had to admit the boy was getting good. He was making it so that Stephen had to add real challenge to the mix. Actually, he was beyond tired—he was downright exhausted. He fought to stay awake as he and Phoenix sat together and ate a rabbit a piece. They weren't going to eat them all just now—that would be greedy. They would sling the others into the back of the car and have them later for when they couldn't get out and hunt.

The air was cold around them. The sky held only stars, no clouds, giving promise to a frost overnight. They could choose to sleep in the car or in the woods—Stephen had voted for the latter. They would sleep as their animals tonight. It was warmer that way, their fur, and the way their blood ran higher, giving them protection. Stephen was a little unsettled about it, though. It was one thing to be able to shift to animal, but another to stay for a long time. For him, it wasn't a bother, but he had grown up with the warnings that if he started to sleep as his *tiger*, eventually he would become more animal than man. It was Phoenix he was worried about—the half-breed—the one who wasn't used to living this way. Yes, he had had two years of it, but he had never slept as his *wolf* before. Hopefully, nothing bad would come of it.

When they were done eating, Stephen made a very feeble attempt to clean himself, the effort great. They both found a spot where one of the trees had fallen, its roots standing vertically, giving some shelter from the cold. Stephen curled up into it and let the small *wolf* tuck himself into him. They fell asleep like that, curled up together, their body heat keeping each other warm.

Stephen was asleep in seconds.

He had no idea how many hours had passed when he woke, but he felt refreshed. He often did when he had slept as his *tiger*, everything inside him replenished with such greater speed. He stretched his paws out in front of him, to shake out the tension from sleeping so still and suddenly froze. Phoenix was no longer curled up beside him. His heart missed a beat and he sprung up.

"Morning." Phoenix had shifted and stood a few feet away. It wasn't quite light yet, but the sky wasn't as dark as before. The sun was just around the corner, giving off a warm glow. Stephen nudged him with his snout, telling him off. "I couldn't sleep as my *wolf*. It was too weird. I had strange dreams."

Stephen growled in response. Yeah, he had forgotten those—the dreams. Being one's *tiger* or *wolf* brought you deeper inside yourself, closer to what was there—closer to the very thing that made a person who they were. The soul communicated through dreams. That was what he was told anyway. His glance fell to the pile of rabbits. It was one less meaning Phoenix had eaten another. Stephen slid one away from the others and sat back to chew on it. It wasn't as good as it would have been the night before, the freshness gone, but it was still better than that defrosted shite that Cade ate. God, how could he stand it?

When he was done, he shifted back and got dressed, then stretched. He always felt so good after a shift, his entire body brand new.

"We'll go and meet up with Cade and Gemma now?" Phoenix asked, plonking himself down on the ground and leaning against the trunk of one of the trees. Dark circles had formed underneath his eyes, even though he claimed to have slept.

"Yes," replied Stephen, pulling his watch from his pocket. "Be about a four-hour drive, three maybe if there is no traffic and we make good speed."

Phoenix was quiet. He had said very little about the incident with his father, but it had to be on his mind. Anything he spoke about was Cade or Gemma, and even that was just on the surface. Stephen guessed it was his right, though. "Shall we go?"

The car was parked along the embankment. Stephen almost couldn't believe it when he had

Mason Sabre

managed to find a place for *Others*. It wasn't the best of places, he had to admit. Shabby at best, but there had been rabbits to catch, so that was something. What he wouldn't give for fox, though. Stephen was glad to see that the roads were quiet. Everyone was still tucked in at home, the day's commuters not having hit the road yet. It meant that he could put his foot down and maybe they would make good time.

*   *   *

They made only one stop on the way, and that was to use the bathroom and to grab coffee. Stephen used the break to call his dad and check in with everything. He knew he'd be up. He was always up at such an ungodly hour. The best way to keep Malcolm thinking that everything was normal was for Stephen to act normal—and calling early would be normal. Stephen wasn't much of a sleeper himself, which was why he knew his dad would be up. "We'll be home in a day or two," he told him. It was enough to buy Cade, Phoenix and Gemma some time, he hoped at least. He would meet them later and send them on their way, then take a long drive home. It would be strange to go home and the three of them not to be there. He could feel the emptiness of it just waiting around the corner to catch him.

Phoenix fell asleep half an hour into the last stretch. Stephen watched as the world went by him and the sun rose high in the sky. The roads began to get busy again, the exhausts and revving of engines filling the air as cars started to pour onto the motorway. He didn't wake up until Stephen slowed the car down and took the exit for the motorway services where they were to meet. "Are we there?" he asked, yawning.

"Just about." Stephen squinted. "I can't see Cade's car."

Phoenix pushed himself up in his seat. "They're not here yet?"

Stephen reversed the car into a spot just in front of the coffee shop so that he could see any cars coming in. He cut the engine and put the brake into position. "No." He yawned then pushed his seat all the way back and crossed his arms over his chest. "I'm going to close my eyes while we wait."

Phoenix was left sitting there staring at a slumbering Stephen. He scowled then rummaged through his bag to pull out a book. He might as well read. There was nothing else he could do really.

Stephen heard the flap of pages and smiled inwardly. The damn kid could devour an entire library. He certainly was the child that Cade had not had yet, he mused as he started to drift into sleep.

The car door banged closed and Stephen jumped awake and had his hand around Phoenix's throat in a matter of seconds.

Phoenix gasped, staring at him, wide-eyed. "Sorry," he croaked, hastily holding up two paper cups. "I went to get coffee. "

Stephen let go fast, swearing softly. "You had money?"

Phoenix suddenly looked sheepish as he rubbed his throat. "No ... but you did."

Stephen patted his pocket where his money had been. "You pickpocketed me?"

Phoenix grinned and then pointed to one of the cups. "It's nice coffee. I got you one, too."

The scowl that crossed Stephen's features wasn't because he was mad at Phoenix—it was mostly for show. He took one of the cups and sipped the hot liquid. "You're damn lucky it is," he muttered. It wasn't that Phoenix had taken the money that bothered him, it was that he hadn't woken up when he had done it. In fact, he hadn't woken up when Phoenix had left the car, either. That, on its own, was worrying.

He rubbed his eyes then glanced at the clock. They had been waiting there for an hour now. "No Gemma or Cade?"

"No. I haven't seen them."

"You've been awake this entire time?"

"I was reading." Phoenix picked up some paperback he had open in the middle.

Stephen swore under his breath. "You might have missed them?"

"No. Every time I heard a car or something, I checked. Couple of cars, some big lorries and vans ... that's about it."

"Shit." Stephen shoved his cup into the little holder near the handbrake and climbed out of the car. The car park was pretty much empty, like

Phoenix had said. It was too early for people to be stopping just yet. "Shit."

"This is the right place?" Phoenix asked as he got out of the car after Stephen.

Stephen nodded. "Yep. We meet up here all the time." He leant on the bonnet of the car and rubbed at his face.

"Maybe we can go to where they're staying? You know where it is, right?"

Stephen narrowed his eyes at Phoenix. "Can you feel Cade?" He was referring to the bond Cade and Phoenix shared. When Cade had found Phoenix, he had bonded with him, making them inextricably linked.

Phoenix shook his head slowly, fear suddenly flitting across his face. "There's nothing there."

"Fuck, we need to go. Get in the car."

Chapter Fourteen

Cade rolled onto his back and tried to stretch out his arms and legs, but they were as heavy as lead. With great difficulty, he managed to open his heavy eyelids. Flashes of light came in, stinging his eyes. His jaw ached from where someone had kicked him in the jaw. A shiver ran down his spine from the cold air around him. He blinked a few times and forced his eyes open, but he couldn't focus them. The world had been transformed into flashes of white and silver.

Despite his weakness, his senses prickled. There was someone else in the room.

"I think he might be waking up," a voice said from somewhere on his right.

"Gemma …" He tried to push himself up into a sitting position, but it proved impossible. His body was so heavy, a deadweight he couldn't move, his mind fuzzy.

"Let me help him," another voice drawled. Cade cracked his eyes open and squinted towards the unfamiliar male voices. There was a blur of movement and then something cold and wet splashed into his face. He sputtered as water gushed into his mouth and streamed down his chest, soaking him. In a weak attempt to shield himself, he lifted unsteady hands up in front of him, but they got brutally knocked away. He tried to turn his head to breathe, but the powerful spray was relentless.

"Maybe we woke up the big, bad wolf," one of the voices mocked, which brought with it a chorus of laughter. Three people—Cade was able to distinguish the number of voices when the water ceased. With great difficulty, he finally managed to roll onto his side so that he could get up into a sitting position. His back ached, his head so heavy he was unsure how he was even holding it up himself.

Metal clanged to one side of him and something squealed—rusty hinges perhaps. He was in a cage? He peered through weary eyes to take in his surroundings. The gate was open and a man crouched down in front of him, a lopsided smile on his face. He had a scar just along his chin, making it look like some kind of deformed dimple.

Cade gulped for breath, his body shivering from the cold and weakness. "Wh-who are you?"

Cade's teeth chattered from cold. The man sneered at him and rose, giving him no reply. "Where's Gemma?"

"Did I give you permission to speak to me?"

Cade had no strength to react as the man brought his booted foot forward and kicked him square in the jaw. Cade reeled back, the world spinning around him.

"You *dare* to fucking speak to me again, and I won't be so easy on you," the man barked before turning the water onto Cade once again. His heartbeat pounded in his temples as he tried to breathe and get air, spluttering as the water hit him hard and fast. His *wolf* thrashed inside, pushing against Cade's skin, wanting out, the need to protect and to fight consuming. He did not cower in the face of danger, least of all to *Humans* who stood behind weapons. His *wolf* was ready to eliminate any threat. Cade gritted his teeth and tried to hold him back—he couldn't risk getting himself killed before he had made sure Gemma was safe and sound.

Cade rolled onto his stomach, head down. The water pounded onto his back, whipping his flesh. His fingers and face began to shift, his claws and teeth elongating. "Oh no, you fucking don't," the man said when he realised what Cade was doing. The water stopped instantly, the gate swung open again and something heavy pressed Cade down. A sharp sting in his arm told him he had just been injected with something. He growled, the sound half animal, half man as pain tore through him. He slumped onto the wet ground and then everything went dark.

A while passed before he roused and started to feel his body once more. He lay perfectly still, though, not about to alert anyone to the fact he was gradually regaining consciousness. He could sense people there, and he wasn't about to set off another onslaught of whatever shit this was. He needed to be ready for them this time, not half-dazed and helpless. He moved his toes slowly, pins and needles shooting up his legs. Keeping his breathing slow and even, he listened carefully for any sign that the men had realised he was awake. He needed to find Gemma, and that wasn't going to happen if he didn't get the hell out of there.

The ground beneath him was solid and hard, concrete no doubt. Warmth flowed through his limbs as his circulation came back and the blood began to flow properly. It travelled along his arms, then through his entire body, and despite the heaviness in his body, he was sure that if he wanted to, he could move. He peered through hooded eyes, fighting the urge to look for Gemma. He let the world slowly into his vision, just enough so that he could see his surroundings and what was going on. One man came into view. He was sitting alone, his back to Cade, reading a paper. Cade moved deftly so as not to alert him.

There was another cage next to him, not like the ones in the Society basement, which were made of silver, but a normal iron-barred cage. The silver that had been injected into his veins, however, ran through him like fire. In the cage next to him, a mass of auburn hair splayed out across the concrete. Gemma …

Cade shot up without thinking, his heart thundering in his ears. The man sitting outside the cage turned, and then his face broke into a malicious smile. "Hey, you're up." Cade vaguely realised that he was still wearing his jeans, but they were dry now. How long had he been out of it?

The man headed to the door of the room they were in, and Cade twisted himself to reach into the other cage. "Gemma," he muttered. "Gem ..." She was lying on the floor with her back to him, her body deadly still. He reached in and stretched out, almost touching her. He tried to get a grasp on her top—she was dressed at least. That was lucky for the *Humans*, he thought, not for Gemma. If they fucking touched her, they would pay for it, and it would be a long, slow, painful payment.

A man came into the room, clean-shaven, square jaw, with the kind of smile that put you on guard and told you not to trust him. His voice held the charm of a snake. "Patterson," he introduced himself.

Cade's hands balled into fists. He fucking should have known it.

"Don't worry about your little girlfriend there. She's quite okay. Just sleeping. Women," he smiled insidiously, "you know how they are. Get in these places and start screaming like bitches." Paterson adjusted the cuffs to his shirt, pulling his suit sleeves down in place and flattening out the creases.

"What do you want?" Cade ground out.

Patterson smiled. "Straight to the point. I like that."

Cade's *wolf* had perked up, ready, but he was biding his time, knowing the leaping out right now would cost him. Patterson was like prey—watch him slowly, learn his movements, learn what will spook him and what won't. Patterson was a coward, Cade knew that from dealing with him before, but today he had a sense of bravado—the cage. But it wasn't so much the cage that held Cade back, but Gemma in the cage beside him and what they might do to her. "What have you done to Gemma?" he demanded.

"Relax, wolf. She's fine. Just sleeping." He leaned close the bars, his eyes locking with Cade's. "Don't worry," he whispered conspiratorially, "the baby is fine, too … for now."

Cade lunged for him and Patterson laughed and took a step back. He tsked, smoothing his suit down once more. "What do I want? Well, that is the question, isn't it? In good time, my friend. All in good time."

"I am not your fucking friend."

Mason Sabre

Patterson put his hand to his chest, taking on a mock expression of offense. The *Humans* with him sniggered and laughed. "Do you know what strange thing happened to me last night?"

Cade scowled.

"No? Well, I was sitting down with my wife having dinner when I got this phone call. Now I don't normally take calls when we are having dinner, as I consider it rude, but I was very pleased that I decided to take that one. It was one of your type—an *Other* who works in one of my hotels." He paused, watching for an expression on Cade's face, but Cade wasn't about to give him the satisfaction of any kind of reaction.

Cade stood quietly, listening. He'd landed in a god damn *Human* hovel. Figured.

"Anyway, the guy at the desk called me. He couldn't believe it; the queen of the crop had walked in with this *wolf*." He leaned closer. "That would be you if you don't know. And guess what? She's pregnant—fucking pregnant." He laughed, a gleeful, nasty laugh. "He could smell it on her like a whore in heat in the middle of a summer's day. Boy got so excited he could hardly speak when he called me. And then you book into a double room and shit, even I got excited. It was easy to work things out from there on—you, her, a pregnancy, secret room, not one in your Society. It made me wonder, what had I done to deserve such good luck? To be handed you both and not only that, you've broken the god damn laws of your own people." He chortled with delight. "What would you give to avoid persecution, to save your whore from execution? Do you know what I realised?"

Cade didn't answer.

"Anything. That's what you'd give. Do you know that Norton industries would be very interested in a mix-breed baby? All I've got to do is call wee daddy up and tell him the predicament and offer to fix it for him. What do you think he is going to say?" He leaned in closer, a smug expression on his face. Cade's arm shot out of the bars and his fingers wrapped around the surprised *Human's* throat. He yanked him forward and slammed his face into the bars. Patterson clutched at Cade's wrist as the other *Human* in the room scrambled for the keys to get the gate open, yelling for help all the while as Patterson gurgled and choked from the might of Cade's hold.

"Let us go," Cade said to him. "Right now. Or I'll make sure you regret it for the rest of your life."

The *Human* got the gate open, but he paused. Patterson's eyes had grown huge from his struggle to breathe, his eyeballs bulging and he tried to suck in desperate lungfuls of air.

"Come on in, I dare you," Cade growled at him, his eyes at a half-shift.

Another *Human* came barging in, his eyes quickly taking in his boss's dire situation. He rushed past Cade's cage and went straight to Gemma's. Cade's heart skipped a beat. *Fuck.*

"You let go right now, or sleeping beauty gets put to permanent sleep."

Cade and the *Human* locked stares, then with a curse, Cade let go of Patterson abruptly and he staggered back, clutching at his throat as he wheezed and coughed. The *Human* at his cage charged in, bat in hand, knowing he was safe with the threat of Gemma hanging over Cade's head. He swung the bat and Cade's arm took the brunt of the blow as he lifted it to protect himself. Cade kept his eye on him, showing his dominance despite being unable to fight back. The bat had been coated in silver and Cade's arm burnt where it had hit him. The man swung again and hit Cade in the side on his bare ribs, slamming him into the bars at the back.

Gemma's eyes fluttered open with a start and met Cade's just as he slid down the bars. With terror on her features, she reached out for him but the man caught him with the bat against his face. Pain shot through his cheek as he pitched to the side. "Please, stop it," Gemma cried. "Please don't hurt him."

The *Human* stood over Cade, bat hanging at his side and beads of sweat rolling down his forehead. "Your bitch is going to watch us kill you for that little stunt."

Cade swayed where he sat and tried not to pass out from the blow to the head. He called to his *wolf* but the silver had slowed him down and dulled his wits.

Gemma's cage opened and the *Human* entered. It was all Cade needed to wake his *wolf*, silver or not. His mate was at risk—nothing would hold him back.

Cade snarled as the man lifted his bat again.

Chapter Fifteen

Stephen didn't know what was happening. One moment he was driving along the motorway, and the next, Phoenix was having a convulsion next to him. His head lolled and his eyes rolled back in his head, choking sounds gurgling in his throat. Stephen's arm shot out to hold him in place, a steel barrier against his chest. He pulled the car onto the hard shoulder abruptly and quickly unfastened the boy's seatbelt. Phoenix wheezed, his eyes open wide, unfocused.

Stephen gave him a firm shake. "Phoenix."

"I can't breathe …" he managed.

With an oath, Stephen pushed Phoenix's head down and ordered him to take deep breaths. He had no idea what the hell was wrong.

Phoenix's head jerked back up after a minute, his face contorting in pain. "I … Cade …"

Stephen's blood ran cold. "Something's wrong with Cade?"

A slight shake of his head and then he tensed again. His body shook as if he were being electrocuted by some invisible force. Stephen unfastened his own seatbelt and grabbed Phoenix's wrists to try to steady him. But it was a mistake. Whatever it was riding Phoenix fed into Stephen, and the moment his hands connected with Phoenix, Stephen couldn't breathe, the breath knocked from him. He had to focus himself, remind himself where he was and what he was doing. He was sitting in the car, going to meet Cade. When he got his bearings, he let go of Phoenix and let himself breathe a moment. Cool air wafted in through the window he had wound down, the sounds from the outside helping to ground him somewhat. Phoenix began to calm as well, but his face remained flushed, his eyes watering as he leaned back and sat there silently watching the cars speed by them.

"Are you okay?" Stephen asked after a moment.

Phoenix licked dry, parched lips and Stephen grabbed a bottle of water from the backseat, quickly uncapping it and offering it to Phoenix. Phoenix gulped the water down until he had drained the bottle. Panting as if he had run a marathon, he said, "Something is wrong … his *wolf* …"

"Whose *wolf*? Cade's?"

"I saw it … but not Cade. Like …"

"Like?"

"It's like they aren't together." Phoenix tilted his head and looked at Stephen. "When I see Cade when he talks to me through the bond, I can see whichever one it is, but the other is there, you know? Like in the background."

Stephen did know. It wasn't easy to explain, but he knew what he meant. It was like there was a piece connecting them both and they always came together. He nodded for Phoenix to carry on.

"Now it is like they aren't there. Cade isn't there … but his *wolf* is."

Stephen frowned. "Are you sure the *wolf* is *his*?"

Phoenix nodded. "I know his *wolf*. I know all of the markings."

Stephen had no doubt that he did. He reached a hand out to Phoenix, but avoided touching him. He wasn't doing that again just yet—those shakes and visions were enough. Touch always made the voices in his head worse, opening

some door for them to break through. But then
again, maybe he could see things Phoenix couldn't.
His fingertips hovered just above Phoenix's hand,
not making that last move.

Eyes fever-bright stared back at him. "Do
you want to see?"

For someone who was only sixteen, he
seemed to know an awful lot. His eyes took in
everything, even though he stayed quiet. He must
have caught on to Stephen's 'ability'. "I'd like to try
if that's okay."

Phoenix offered his hand to him and Stephen
simply stared at it for a moment. What was going to
come of this? He had no fucking idea. "If something
happens with me, let go."

Phoenix nodded and Stephen took a deep
breath and clasped his hand tightly. He kept the wall
inside up this time—he had been ready for the
onslaught in his mind. He let it down slowly,
opening the door between his mind and Phoenix's
with caution. Beyond it was what looked like a
sterile, white room, but as Stephen gradually let his
guard down, colour was added. A bit here, a little
there. The *wolf* was at the far side, but he was faint,

more like some faded picture than anything real that he could touch. "Cade?" Stephen spoke in his mind rather than out loud. "Cade, is that you?" The *wolf* didn't move nor did it indicate that it had heard him. Something dark and malevolent pushed on the edges of Stephen's mind, and he tried to throw a shield up, pushing it back and burning the feeling of sorrow with it. "Cade ..."

He walked toward the *wolf*, a feeling of weightlessness surrounding him, but his chest grew tighter with each step he made. A sense of paralysis seeped into him and spread through his body, starting in his feet, then up his legs. Still, he kept moving, trying not to think about how hard it was to actually move. He focused on the *wolf* ahead and tried not to make sudden movements. As he approached, he noticed that the *wolf* wasn't breathing.

Maybe he is dead.

The thought hit Stephen like a truck. He faltered, gasping and fighting as the world tried to jump into his mind all at once and control him. He dropped onto his knees and clutched at his head, refusing to let it in and take him over. Pain lanced through his jaw and it started to lock into place. He could hear muffled voices ... someone was crying ... screaming. His stomach twisted with a sickness that he didn't understand. Panting, his palms flat on the ground, his head down, he desperately tried to put all the pieces of his mind back into one place.

He slowly lowered himself onto his stomach, and then he was moving slowly, slithering rather than a crawl. He had to get to the *wolf*—he didn't know why, but he knew that he had to. When he reached out to it, he expected to feel nothing more than the cold tiles of the floor, but what he touched was warm fur, the softness of it wrapping around him. "Cade?" he said, his voice hoarse. "Cade, is that you?"

The *wolf* moved slowly, turning its head to the side so that Stephen could see its eyes. They were Cade's eyes, blue, but not the *wolf* Cade, but Cade as a man. It was like they had swapped somehow. Was this what happened inside when they shifted? Did the animal become the man? Shit. He had a temporary shift somewhere. Stephen caught the *wolf's* face in his hands, pulling him around by the fur so that he could look right into his eyes. Maybe he could reach Cade through Phoenix. "Are you there? Cade? Can you hear me?"

Silence. Absolutely nothing—not even the sound of his own breathing. Maybe it was the shields that he had thrown up in his mind. He let them down a little, using everything he had to control them and prevent the world rushing in. Running a hand through the *wolf's* thick fur, he brought the *wolf* closer to him so that his snout rested against his shoulder. He held him in an embrace and closed his eyes, taking in the familiar earthy scent that was Cade and his *wolf*. He let his mind slip into Cade's. It was dark in there, the opposite of Phoenix's mind. There was something else in the darkness ... something sinister ...

Shit. It was silver.

No sooner had the thought entered Stephen's mind than his skin started to burn. His mouth filled with water and suddenly he couldn't breathe. He clutched at his throat as his chest constricted and his airways shut down.

Stephen's eyes snapped open and met with Phoenix's panicked ones, his face sickly pale. His mouth was dry, not wet, his heart pounding loudly in his ears. He hadn't moved, still sitting in the driver's seat of the car. Phoenix sat there watching him, not saying anything. Stephen let his eyes close and when they did, it was all there again—all of it. He was in a cage … *the* cage? He couldn't be back there. Maybe this was just a bad dream. Nothing more than a memory of the time Cade and Gemma had spent at Malcolm's.

But no, it wasn't the same. He cracked open heavy and tired eyes. Gemma was there, next to him. She was sitting, up, but her eyes were filled with unshed tears. Her matted hair clung to her face and she had a bruise across her check. Stephen tried to reach out to her, but he couldn't make his arms move. Someone else was there, too. Someone darker … someone *Human*. He squinted to try to focus better, but it wasn't working. Two men—no three—none of them made any sense. One of them came closer, the thick fog making it hard to distinguish any features.

Suddenly, Stephen's head snapped back, gasping as he came free of his mind's hold, his heart beating wildly in his chest.

Phoenix started and let him go. "What is it?"

The rush of air made it too hard to speak.

"Stephen?"

"Did you see? Can you see what I did?" he rasped.

Phoenix hesitated then nodded slowly. "What was it?"

"*Humans ...*" He swore violently. "Fucking *Humans* have Cade and Gemma."

Chapter Sixteen

The car wouldn't move fast enough for Stephen. He had the pedal jammed to the floor of the car as he manoeuvred his way around the cars that filled the motorway. He shot a look at the speedometer. "Come on. For god's sake, move." He swore and slammed his hand down on the horn several times. "Get out of my way," he yelled at the cars blocking his way. Stephen didn't give a shit how many laws he had just broken or how many road violations he had just committed. All that mattered was getting to that damn hotel and finding what had happened to his sister.

He had no idea how the *Humans* had found them there. It was meant to be a secure place—one that helped strays. Maybe they hadn't been careful enough and someone had spotted them. Whatever it was, he needed to get there and fix it. Guilt urged him forward, cursing every time he had to slow down so as not to plough him and Phoenix into the back of some slow, dawdling driver. He was the one who had booked this room for them. His mate, Raven, a panther, rare in the shifter world, had told him about the place. He was one of the few friends he trusted with his life.

Raven ran one of the bars that was a balance between Society and strays. He played both sides and he played them well, but he was honest and decent and trustworthy—qualities scarce in a person. The lack of spots in panthers was considered a leopard deformity, one which made panther shifters die off quickly. They didn't tend to make it through infancy, but Raven had.

Stephen screeched the car to a halt in the courtyard of the hotel—it was more a stately home than a hotel really. The restaurant built to the side of it was for *Others* who weren't shifters, although some restaurants did specialise in raw meats, but they were expensive and mostly under the radar of *Humans*. Eating there was usually by booking only. It was where he was supposed to be meeting Cade and Gemma this morning. Stephen stopped the car right outside the reception office. Who cared if it blocked the way … Stephen certainly didn't. Stephen knew the room number so he didn't bother to check with reception. He took the stairs two at a time with Phoenix close on his heel. When they got to the room, he found the door locked.

He pounded on the wood with his fist, even though he knew there was no one inside—he could feel it. "Cade? Gemma?" They had been there, though; he could smell their scents. They hung in the air like a trail of invisible breadcrumbs for him to follow.

"They're not there," Phoenix said, his face full of concern.

The putrid stench that *Humans* always left behind like some kind of toxic bio marker was rife in the air. Without preamble, Stephen twisted the lock with his bare hand and broke it. The door swung wide open to reveal an empty and clean room—too clean. The scent of bleach was suffocating—only *Humans* would think that it was enough to cover up scents. The bed had been made, the sides polished and fresh towels hung on the rack in the bathroom, all the patterns lined up perfectly. New cups sat on the side and a fresh toilet roll had been placed on the back of the cistern.

"Smells like they were just here," Phoenix remarked.

"Yes. That's what I was thinking." Stephen laced his fingers together behind his head as he paced for a moment. "Shit." He turned back to Phoenix. "You know your link thing? With Cade? Did you see where they were? Did you see the *Humans*?"

"No. I tried when you were driving, but it was like he is gone."

Stephen struggled to keep his frustration in check. He rubbed at his face. *Think, think …* "When Cade was in the cage two years ago, you couldn't feel him then, right?" At the time, Cade had been stuck in Malcolm's cage for twenty-four hours for breaking Society law.

Phoenix was busy rummaging through the drawers in the room. "No, but it was like he was gone."

"Like now?"

Phoenix contemplated that for a moment before shaking his head. "No. When he was in the cage, it was like before the bond. Just me in my own head."

"And right now?"

Stephen knew the answer, but he had to ask anyway.

"He's here. I can feel him, but it's what I said. It's just his *wolf,* and the Cade part is missing."

With a colourful oath, Stephen went back to his pacing. Cade couldn't be in a cage of silver, maybe that was the difference. Maybe this was just a plain cage. But if that was the case, why didn't he break out? *Others* were strong enough to manipulate and bend man-made iron or steel bars. Why was Gemma crying? He tried to piece everything together—a jigsaw puzzle.

The hotel management had to have answers. They'd know if they had checked out or whether people had come looking for them. Stephen turned abruptly and strode out of the room, leaving Phoenix to follow.

There was a woman sitting behind the desk at reception. Pretty little thing—blonde hair, long nails, perfect kind of bimbo look—but only a fool would believe her harmless. She wasn't shifter, but she was *Other*—Fae. They were magical "hippies", creatures that could control the elements—earth, fire, water and wind. They might not have the physical strength of shifters, but their powers were great.

"Excuse me, miss."

She looked up from where she sat delicately filling in some paperwork, and Stephen vaguely wondered how her long nails didn't piss her off when she was trying to write. Her gaze travelled over him appreciatively and she sat up a little straighter, a sensuous smile spreading over her face. "Yes?"

"My friends were in room 103. Have they checked out?"

The smile turned to a grimace at Stephen's cold, no-nonsense tone. The woman sighed loudly and flipped open the ledger in front of her. She located the number and then shook her head. "One hundred and three is empty."

"I know that," Stephen bit out. "I asked if they had checked out."

"Well, if it is empty, it would suggest they had, wouldn't it?"

Stephen ignored her scornful tone. "When did they check out?"

Mason Sabre

She lifted the ledger and put it in front of him. "See there? No one has been in that room all week."

"No, that's bullshit. I booked the room myself." Phoenix shifted from one foot to the other from beside him, uneasy and anxious.

The blonde took the book back, closed it and shrugged. "Maybe they had a different room."

He gritted his teeth and tried to keep a lid on his temper. Flying off the handle was not going to help him. "What time did you start? Switch over is 8:00, right?"

"No. I came in at 7:00, then Andy left."

"Andy was the guy on last night?"

The woman gave him an exasperated look. Stephen simply stared back at her and waited. She rolled her eyes. "Yes."

"Do you know where I can find this Andy?"

"I can't tell you that. I'm sorry."

Stephen was sure she wasn't. "The hell you can't. This is important."

"It isn't our policy to give out details like that."

"I don't give a shit if it is in your last will and testament. I need that address."

Dark Veil

"I've told you …"

"I don't care what you've told me. Now, where can I find this Andy?"

"I …"

Stephen leaned over the counter, his eyes locking with hers. She froze and a flicker of fear flashed over her features. "Do you know what I am?" he said in a dangerously low tone.

She gave a meek nod.

"Good, then you know that I will get that information from you. Now I can come behind there and find it for myself, or you can tell me where he is. Because my sister was here last night and now she isn't. I need to talk to Andy."

"Maybe she stayed in a different hotel," she croaked weakly. When he didn't back off, she quickly added, "He lives on the grounds. There are some staff quarters at the back. He lives in room six …"

Stephen was already heading towards the door before she could finish her sentence, a bewildered Phoenix quickly running after him and wondering what the hell had just happened.

The staff quarters looked like they had once been some kind of barn that had now been converted into flats. There was a main door at the front—basic, but big—going all the way to the next level. Beyond that was a flight of stairs. Stephen tried the handle and found it unlocked. The stairwell, which went up three floors, was in the middle, and on either side were two doors, room numbers one and two.

Great. The guy's room was at the top.

Stephen raced up the stairs, and Phoenix followed. There was no response to his loud knocking, or any answer when he called out the man's name. "He's not here," Phoenix said, breathing in. Stephen agreed, but it was better to check. He grabbed the handle and twisted the lock, this one stiffer than the one in the hotel room. It cracked in the carriage, the wood splintering. "Whoops," he said to Phoenix.

An empty, untidy room greeted them. Stephen swore.

"Maybe he works the night shift tonight," Phoenix offered.

That wasn't good enough for Stephen. "We don't have until tonight." Something in his gut told him there was a clock ticking over all of their heads. "Come on. I'm going to go and chat to my mate … see if he knows."

They were at the last set of stairs when the door to the building opened and in walked a young-looking shifter—a *tiger*. "Shit," he muttered under his breath, and that was all Stephen needed to hear to know this was the man they were looking for.

He turned and bolted out of the door, heading for the main carpark. Stephen raced after him, long, heavily-muscled legs carrying him quickly and effortlessly towards his mark, covering the distance between them within seconds. Did these little shits never learn that they couldn't outrun him? Stephen lunged forward and tackled the *tiger*. They fell to the ground and landed in the dirt and gravel, rolling from the momentum with which Stephen had thrown himself on the man.

Stephen gripped the man's hair and then slammed his face down into the ground.

"I don't know nothing," the man spluttered.

"If you don't know *nothing*, why are you running, Andy?" Stephen yanked him up by his hair. He clutched at Stephen's hands and let out a howl of pain.

"I-I don't know. You m-made me afraid ..."

Stephen swore then muttered, "It's *I don't know anything*."

"What?"

"And that is *pardon?* Doesn't anyone know how to fucking speak properly anymore? Room 103 ... there was a couple staying there last night. What happened to them?"

"N-No. No one there ..." His words died on his lips as Stephen slammed his head back down again.

"Don't piss me off." Stephen pushed his knee onto the guy's back, causing him to call out in pain. "My sister and my friend. You're *tiger*. Do not even try to tell me you don't know who she is."

"Ohhh ... your sister ..." The man gave a pathetic, cockeyed smile. "She w-was here, but she didn't stay. She didn't like the room."

Stephen's arm twitched to slam the man's head down again. Phoenix was certainly expecting it because he tensed, readying himself for it, but instead, Stephen yanked the man to his feet and pulled out the car keys. He tossed them to Phoenix. "Go to the car and open the boot."

"The boot?" The man squirmed in Stephen's grip, but Stephen held on tighter, his other hand going around the man's throat and choking him.

"I wasn't speaking to you." He dragged the man along with him as he followed Phoenix to the car. Phoenix glanced over his shoulder, but said nothing. He unlocked the car when they got to it and then the boot.

Stephen shoved the man against it. "Get in yourself or I push you in. On the count of three."

"I told you, I don't know no ... anything."

"That would be one ...," Stephen said, pinning the man with a glare.

"Please."

"Two ..."

The man went to say something else, but seemed to reconsider. He placed his hands on the edge of the boot and lifted his leg to climb in.

* * *

Raven's bar wasn't that far away from where the hotel was. It was situated on the edge of town, where it became a city. Even though it was out of the way and could only be reached by car, it was always packed with patrons. Stephen pulled the car to a stop in one of the staff spots. The bar was closed, but he knew Raven would be in there setting up. The *panther* was married to this damn bar.

He looked over at Phoenix. "You can stay here if you want to." This probably wasn't a show for a young *wolf*, but it was Phoenix's choice. He'd have to see these things sooner or later.

"I'll come." Stephen felt a surge of pride at the young wolf's declaration. He was a watcher, he thought with approval. He took in everything that went on around him but said nothing.

Climbing out of the car, he hoped like hell Raven could help them. When he opened the boot, Andy cowered away, his submissive *tiger* recognising full well the dominance of Stephen's. Stephen wasn't giving him a choice this time. He grabbed him by the hair and pulled him out of the boot, then strode towards the bar. The man scrambled along the ground as he tried to keep pace or lose his scalp. When they approached the main door, Stephen launched the young man at the large metal doors, sending him crashing into them. The man bounced off the metal shutters, making them rattle violently from the force. Blood trickled down from his nose but there was no pity from Stephen. He pulled him back up to his feet and the man yelped.

It was a good minute before they heard the clank of the bolts on the other side. Raven slid the heavy door back and squinted against the rays of bright sunshine. He gave Andy a visual once over and then looked at Stephen. "Couldn't ring the bell like a normal person?"

"Brought you a present." He tossed him though the open door and Andy went sliding across the wooden floor inside.

Dark Veil

Raven gave Andy an impassive look and then motioned his head towards Phoenix as he slipped in with the rest of them. "And who's this?"

Stephen followed Raven's gaze to Phoenix, who was casting uneasy glances at the dangerous-looking *panther*. He didn't blame the kid. Raven exuded a menacing aura, one that warned you not to dare mess with him. He was tall and well-built, muscles bulging under his shirt and snug-fitting jeans, indicating an incredible physique. Black eyes stared out from a ruggedly handsome face—which might not have been so pretty considering how many times he'd had his nose broken and face and lip cut open from past heated 'arguments'. Fortunately for him, shifters healed amazingly fast, and physical scars were something an *Other* would only ever bear if they had not healed from inner pain that had been caused. A scar that ran down the side of his right eye hinted that Raven had experience of this, but the mark only served to make him seem even more threatening. Despite this, his incredible good looks, and the danger he emanated, ensured he was never lonely for female company.

"This is Phoenix," Stephen said. "He's with me."

That was good enough for Raven. Phoenix got dismissed as any kind of threat instantaneously and given no more thought. He pulled the huge door shut

Mason Sabre

behind them again, blocking out all sunlight and leaving the room in dimness.

"My sister and Cade are missing. This shit knows why and he isn't talking."

Raven shook his head slowly, tsking. "Why didn't you say so?" He pulled out a pair of black, leather gloves from the back pocket of his jeans. "It's been a while since you brought me a present."

Stephen held his hands out. "I know. I'm a shitty friend. Still got the last one?"

Raven shrugged. "Just the head."

"Trophy?"

"Dart practice."

Andy's eyes grew huge, and he quickly backed up along the floor. "No ... please ..." His back hit the snooker table and he whimpered as he watched Raven roll his sleeves up and reveal a tattoo of a pendulum on his arm with the name Poe written on the top of it. He gulped hard. "Y-You're R-Raven?"

"That's correct," Raven said calmly.

"*The* Raven?"

Raven slapped Stephen on the back. "Fucking hell, mate. He sure is fast. Where did you catch this one?"

"Please," Andy begged. "I'll tell you anything you want to know."

Chapter Seventeen

"P-Patterson." Andy sat on a chair, unbound and uninjured, but too afraid to make a run for it. He'd not make it two steps, and he knew it. Piece of shit. He was a disgrace to his kind. He was spilling his guts without any coercion, one of the negative aspects of hiring a coward to do a job. They'd turn their own mothers over just to save their own necks.

"Patterson?" Raven asked him. "As in *the* Patterson?"

Andy nodded his head in earnest. "Yes … he … he …"

Fucking Patterson. It had to be him, didn't it? Who else would pull shit like this?

"What does he want with Cade and Gemma?" Stephen growled.

Anyone would think Andy was *Human* the way he reeked with fear. He huddled in his chair, shaking. He was worse than a *Human*. His gaze wandered over to Phoenix, who was sitting on a stool next to the bar watching them interrogate him.

"Don't you look over at him," Stephen snarled, grabbing Andy's jaw and forcing his gaze back to him. "You look at me when I am talking to you."

Stephen grabbed one of the chairs close to him, turned it so the back faced Andy, and straddled it. The proximity did exactly what Stephen had wanted it to—it made Andy even more ill at ease. "What does he want my sister for? And my friend? You need to start giving me answers."

Andy's eyes grew wider and he swallowed nervously. "I … I don't know."

"You don't know or won't tell me?" Stephen glared at him, his eyes dead set on his. Andy couldn't hold the gaze, his eyes darting from Raven to Phoenix. "What do you think?" he said to Raven. "Do we believe him?"

Raven came to stand next to Stephen and leaned down to peer at Andy, his long, black hair falling forward and making the scars on his face appear even more menacing. Raven's heavy build was intimidating—he was almost as big as Stephen and stood out when he walked into a room—but it was his black, penetrating eyes and crazy-ass tattoo that could scare the shit out of people.

Andy shrunk away from him, gulping. "I don't know," he whispered pathetically.

"Did they know my sister was coming?"

Andy shook his head.

"Then how did they find out?" Stephen narrowed his eyes at him.

Andy fidgeted in his seat then sat on his hands as if to stop himself from saying anything further. A nervous shaking started in his leg as he started to tap his foot on the floor.

Stephen slammed his hand onto Andy's thigh to stop the tapping, making Andy jump. He cocked his head to the side, his voice predatorily low. "I assume it was you?"

"No ... no ..."

"You saw the daughter of the alpha and fucking sold them out ..."

"No ... I swear ... it wasn't like that ..."

Dark Veil

Stephen gripped Andy's knee and used it to pull him and the chair closer, their faces inches apart. "Tell me how it was."

Andy's eyes darted from Stephen to Raven. "Please ... I don't know anything."

Stephen squeezed his knee tighter, his grip threatening to crush the bone under his fingers. "You're really starting to piss me off, Andy."

Andy nodded, his face contorting in pain. "O-Okay. I called them ..."

"Who did you call? Patterson?"

Andy shook his head. "My mate. I called him and told him who had come in. I couldn't believe it was Gemma Davies. I mean, shit, she's like— "

"She's like what?"

"Nothing ... I just mean ... well, she's goddamn Gemma Davies." He looked at all three of them as if that statement explained everything. "Then this morning, before I finished my shift, Patterson suddenly shows up with his men. I couldn't do anything. You have to believe me."

"Then what?"

"They want the keys. To your sister's room." He gulped hard. "I tell them that I don't have them, but they don't believe me. They made me give them the keys. Then the next thing I know, they're carrying them out. My shift was over by then so I just went home. I swear."

Raven leaned in closer, his *panther* flickering in his eyes. "You went home? Someone gets kidnapped and you just go home?"

"I was going to call the authorities," he spluttered.

"Where has he taken them?" Stephen demanded.

"I don't know. Maybe his house."

"His house?" Raven scorned. "Even a *Human* like Patterson isn't that stupid."

"That's what he said. He told the other man to take them to his place."

Stephen stood up abruptly, and the chair toppled to the floor. Andy relaxed for a moment, but his wild eyes continued their crazy darting around. But as Stephen backed away, Raven picked the chair up and slammed it back down again, smacking it into the insides of Andy's thighs before sitting down. Andy cried out as the wood dug into his flesh. "Would you be lying to us, Andy? So that we can let you go?"

"No, I wouldn't … I promise." He glanced over at Stephen, his eyes pleading. But there was no help coming. Raven grabbed Andy by the jaw and made him face him. "I promise, it's the truth. It's all I know."

"If we let you go, are you going to call Patterson and warn him?"

"No … no … I'd never do that."

Stephen didn't think that Andy had the nous, let alone the balls, to call Patterson and warn him, but still, there was a certain unease at letting him go free. How could they trust him? Raven strode over to where Stephen stood with Phoenix. Andy didn't budge, not even moving the chair that Raven had left there purposely. "What do you want to do with him?"

"We take him with us," Stephen said matter-of-factly. It was the best way. They didn't have time to make sure he was secure. Killing him was an option, but that went back to time and also to the fact that if he was telling the truth, the only actual crime he had committed was stupidity, and while Stephen was all for offing the idiots, he also knew Society would probably not quite approve of it.

Raven frowned, obviously not agreeing with Stephen's sentiments. Even Phoenix was staring at Stephen with an expression of concern on his face at his decision.

"If we take him with us and he has lied to us, then we can just beat the shit out of him until he talks. If he has told us the truth, however," Stephen shot a glance to Andy to gauge his reaction, "then maybe we just toss his blabber-mouthing ass over to Patterson to deal with."

Raven snorted. "And you call me the harsh one."

"We're going to Patterson's?" Phoenix jumped in. It was the first time he had spoken since they got there. He had just quietly been sitting and observing. Stephen had had his eye on him throughout, but the boy had seemed fine. He hadn't looked away or flinched from anything. There was a true fighter behind those young eyes. Malcolm and Trevor would do well to realise it and utilise him.

"Yes, but I don't think he will be there. He's an asshole, not an idiot."

"This is because of me?"

It would be natural for Phoenix to think that, especially as Patterson had wanted his head a couple of years back for the murder of a *Human* boy. But that had all been dealt with now.

"No," Stephen assured him. "It's because he is an idiot."

"What if it is?" It wasn't fear that marked Phoenix's expression as he asked. Stephen wasn't sure what it was really. It could be a sudden realisation that he would always have to be looking over his shoulder. Maybe that was why he had been trying so hard for the past two years to tone himself up.

Andy still hadn't moved. He sat there on guard, waiting. Stephen didn't believe him, but going to Patterson's was the only clue they had. They'd start there and move on from there. He did believe that Patterson had something to do with it, however. The *Human* was an ass, though he had upgraded if this was his job alone, and Stephen doubted that very much. This wasn't how Patterson danced, but Stephen was sure as shit going to crash his party. He'd even bring the booze, light a bonfire and offer him the first round. "He wants something. I don't know quite what it is. But don't you dare think that this is because of you. Okay?"

Phoenix gave an unconvinced nod. He'd see sooner or later, Stephen thought. He would realise just how bad these *Humans* were. Phoenix still held faith in them. He still believed that there was goodness in them, but that was because he never made it to adult *Human*. His conditioning was still in its infancy, and his being turned washed almost everything away. But he would eventually see.

"You know where he lives?" Phoenix asked.

"Oh, I sure do." If it weren't for the fact that his sister and best friend were missing, Stephen would have let himself smile at the memory. Two years ago, Trevor had set up Phoenix to be killed, but his plan had been shot to hell when Stephen and Cade had shown up and stopped his plans. Stephen had then hand delivered the dead body of an *Other* to Patterson so that he would drop his manhunt against Phoenix for the murder of a *Human* boy. However, Patterson had not been pleased to encounter a dead body at his door, his throat missing after Stephen had ripped it from the shifter's throat.

Patterson's house was one of the largest houses in the countryside. It was one of those that had been there for years, like an old farmhouse, but appeared more like a stately home. The grounds surrounding it were lavish with greens, and even at this time of year, when the trees shed their leaves and stood out on the horizon as twig-covered skeletons of mother nature, it still looked beautiful. The wildness of it called to Stephen's *tiger*. He was ready for the hunt and the run.

He pulled the car up a little way from the house and let himself inhale the country air for a moment. Phoenix didn't say much from where he was sitting beside him in the passenger seat, but his eyes took everything in. Raven sat in the backseat with a bound Andy next to him. His hands had been tied and tightly secured to the car door. He was not getting out anytime soon.

There were no cars on the driveway to Patterson's—no lights on in the house, no smoke from the chimney. In fact, the house looked deceptively empty to anyone who was *Human*. But Stephen was *Other*. Life hummed against his ears like the gentle buzz of a distant bee. He could pinpoint the exact location of each and every person inside.

"Do we go in?" Phoenix's eyes were transfixed on the house, his anxious eagerness palpable.

"No ... not we. Me."

Phoenix shot him a look, but it was Raven who spoke. "You're not going in there by yourself?"

"I'm not going in. I just want to see who is there ... sniff the place out. I can pick up Gemma's scent easily." If he couldn't, he'd be in trouble. She was the one he should be able to pick up no matter what.

"I'll come with you. Who knows what shit you're going to come up against," Raven said.

"What about him?" Stephen motioned to Andy. They couldn't take him with them.

"Phoenix can stay here." He turned to Andy. "You aren't going to try any shit are you?"

Andy shook his head animatedly.

"You can handle him, can't you, kid?" Raven asked Phoenix.

Unease settled inside Stephen as he waited for Phoenix to answer. He wasn't too happy with leaving him alone with Andy, even if he was tied up. And he sure as hell didn't want Phoenix saying yes to Raven just because he felt he had to. If he couldn't handle it, Stephen would rather know. If Cade and Gemma were in there, though, he'd rather not have to worry about getting Phoenix out, too.

"I can do it," Phoenix said with determination.

"Are you sure? Don't just say it if you have any doubts."

Phoenix shrugged and glanced over at Andy, who was glaring at him. "He's tied up. He isn't going anywhere."

That he was, but even Stephen knew that people could get out of anything if they wanted to badly enough. "If we leave you and he starts anything, even just the slightest inkling, you knock him the fuck out. Okay?"

Phoenix nodded. "He isn't going to be a problem." But maybe that was the problem. Were they hardening Phoenix up a little too much? Had his father's cruelty done this to him? Something had changed in the boy. There was a hardness in him that was more than just an act, a hard resolve in the way he looked at Andy. Even Andy sensed it, because his expression became less complacent as he at looked Phoenix.

"We'll make sure he is secure," Raven said. "Have you got some tow rope in the back of this thing?"

Stephen got the rope from the boot and they quickly secured Andy enough that Stephen felt a little calmer about leaving Phoenix in charge. Raven had tied Andy's hands so that they were on either side of him. He wouldn't be able to get them together to do anything. He had secured his feet, too, so there was no way the shit was getting out of this, at least not on the sly. Stephen gave him a once-over, pulling at every tie, every knot and piece of rope—anything that would ease the niggle in his mind. He leaned over the seat to Phoenix. "If you need to, if something happens and you need to go, I want you to get out of here. Forget this piece of shit in the car. If anyone comes, I want you to run. Do you understand?" When Phoenix hesitated, Stephen's face set in a grim line. "Do you understand?" he repeated sternly.

Phoenix nodded, but it didn't calm whatever it was that was bugging Stephen. Something wasn't right and, for whatever reason, he couldn't put his finger on it. Stephen's *tiger* stirred inside with unease, the same way he did when he knew there was a hunt coming. It was ready and waiting, but for what exactly, Stephen was unsure. With a cursory ruffle of the kid's hair, Stephen turned and headed towards the house with Raven, forcing himself not to look back like a fucking mother hen leaving her chick behind. The kid would be okay. He was smart.

The gravel crunched under his heavy boots and he paused, listening. No guards rushing out. No alarms going off due to intruders on the property.

The house was surrounded by a large hedgerow, at least eight feet tall, behind which was a brick wall. It was about the same height, but nothing Stephen couldn't climb over. That would

Mason Sabre

put him in full view of the house, however, and he wasn't going to risk that.

He walked the parameter of the outside and Raven went the other way. They were looking for an opening—broken wall, damaged hedges—it didn't matter, as long as it got them inside. There had to be one. What Stephen did eventually find was an old gate. It didn't surprise him—most old houses had these. It was an escape for the residents to run into the woodlands behind the house. The door was covered in ivy, clearly unused in a long time. Stephen reached in, ignoring the thorns and twigs as they bit and clawed at his flesh. He clicked the lever under the handle ... it was unlocked. He gave it a hard shove, but nature had tightly sealed the exit and created a barricade. He closed his eyes for a moment, and called to his *tiger.* He was already close to the surface, sensing the danger they were both in. His claws slid out and he sliced through the vines with little effort. He pulled them away, tossing brambles and weeds behind him as he cut and pulled until he could see the door. With one claw, he traced along the edges, breaking away the remaining vines until he could ease the gate open.

It opened onto the back lawn of Patterson's house. The garden was lavish and luxurious, more for show than actual practicality. Typical *Humans*—all money and no fucking sense. There were statues of no use, opulent-looking plants and trees, and a pool that probably never got used. This was fucking England, not the States. Swimming outside in the north of England was something that only ever happened in the movies. But for Patterson, and others like him, it was all about money, status and social standing—establishing their eminence and power. That was what his father had always taught him. No matter what, it didn't matter if you were down to your last power, act rich, act like you own the world, and you will own the people in it. People were greedy, *Humans* and *Others*. Those with money held the power, and they showed it off like idiots.

There was a hatch at the back of the house—the kind of hatch where the wooden slatted doors opened outwards and the barrel men would roll the ale for the bar. Except there was no bar here anymore—there may have been once. That was Stephen's way in, but the problem was getting over to it. The back of the house was lined with windows that reflected the sunlight and gave them the appearance of darkened holes in the brickwork. It also meant that it made it impossible for Stephen to make out any movement from behind any of them. That didn't mean no one was there, though. If that was the case, he was in danger of being seen the moment he tried to sprint across the lawn. He muttered a curse under his breath. The risk wasn't worth it. He needed to find Gemma and Cade, and he couldn't do that if he got himself caught.

He slipped in through the gateway and kept low, his back to the wall. His *tiger* roamed at the surface, like a comforting growl just under his skin. This would have been so much better if he had been able to shift. His senses as a man were sharper than that of a common *Human*, but as his *tiger*, his skills were greater, his senses keener.

From where he stood, the house appeared empty, but he was careful to keep himself pressed up against the wall as he slid sideways. His attention stayed focused on each window, making sure to notice any peculiarity or catch the slightest movement. When he reached the part that had the shortest distance between wall and house, his eyes ran over each window once again before silently racing towards the house. He kept low as he moved, ducking under the back window and shimmying along the wall towards the hatch when he reached it.

There were no locks on the doors. He quietly laughed at their overconfidence in their own power and complacency that that they had nothing to fear from *Others*. They actually believed they didn't need locks. Didn't they realise that if all *Others* came together and there was a revolt, they'd be screwed before they even realised it. On the other hand, maybe they realised that no lock or gate would really stop any *Other* who wanted in.

He eased open the door, half-expecting the hinges to creak and give him away. The putrid stench of *Humans* hit him with a force, leaving a bitter taste in his mouth. He curled his lip in disgust then cautiously peered into the darkness, his acute eyesight giving him the ability to see despite the black obscurity.

Finding no one down there, he lowered himself onto the clean concrete. The place was packed with masses and masses of boxes. Boxes of greed, that's what this was. Rows upon rows of so much shit that they didn't need. He caught a glimpse of some of the labels—Christmas decorations, books, clothes. The *Humans* and their ever-consuming gratifications of just one more thing, one more want and demand, all cast aside in boxes where they would be forgotten. They were all the same, like termites. They devoured and consumed, buying more and more paraphernalia, decimating the earth and all that it had to offer, polluting it, destroying it. One day it would turn in on them, and they were so oblivious they would never see it coming.

Andy had lied. There was no Gemma or Cade here, and they never had been. Stephen didn't pick up any of their scents, and if they had been there, he would have. There was a door at the end of the basement, but there was no need to go for it. Stephen turned to leave, but the logo on one of the boxes caught his attention. He shoved the other boxes out of the way so that he could read it— *Norton Bio*. His blood ran cold and heat seared his skin, leaving a trail of cold sweat. Norton was one of the up-and-coming corporations which made biological weapons against *Others*. They were the creators of war and everything filthy and sordid. So this was what Patterson was into. Stephen pushed the box out of the way and read the next. It was the same—in fact, all of the boxes lying behind them were branded with the same company's name. He pulled one down, but by its weightlessness, he could tell it was empty. He tore it open anyway then swore when he found he was right. "Fucking piece of shit," he muttered under his breath. But what did this all have to do with Gemma and Cade? Why take them? For money? It didn't make sense. He'd be an idiot to announce that he had taken Gemma.

Giving the rest of the boxes a heave, he realised they were all just as empty. Deciding he was wasting his time here, he climbed out the same way he had got in. But as he was hauling himself out, his skin suddenly prickled with unease and his senses went on high alert. Cautiously scanning the area for a moment, he hesitated before eventually turning to shut the door once more. It wouldn't do to alert Patterson to the fact that his alliance with Norton had been discovered.

Something struck him hard on the side of his head and he stumbled sideways, then fell back into the basement and landed on his side with a thud, knocking the breath from him. Pain speared through his head and ricocheted down his body. He rolled instinctively, ready for the next attack. It wasn't a *Human* who stood there, or even a Shifter.

Mason Sabre

"Fucking witches," he muttered as he glared up at the woman standing there. God, how he hated them. This witch was young, maybe Stephen's age, her powers still in their infancy. Stephen raised a hand to his head, expecting to see blood, but there was nothing. Not even the indent of whatever she had used. It wasn't even tender. She flicked her hand up in the air, making a circular motion, and when she flung her hand out, something slammed into his jaw, sending him reeling and sputtering.

She leaned into the doorway. "Mind your manners," she said sweetly.

Stephen rolled back, sitting against the boxes. He cradled his jaw in his hand. "Oh, I'm sorry. What a beautiful fucking witch you are."

She lifted her hand again and he laughed. "This is your idea of how to get people to be nice to you? Hit them until they are? You're a witch, get the fuck over it and get out of my way." He pulled himself up and brushed himself off, paying no further mind to the witch standing there. She could cast all she wanted, but he'd get back up and he'd wish she had never come down there.

"Do you know who I am?" the witch asked.

His eyes raked over her, flickering gold. He cocked his head to the side. "Can't say I do," he drawled in a bored tone.

Something crashed behind the door at the other end of the basement, and Stephen spun around.

"Oh, don't worry. No one is coming," the witch said. "Do you really think that they didn't know you were here?"

"If they know I am here, why did they only send you?" Realisation suddenly dawned on him and he laughed. "It is you who doesn't know who I am, isn't it? You have no fucking idea."

"You're a trespasser. That is who you are. And you are on *Human* property."

"No, darling. I fear you have been gravely misled. I am Stephen Davies."

A flash of fearful recognition crossed the witch's features and she froze.

"That's right, darling. You've come to fuck with the wrong shifter."

Mason Sabre

Chapter Eighteen

Stephen couldn't be certain whether the shocked expression on the witch's face was because he had told her his name, or because Raven had come up from behind her and wrapped one of his big hands around her throat. Wide-eyed, and a look of *Oh* shit, *I'm screwed* on her face, she raised her hand in a desperate bid to cast another blow at Stephen.

Raven's grip tightened around her throat, forcing her head back. "You might want to reconsider," he said silkily, leaning in close to her ear. "My fingers will be in your throat before the last of your spell is cast."

She paused mid move as if she was still considering her options. Her eyes darted to Stephen and Raven dug his fingers in deeper, making her gasp for air and rise onto the tip of her toes or choke.

"I'd do as he says if I were you. He doesn't tend to ask twice," Stephen said as he lifted himself out of the basement once more. She quickly dropped her hand. "Smart girl."

Dark Veil

Stephen dusted himself off and then tilted his head to the side, eyes narrowing. "Do you hear that?"

Raven frowned, his hand still gripping the wheezing witch's throat. "Hear what? I can't hear anything."

"Exactly." They had made a lot of fucking noise, yet no one had come running. Stephen stared at the wide-eyed witch with disdain as she struggled to breathe. They had had it right years ago, burning them at the stake. "Did you come here of your own accord or were you sent here to deal with me?"

The witch tried to talk, but Raven's grip was making it virtually impossible. "Let her breathe a second, will you?"

Raven scowled, his displeasure at easing her torment evident. "Just for a second," he muttered. Stephen might hate witches, but Raven straight out despised them—and with good reason. It was rumoured that his mother had been a witch, and she had offered him up to the *Humans* to spare her life. Raven refused to talk about his childhood to anyone—even Stephen, with whom he'd been friends for years, had no idea about his upbringing. All he knew was that it must have been a shitty ordeal.

"Answer me, witch," Stephen demanded. They were running out of time, but his gut was trying to tell him something. "How did you come to be out here? Was it by chance that you stumbled upon me?"

The young witch stiffened as if someone had just rammed a steel pipe up her spine. Her expression hardened and her mouth set in a determined line. She was going for anger, but the scents emanating from her were so rich with fear that they were almost palpable.

Such a façade.

"I don't have to answer your questions," she grated out.

Stephen inched closer so that she was forced to tilt her head back to look up at him. Being stuck between two big, dangerous shifters was a precarious place for a witch to be—especially when both shifters shared an intense dislike for her kind. "They sent you out here, didn't they? All by yourself, I bet, too."

She didn't flinch, her gaze unwavering as she stared back at him.

"I wonder," he murmured thoughtfully, "were they sending you to end me … or sending you so that I could end you?"

Her stare wavered for a fleeting second before she swiftly slammed shutters down over her features. It was the only indication that his words had startled her. He watched the calculation flicker in the depths of her hazel eyes and then the tightening of her jaw as realisation settled in.

"It's the latter, right?" He didn't need her to answer. Her reaction had been enough. This was so fucking typical of *Humans*, he mused. Use *Others* and then off them at the first chance. Stephen took another step towards her and she instinctively tried to move back, but she was met with the large, solid wall that was Raven. She stiffened, and Raven chuckled from behind her, taking pleasure in her distress.

Stephen took a deep breath, then lifted a hesitant hand to hover near her face, making her shrink away even though she had nowhere to go. The answers were in there, but did he really want to do this? Did he really want that part of his mind fucked up this way? "What does Patterson want with my sister and Cade?"

"How should I know?" she muttered breathlessly.

He hesitated then slowly nodded in acceptance. "Then I guess we have no further need for you," he said flatly before looking at Raven. "She's all yours, mate."

The young witch tensed as he turned his back on them and left her to Raven's mercy. "Wait," she shouted out hastily, and the *panther* behind her sighed disappointedly. "They don't want your sister ... or Cade."

Stephen slowly turned back to her and waited.

"You really think that is their goal? They were just an opportunity that came up. Like fate."

He frowned as he listened. "What the hell are you talking about?"

The witch gave a short laugh. "Maybe it is you who doesn't get it after all. They don't want your sister ..." She looked him straight in the eye. "They want the kid ... the half-breed."

Stephen's heart plummeted. "Phoenix?"

The malevolent smile that formed on her lips made his blood run cold.

Fuck. He had left him on his own, defenceless and unprotected. He heard Raven's soft oath from behind the witch but he was already running in the direction of the car.

When he neared the car, Stephen forced himself to slow, putting out feelers for any danger lurking about. After he was satisfied no one was waiting in the shadows, a gun loaded with silver pointed at his head, he ran for the car. Before he had even reached it, he could sense that everything was just ... wrong. "Phoenix," he shouted, heart thumping wildly in his chest.

No reply.

The back door was wide open, and no one seemed to be around. He ducked his head to look inside and swore viciously at the sight before him. Andy sat in the car, or at least the remains of what looked like Andy. Where his eyes had once been, there were now two bloodied sockets of nothing. Blood poured from his eyes, nose and ears, and one of his limbs were missing. He was still tied up, his hands bound to the door, but one of the arms was no longer attached to his body.

He spun around, scanning the area in desperation just as Raven sided up to him, the witch still in his grasp. "The boy?"

"He's fucking gone," he growled. His arm shot out and he grabbed the witch, snatching her from Raven's grasp as if she were nothing more than a rag doll. Her short, dark hair whipped across her face as he jerked her around. "Where is he?"

But the witch wasn't listening to him. Her eyes were riveted to the sight that lay behind him. She shook her head desperately, and Stephen could feel her pulse throbbing under his grasp. She pushed back against him, trying to get away. "No," she breathed. "Oh god ... Andy." She lunged for the lifeless body in the car, but Stephen jerked her back. She started to struggle wildly in his arms, her eyes filling with tears. "Andy," she cried out, trying to reach him.

"He's dead," Stephen told her harshly. "There's nothing you can do for him."

"You fucking did this," she yelled at them. "The both of you. It's all your fault." She glanced at Andy once again and covered her mouth with the palm of her hand. "Why? He ... he was my friend."

"We didn't do this to him. This was done by the people you call friends. The people you're protecting," he spat.

She tried to pull away again but Stephen yanked her back around to face him, his patience worn. "Tell me where Phoenix is."

"I don't know," she cried. "Let me go."

"Phoenix is nothing to them. Tell me why they want him," he demanded.

She glowered at him. "He's a damn half-breed. Why do you think they want him?"

He scowled. "They want him because he is a half-breed?"

She snorted. "And I'd heard so much about the great Stephen Davies. Maybe the rumours were wrong."

Stephen's mind worked like a puzzle, trying all the pieces into place and then discarding the ones that didn't fit. What did Patterson want with Phoenix? What did Phoenix have? It couldn't be because of the dead *Human* boy a couple of years ago. Patterson had no idea that Phoenix had been the one to kill him. They had handed him Phoenix's maker, who had the same tracer—or else, shifter DNA—as Phoenix, and so Patterson believed they had taken care of the culprit. The blood samples had been a match. Case closed.

"He wants him because he is a half-breed," he said thinking aloud. "Because he is different. He was *Human* ..." Stephen's mind went back to Patterson's basement and the boxes. Suddenly the word Norton stood out like a fucking flag in the middle of an empty field.

"He is more powerful than you. More powerful than pures," the witch said. "Why do you think they don't allow you lot to mix your breeds? Could you imagine? A *Human* bred with an *Other* is one thing, but what if you had a mix? The fact that this half-breed made it and didn't die shows them that it is possible. Something in the boy made him survive ... imagine the possibilities."

He did. Phoenix was something new, something that no one had thought possible. But what if incongruent *Others* could in fact mix this way? That would scare the hell out of *Humans* because, while half-breeds had the best of both worlds, mix breeds would have power beyond belief.

Shit. Gemma and Cade. Did Patterson know she was pregnant? He wasn't going to ask the witch and give it away. They wanted Phoenix because he could hold the strain. If he held the powers of both sides, what power would Gemma and Cade's baby hold?

"Shit," Stephen repeated aloud, turning to Raven. "We have to get to my sister."

"What about the witch?"

"Bring her with us. If she tries anything, just put her out." She glared at him, her eyes shooting daggers. He had no qualms about ending her life— sometimes shit just needed doing.

Mason Sabre

Before he realised what she was planning, the witch brought her knee up in the perfect way that women always managed to do, slamming her thigh between his legs and sending pain spearing through every inch of his body.

With a grunt, he let go of her and fell to his knees, cupping his brutalised manhood with both hands. "Bitch."

She raced away from them, but Raven was on her fast, his strides bigger than hers. He leapt and tackled her down to the ground, rolling with her as he did so, so that she landed on top of him and his large frame didn't crush her.

"Let me go," she screamed, smashing her fists into his chest, but Raven grabbed her wrists and held them in one big hand, the other locked around her waist.

"Are you that stupid that you don't realise we did not do this to Andy. *They* did," Stephen croaked, still clutching where she had kneed him. "What do you think they are going to do when they get hold of you?"

"You are the one who is stupid," she spat. "You just hand delivered them the half-breed."

Chapter Nineteen

Cade leaned against the bars between his cage and Gemma's, feeling her presence right behind him as she mirrored his stance. His chest rose and fell slowly, his breathing laboured. *How long had they been here?* His limbs ached and his bones were stiff, his body heavy, every movement slow and sluggish. His head thumped to the rhythm of his heartbeat, ready to explode.

He let his eyes stay closed, letting them think he was sleeping. It was easier that way. *Humans* and their all-so-powerful weapons. The silver they had shot him with made him burn hot on the inside, but his skin was ice-cold on the outside. Cade held onto Gemma's hand through the bars behind him, keeping the touch hidden. The moment his senses told him he wasn't being watched, and the guards' presence felt a little further away, he peered through his lashes at his surroundings. It looked like they were in some kind of a converted barn or basement, but the loud bangs and crashes that echoed through the place made Cade approximate that the place had to be much larger and much deeper.

Three *Humans* were sitting in the corner of the room, eyes on the tiny screens there as they laughed and gibed at each other. As far as Cade could tell, the monitors were linked to security cameras that seemed to show different angles within a large warehouse, as well as the immediate area around the outside of the building. It didn't show enough for him to have a clear idea of where the hell they were exactly, or why and who the hell had brought them here.

One of the men suddenly swore and the other two jumped up and raced out. Cade forced himself to stay put and not react. He didn't want to call attention to the fact he was conscious. He felt Gemma grip his fingers and he gave her a reassuring squeeze in return, glad she was following his example and staying as quiet and motionless as possible.

Fuck, he hoped to god that it was Stephen who had somehow found them. He would have realised they were missing by now since it had to be hours from the time they had agreed to meet at the service station. Then again, if it was Stephen, it definitely wasn't a good sign that these *Human* asshole guards had just spotted him on their screens, he thought with a curse.

Letting his eyes close again, Cade shut out the outside world, closing his ears and his mind to everything. He pictured a stark, white room, the one where he and Phoenix could go to and connect in their minds. He called out for the young *wolf,* asking him to respond, but it was like searching in the darkness for a speck of dust. Phoenix was nowhere to be seen.

A good few minutes passed with Cade deep in his mind, desperately searching and calling for the *wolf,* pushing himself beyond his limits despite the weakening effect of the silver coursing through his system.

The door to the room they were being held in suddenly burst open, and Cade felt Gemma jolt from behind him. He stroked a thumb over her knuckles in the hopes of calming her and she grasped his fingers more tightly. He swore inwardly. He hated feeling helpless when it came to protecting his mate—worse so when his mate was carrying his child.

"He's still out of it? How much did you give him?" Cade recognised the voice immediately. Patterson was the key representative and alliance between *Humans* and *Others*. Power and money defined him, as well as his hate for *Others* and his belief that *Humans* were the superior race. Despite this, however, he had shown enough acumen so far as to know that starting a war with *Others* might not be the smartest move. *Humans* may vastly outnumber them and hold powerful weapons, but the strength and danger of an *Other* was not to be scoffed at or taken lightly. For every fifty *Humans*, one *Other* was needed to take them down.

Did Patterson have any idea he had just kidnapped the *Other* alpha's daughter? Cade would bet his life he did—nothing would be accidental or pure luck with Patterson.

Something metal rattled against the bars. "Hey, *wolf* boy, wake up."

Cade opened his eyes slowly and fixed them on the well-dressed diplomat. He looked out of place standing there with his expensive suit and shoes and groomed hair. Patterson moved in closer, but made sure to keep a safe distance from the cage. Perhaps he wasn't a complete idiot. "With what right do you hold us prisoners here?"

Patterson gave a faint smile then inclined his head at him. "You are free to go," he said smoothly, his face giving away nothing.

The *Human* next to him bashed his bat against the bars, the thud reverberating around the cage. "Hey, *wolf* boy, you can go," he jeered, but Cade kept his eyes fixed firmly on Patterson. He didn't for a minute trust Patterson or believe he had gone to all this trouble to catch them, just to let them go this easily again.

"I'll leave it in your capable hands. Don't screw it up," said Patterson to his lackey and then turned and left the room without sparing Cade another glance. Cade got to his feet slowly, all his senses on high alert. He heard Gemma's shaky breath as he rose, but he dared not take his eyes off Patterson's minions. Losing sight of a threat for even a second was never a wise thing to do—it could prove lethal.

"You're letting us go?" Gemma breathed hopefully.

The *Human* scum laughed unpleasantly. "Your boyfriend can go, sweetheart," he drawled, his eyes roving over her lasciviously, "but not you." His grinned widely, showing off a set of yellow, crooked teeth. "You'll stay here and keep me … company."

Cade roared and hurled himself against the bars, his arms shooting out from between them and grabbing for the man. "You stay the fuck away from her," he snarled.

The man sprang backwards and chuckled. "Don't worry. We'll take good care of her." There were two men in the room. Cade could take them, silver bat or not, they'd have to kill him to get him to leave her there.

"How shall we do this?" one of the men asked. He had a deep accent, one that was from the east—not too bright then.

"Cade, just go," Gemma beseeched him softly. "We have a better chance of making it if you are free. You can come find me. It's no help to us if we are both stuck in here." She spoke so quietly that only he could hear her words with his enhanced hearing. He inhaled deeply, then stepped back close to her again, snaking his hand through the bars and cupping her face in his hand. He didn't know if he should tell her that they had no intention of setting him free. He stroked the smooth skin of her jaw with his thumb and she turned her cheek into his palm.

"I'm not leaving you, Gem. Don't ask me to." His hand fell from her face and he slumped to the ground weakly. He leaned against the bars, breathing heavily, his head slumping forward.

"Cade," Gemma cried out in alarm, reaching through the bars for him.

"He's been out of it for ages. I think you gave him too much of that shit."

"If it was too much, he'd be dead," the one with the deep accent said. He unhooked the keys from his jeans and cautiously opened the cage that Cade was in. He didn't go all the way in, but extended the bat forward and prodded Cade. Cade murmured in response and pushed the bat away. The *Human* laughed. "He's fucked, look at him. I say we just bag him and dump him like the others."

Gemma gasped. "What do you mean? You said he's free to go." Her voice was bordering on hysterical.

The one behind had a gun out, ready and aimed at Cade. The *Human* with the bat inched in, little by little, ignoring Gemma's cries and pleas as she clutched at Cade through the bars. "Please don't hurt him," she wailed. "I'll do anything. Please. I'm begging you."

"Let go of him," he barked at her.

"No ... please," she begged him.

With a grunt, he stepped closer and tried to grab hold of her arm to yank it off Cade. Before he could so much as lay a finger on her, Cade's arm had shot out and seized him by the throat. He got to his feet slowly, claws digging into the man's flesh as he steadily squeezed and threatened to crush the man's windpipe. The bat dropped to the floor with a thud as the man flailed weakly. Gurgling, his eyes grew wide in fear and terror as he stared into eyes that had gone *wolf*.

Shouts and blasphemies came from outside the cage, and the one holding the gun raised it and pointed it at Cade.

"You shoot me and your friend is dead," Cade growled, his voice dangerously close to his animal. "My claw is the only thing keeping him from bleeding out. You shoot me and he's fucked."

The *Human* raised the gun higher, cupping his hands together to steady his shaking grasp. "Fuck … fuck …" he chanted. He slowly edged forward and grabbed the keys from the lock. "Leave them …" Cade demanded, but the man was already hastily backing away with them and heading for Gemma's cage. It was Cade's turn to swear now as he pushed the *Human* he had hold of forwards and advanced on the gun-toting one. He had found and unlocked Gemma's cage before Cade could reach him, locking himself in with Gemma.

"What are you doing?" she sobbed as he aimed the gun at Gemma.

"Seems now we have a little bit of a problem here, *wolf*," he said. "Let him go and she doesn't get hurt." When Cade didn't move, he stepped forward and aimed the gun at Gemma's head. "Down," he barked at her, forcing her down onto her knees. His eyes flicked from her to Cade. Cade stayed where he was, at the gate with his claws still digging into the wheezing *Human's* jugular.

Mason Sabre

Cade's *wolf* bubbled at the surface like a raging bull waiting for the gate to open as the *Human* ran a knuckle along Gemma's cheek. "You can kill him if you want, but you ain't getting in here. All you can do is watch," he sneered, licking his lips.

Cade roared, baring his teeth. "If you touch one fucking hair on her head, I'll …"

The *Human* leaned in, ran his hand down to her collarbone. "You'll do what?" Gemma's features were tight with fear, and Cade knew her fear was mainly for him and their baby. She was afraid that the slightest wrong move would put the baby at risk, and that was enough for Cade to finally believe that she wanted this child just as much as he did.

"Let her go," he ordered, his *wolf* going crazy inside.

"What do you think you can do other than watch me?" His hand opened around Gemma's throat, and she lifted her hands to stop him. "Don't even think about it," he said to her. "Let go."

"Fuck you," she rasped. Furious, the *Human* brought his hand down across her face, smacking the butt of the gun into her cheekbone. She cried out and slumped to the ground.

"Gemma," Cade called out.

"That is not how we play," he said to her. "Now tell your *wolf* to back the fuck off."

Gemma laughed. "Do you think that I can make him do anything?"

The *Human* leaned in closer, his face in Gemma's as he sneered. "Maybe you can't, but perhaps this will." He lowered the gun, not to her throat or her chest, but down to her abdomen. She inhaled shakily, terror in her eyes as he pushed the nozzle of the gun into her flesh. "Tell me, do you think an unborn baby can survive silver poisoning? Now tell the *wolf* to let go."

She didn't need to. Cade let go of the man and he fell to the ground clutching his neck and sucking in lungfuls of air. Cade held his arms up in the air as a show of surrender. "Okay, you win. Don't hurt her," he ground out.

The *Human* hollered for help and the door to the room opened and Cade waited for the inevitable. Something whacked him hard on the

Mason Sabre

back of his head and Cade collapsed to the floor.
The world went dark as someone pulled a sack over
his head, yanking a cord around his throat and
tightening it. So many hands, so much noise, so
much shouting. His *wolf* was coming loose now—his
hands shifted and he felt his bones move and start
to realign. His growl echoed so loudly in the room
that it was hard to hear anything above the sound.

He had to get to Gemma, to his mate, to his
child.

"I'm fucking dying," the *Human* Cade had
held rasped.

"Hold your hand over it and apply pressure,
you idiot," someone else shouted.

Another blow to the gut knocked the wind
out of Cade and made him double over, wheezing.
Someone grabbed hold of his hands, pulling them
behind his back and forcing them into an awkward,
painful position. He fell to his side, grunting as
someone bound his hands in that position, sending
pain through his shoulders and his neck all at the
same time. It felt like his arms were going to be
ripped off. The wolf tried to come, tried to shift, but
his arms were the wrong way and they would surely

pull the *wolf's* chest in half if he even tried to shift. Cade's rib cage bulged, his sternum pressing tightly against his skin. Someone hit him again and he went down once more. Blow after blow came until he couldn't feel them anymore. His skin felt numb, every ounce of pain that he felt blurred into nothing. His mind swam, drifted away to the white room. He could hear screaming, but it wasn't his own, it was Gemma's.

He tried to shout back, tried to speak, but his voice was gone, he couldn't breathe. Hands pulled him to his feet and pushed him forwards, making him run. "Gem—," he uttered through the cloth over his head.

She screamed his name back, guttural sounds filled with pain. His *wolf* howled, its cries desperate. He was pushed onto his side, onto something hard, but he was moving fast ... on wheels.

Cold air blew over his skin and the smell of something wet, damp and musty filled his senses. They were underground—somewhere dark and damp. But as they moved on, he picked up another scent, something familiar.

Phoenix …

All at once it was there, the scent, a piece of home in the place of horror and death. He tried to grasp onto it, but just as fast, the scent had gone and he struggled to make out if it was real, or just a passing memory.

The clank of a large, metal door opening, and then they were outside—the breeze was faster, colder against his skin. Whatever he was on, a trolley of some kind, stopped suddenly as it hit something, and then he was tilting, head first. He started to fall, and he instinctively pulled himself into a ball, not knowing where he would land. He held his breath, ready for impact.

He landed on his back, something smacking him hard and knocking the wind from him. It was cold … freezing.

He was in water.

He was tied up.

Water started to fill his mouth.

Chapter Twenty

Phoenix stayed in the car and watched as Stephen and Raven walked off into the sunset like heroes —something that he would never be. He watched them with a mixture of contempt, envy and fear. He would never be like them, and they would never treat him like one of them. Not fully. Not really. Not like he actually belonged and had a place in their world. He would always be the one left behind, the one seen as having a weakness because he had once been *Human*—the one who needed protecting.

He watched them wander off into the danger that was beyond those hedges. Would they even come back? They were the last threads of his life—he'd be left alone again, the outcast of two worlds, living in some kind of limbo and waiting to die or find his place. Whichever came first. It didn't matter what he did or who he was. Would he ever fit in or be seen as something other than the little half-breed.

Cade ...

The very thought of him brought about so much inside Phoenix. It pulled heavy against his chest. In his mind, Cade was slipping away into darkness—their white room was nothing more than an empty chamber now. The man who had saved his life and given him a home had disappeared into a dark cave, and Phoenix had no idea he was ever coming out again. The still *wolf* was fading.

What would happen to Phoenix if Cade died?

Phoenix curled his fingers tightly around the door handle as the thought rose unbidden to his mind. The *Others* wouldn't protect him forever. He was the burden in their lives—he was a burden in Cade's life. All he had brought him was problems and tribulations, he thought gloomily. It would be better for everyone if he just left.

He could run again—he knew how to do that. He'd be long gone before anyone even noticed. Maybe they wouldn't stop him even if they knew. He'd made it this far—made it into the woods that day. He could make it again.

Stephen and Raven had stopped at the edge of the hedgerow that surrounded the property and were talking for a moment, Stephen pointing in different directions as they made plans for them to split up and search. Phoenix would never be one of them. He would never stand there and be called upon to be the fighter. Even from this distance, Stephen and Raven's large frames emanated dominance, power. They knew their place in this world—they *had* a place.

Stephen's trained mind was razor-sharp and he had a confidence that Phoenix could only dream about. Phoenix was just … nothing. *Human*. He would always be this way. His body could grow, his muscles eventually shape and tone and his bulk transform to man, but he would never be like Stephen and Raven. Even Raven, a part stray, had a place and a purpose in this world. They were both wanted and needed.

Phoenix scowled at himself in the mirror at the centre of the visor he had pulled down to keep an eye on Andy. Childish blue eyes stared back at him, filled with innocence and weakness. The scar that ran through Phoenix's eyebrow was more vivid today, alive with colour and pain. He'd never be accepted if Cade died. Two fathers—two species— and he would ruin them both. Maybe it just wasn't meant to be.

Andy coughed, startling Phoenix and pulling him from his thoughts. He automatically gripped the door handle harder and mentally chastised himself. He needed to stay focused.

He glanced back towards the hedgerow—Stephen and Raven had disappeared from sight now. They were off doing what was needed of them, and he was sitting in the car because they couldn't take him with them. He was too weak and too much of a problem. He didn't blame them really—he'd not want him tagging along, either.

They were different. They were *real* men—real men who didn't kill their mothers and cause their fathers to hate them. Phoenix crushed the handle in his hand and stared at himself in the mirror with hatred. He clenched his jaw and turned away abruptly, not bearing to look at his pathetic reflection any longer.

If Cade dies …

Andy was still coughing. Wheezy whistles punctuated the onslaught as he tried to breathe, his face turning red from the effort.

Phoenix twisted around in his seat. "Are you okay?"

The man in the back strained forward against the binds that held him in place, the ropes pulling tighter and digging deeper into his flesh.

Phoenix should have just gone, he knew it. He should have got out of the car and run when the thought first came to mind. That was his problem, wasn't it? He never acted, never did what was right. He just stayed there and let everyone die around him. This man was going to die. He was going to sit in the back of the car and choke to death.

"Untie me," Andy spluttered. "Fucking untie me, half-breed. I can't breathe."

The name grated against Phoenix. "No."

He wanted to. He twitched in his seat to lean over and let the man go so that he could deal with whatever this cough was. But that would just be a trick … wouldn't it? A ploy to let the stupid *wolf* who had once been *Human* fuck up. Andy would get away and then Phoenix would be screwed, exposing him for what he really was—a failure.

He should have just left before he let any of them down—before they all ended up looking at him with the same hatred that his father had yesterday. He could already see it in some of them—Trevor especially. It wasn't Cade's father's fault, he mused. The *Other* just wasn't good at hiding it.

But Malcolm and Emily? They would see eventually. Malcolm only spoke to him when he had to, and Emily probably only tolerated him, too.

He should have left.

Andy coughed harder, the blood vessels in his eyes started to burst. Phoenix started to panic. Maybe he should go around to the back and hit Andy on the back. But as Andy retched and coughed and choked, all Phoenix did was sit and watch like some helpless half-breed that they all believed him to be.

"Let me out," Andy wheezed through another coughing bout. "Untie me."

"I can't."

Spittle flew from Andy's mouth and saliva ran down his chin and dripped onto his shirt. He threw his head back, panting to catch his breath—getting ready for the next round. Perhaps he wasn't faking it, Phoenix thought nervously.

Andy shot forward suddenly, his eyes bulging like those of cartoon characters in children's comic books. He was sure they were going to explode any second, images of flying eyeballs and blood splatter vivid in his head.

This time, Andy's strangled cough was followed by a spatter of blood from his mouth. His chest rattled and expanded with a thud. Phoenix looked on in horror as blood began to pour from his eyes, nose and ears. It stained his cheeks, dark rivers of red mingling as they flowed down his face, his collar growing dark with it. It soaked through the top of his shirt, painting the fabric crimson. Andy opened his mouth through the agonising pain, but all that came out were thick, guttural cries masked by the gurgling inside his chest. "Shit." Phoenix fumbled for the handle of the car just as the car's doors all flew open at the same time. Blood splayed across the seats and windows and hit Phoenix as Andy's arm was ripped clean from his body from the violent force of the car doors opening.

Phoenix stared at Andy's lifeless body, bile rising to his throat.

Before he knew what was happening, he was being pulled from the car and launched onto the dirt. Instinct and Stephen and Cade's training instantly kicked in, and Phoenix rolled over and tried to spring to his feet. A vicious kick to his ribs had him sprawling on the ground again. He grunted and looked up at the three large men that stood over him threateningly. A movement to the side caught his eye as a tall, slim woman with long, black hair approached him. He squinted to see better, still winded from the blow to the ribs. She was pretty, older, and definitely *Other*.

She propped one of her high-heeled boots onto his chest and pushed him back onto the ground. Tilting her perfectly made-up face to the side, she sighed as she studied him. "Handsome little thing you are," she crooned. "What a shame."

One of the men hunkered down next to him, his face an impassive mask.

"What do you want?" Phoenix ground out, glaring at him, and the woman from above him chuckled.

"Ooh, handsome *and* feisty. I like that."

With lightning speed, the man's arm shot out and something sharp pricked Phoenix's neck before he had a chance to stop him.

Dark Veil

His hand flew up to cup his neck while trying to hit the man with the other. His limbs grew heavy and his head fell back with a thud. Darks and greys slipped into the edges of his vision, and everything around him started to blur.

All he had needed to do was watch the car and he couldn't even manage that. The world started to collide. He had failed, he thought dejectedly just before his entire world went black.

When Phoenix opened his eyes, he was surrounded by darkness. He was lying on something hard and cold and fabric. He rolled onto his back, but the place was confined. The surface where he lay wasn't flat or smooth. It had metal ridges and above him was another sheet of metal. His body bounced and jolted suddenly, making him land sharply on his shoulder. He was in a car— in the boot of a car. He rubbed at his neck where they had jabbed him. How long had he been out? He didn't have a clue, but they were moving. No longer at the house.

Great.

Not only did he not fit in, but now he was incompetent. He lay on his back, his knees twisted

Mason Sabre

to the side because the space wasn't high or wide enough to have his legs up or stretched out. Now what did he do? Wait again, for them to save him and get him out like they always did? Maybe this was why he didn't really fit. Maybe this was why they saw him as weak.

There was nothing in the boot with him. No tools, nothing to bang or to smash his way out. He pressed his palms firmly to the roof of the lid, but it was locked. He couldn't do anything with the mechanism. It was housed in metal, and even if he could get to it, he didn't have a key.

The car was moving fast. It went over bumps in the road, which rattled through there back and jarred him. He put his hand out to steady himself and tried to keep his head up, but they went over something big in the road and his cheek smashed off the floor of the boot as his head whipped to the side. Pain throbbed lanced through him, sending lightning through his skull.

He was stuck.

Phoenix lay in the darkness a moment, stilling himself and his mind so that he could think logically about this. There were ways out of this, weren't there? He had read enough that he should have come across something. The boot wasn't in total darkness—light came in from the gaps around the panel that held the car's lights in place. Phoenix shoved a boot against one of them and it moved an inch. He pushed his back against the interior of the car to give himself some leverage and raised his foot again and waited. When the car hit another bump in the road, he slammed his foot against the panel. It took six good kicks for the panel to become dislodged, and when it did, Phoenix moved himself around and pushed the panel out.

He could see the road. It sped by as he peered out. He pressed his face to the hole he had just made and the light panel swung down. They were in no place he recognised. The road was just that ... a road. There was nothing along the way. Nothing to tell him where he was or how far they had gone. There were no other cars on the road. No one else there. And no point in yelling.

Suddenly, the car veered to the side and started to slow when the tyres hit what sounded like gravel. Something beeped and hummed, and then Phoenix heard the mechanical sound of rollers and doors. The car stopped, but the engine was still running. Phoenix held his breath, then the car moved again. They were going down. The car came to another stop and the driver cut the engine. One … two … three doors opened. Phoenix shoved himself back into the boot and waited.

The boot opened after a few minutes. The man standing there was probably around Cade's age, but he had a receding hairline. Phoenix felt half of his face work, the other half seeming numb.

The man angled his head as he looked at Phoenix. "A real half-breed," he beamed. "I never thought I would see the day."

Chapter Twenty-One

Stephen's heart lurched inside his chest with the realisation of what he had done. His pulse thundered loudly, the hum of the world around him paling into nothing. He stared at the empty passenger seat where Phoenix should have been.

Fuck.

"You put the prize right in front of them and then left the box unattended for them to just take it when no one was looking."

His jaw tightened and his hands balled into fists. The witch was right. That's exactly what he had done.

What a stupid fuck he was.

He glanced from the car to the main road, his eyes searching frantically for any kind of clue. With a curse, he ran an agitated hand through his hair. What the hell was he expecting to find—a fucking sign that read, 'Bad guys, this way'?

"God damn fucking shit," he shouted. "How the fuck did this happen?"

Raven got to his feet, hauling the witch up with him. "Behave," he growled at her, and she glared at him mutinously. She squeaked as he dragged her with him over to Stephen, almost stumbling while trying to keep up with his long strides. He let his gaze rove the area. "They can't have gone too far."

Stephen stared hard at the woman. "Taking my sister and my friend ... all this ..." he motioned to the mess around them, "it was all just a lure to get to Phoenix? To get the boy?"

She flicked her hair back and dusted herself off as much as was possible with Raven gripping her arm. He scowled at her and gave her a shake so she would answer. She threw him an annoyed look before casting her eyes upon Stephen. "What need would they have of your sister and friend?"

"What need do they have of Phoenix?" Stephen shot back.

The witch pursed her lips and lifted her chin in defiance, her long, blonde hair swaying behind her. She was beautiful, perfect—a god damn siren of the land—but right now, Stephen would love nothing more than to put his hands around her pretty, little neck and throttle her. "Where is my sister?"

"Gone," she replied with a nonchalant shrug. "It's too late now."

"Too late? Stop fucking with us, witch," Raven said fiercely. "Where are they?"

Her expression twisting into one of hatred, she yanked her arm from his grasp, and this time, Raven let her go. "You," she said, pointing at Stephen, her eyes blazing, "and you," she pointed at Raven. "I don't owe either of you anything. Go find them yourself."

"You owe it to yourself," Stephen shot back. "You know damn well they didn't send you to kill me. They were sending you to your death. This is who you want to protect? When they'd see you dead in a heartbeat?"

"Really?" she drawled. Taking a step back, she flicked her hand at Stephen in one fluid movement. Something smacked him in the ankles and took his footing right out from under him, sending him flying down to the ground and landing on his back with a thud.

Raven lunged for her, but she raised her hand again, palm out, and sent him reeling back so that he landed next to Stephen in the dirt. "As you can see," she said, placing her hands on her hips triumphantly, "I am quite capable of looking after myself. *That* is why they sent me."

"Party tricks," Stephen muttered as he got back up.

Raven got to his feet next to him, murder on his face. She raised her hand again, but he was ready for her this time. With feline speed, he leapt for her, knocking her to the ground and pinning her wrists down so that she couldn't cast any more of her underhanded magic. She gasped and began to struggle beneath his big, heavy frame in vain. "You have no idea how much I enjoy the feel of soft, writhing, female flesh under me," he taunted her silkily. His words had the desired effect and she immediately froze, her cheeks burning crimson.

"Yes, I have no doubt that unwilling, thrashing women are the only type you ever manage to get into your bed," she spat.

Raven chuckled. They both knew that a man that looked like him would never be short of eager women in his bed. "What's your name?" he demanded.

"Fuck you."

In one fell swoop, he had flipped her over so that she was lying on her front. She squealed and resumed her struggles while Raven held both hands behind her, knee planted firmly on her back to keep her in place. He grabbed her hair and pulled her head back, his lips close to her ear. "Your name."

She gritted her teeth then grunted reluctantly, "Anika."

Stephen sighed as he crouched down next to her head.

"Get the fuck off me," she shrieked, trying to buck him off her, but he was bigger, heavier and he pinned her easily. Raven pushed her head down and Stephen frowned.

"What's this?" He shoved her hair out of the way, sweeping it back. Behind her ear was a tattoo—a number—just like the girl he had found at the river. He exchanged glances with Raven.

Mason Sabre

"None of your fucking business. That's what that is."

Raven dragged her to her feet once more, keeping her hands firmly behind her back.

"I found a body—a woman," Stephen said quietly. "She had a tattoo just like this."

"So?" she panted.

"These are the same people who have my sister? They killed that woman."

The witch scoffed. "Like you actually care."

"They have my sister and my friend, and now they have an innocent child," Stephen persisted, "so yeah, I do care."

"Always the way, isn't it? Society doesn't give a shit to what happens out here. We can all rot and it doesn't matter. Yeah, I know who you are, Stephen Davies. Spoilt fucking heir to the god almighty throne of power."

Stephen's features hardened. What the hell did she know? He had his freedom. "If you side with the *Humans*, you are just as bad as they are."

She gave a short laugh. "You don't care about what goes on here until it affects you. Society—all the fucking same. You don't get it, do you? It is *you* in the wrong." She fixed Raven with a glare. "And you're worse than he is. You know that? At least he was born into Society. He doesn't know any better. But you … you tied up one of our own," she motioned towards Andy with her head. "You … you …" Her voice faltered as her gaze fell on Andy's mutilated body once more, chest heaving as she tried to regain her composure.

When she turned back to Stephen and Raven, her blue eyes swirled with emotion. "This is what Society does. They take strays, tie them up and leave them to die like that … like it doesn't matter. It's what you'll both do if I tell you," she rasped. "So why should I? What's Society going to do for me? What have they ever done for me? Nothing … just treat me like some cheap whore and then cast me aside … again."

Both men remained quiet for a moment, then Raven said, "Do you promise not to try anything if I let you go again?" Surprised eyes jumped to his, but he simply stared at her, hard jaw set in a determined line. She blinked away tears and gave a curt nod.

"Okay then." He released her wrists from his vice-like grip, and slowly raised his hands to show her he meant no harm. "We didn't kill Andy."

"You did," she said forlornly. "The moment you forced him to talk." She turned and walked a few feet away from them both, leaving them to both stare at her rigid back.

This was getting them nowhere, Stephen thought frustratedly, and Raven's soft oath from beside him told him he felt the same. They needed to find Phoenix and Gemma and Cade. His *tiger* rose inside him, his eyes flashing gold as it demanded to be let out. Blood pumping through his veins with ferocity, he stormed to the car and sliced through the rope that still held Andy in place with his claws.

"See?" she said. "You're literally going to take him and dump him on the side of the road. Doesn't he even get a burial?"

"My sister is pregnant. Do you know that?" Stephen ground out. "You accuse me of only looking out for my own? Damn fucking right. But not because we are Society ... not because we are some evil gathering ... but because she is my sister ... my *family*. You have a family. You would do the same."

"Do I?" She raised her eyebrows at him.

"To have the powers you do, then yes." That was the way it was with witches. Away from their families and their covens, they grew weaker, their powers faded. They had to have a connection.

Raven was staring at her and she shifted uneasily under his intense gaze. "You were *Human*, weren't you?" he said, coming closer. "That is why your eyes shimmer the way they do. That's why your power is strong." Stephen's head whipped around, and his gaze focused on her.

"You don't know what you're talking about," she denied huskily, moving back.

He continued as if she hadn't spoken. "That's why your powers are strong, like Phoenix's. That's it, isn't it?" He walked her backwards as he spoke, backing her all the way up to the side of the car. His large frame dwarfed hers, and her breathing quickened as he leaned in close. She gasped when he reached out and caught hold of her forearm, pushing her sleeve up to expose her scarred wrist.

Mason Sabre

Old welts and puckered skin marred her otherwise perfect flesh. "They took you, didn't they?"

Anika yanked her arm back, breathing heavily. "It's none of your business," she croaked, refusing to break his gaze.

"Help us find the boy," he urged her softly.

She swallowed hard. "No one helped me ..." she whispered. "No one came. No one. I was six years old ... just six ... riding my bike ..." Her voice rose with emotion. "Do you know what that is like? I was riding my damn bike to school. That was all. Then this van sided up next to me ... the doors opened and lifted me clean off my bike. I ..." She paused for breath. "I screamed, you know? Kicked and fought and shouted for someone to help. No one came. They robbed me of my family ... of my life. I can't even remember what my name was."

"I'm sorry," Raven said softly, but her gaze hardened at his words and she pushed against his hard chest. He let her shove him back, and he stepped away.

"Don't pity me. Don't you even dare."

"He has a tattoo, too," Stephen said suddenly, and both Raven and the witch turned to look at him. Anika's lips parted, her shock at this revelation evident.

"Help us," Raven said, his eyes on her again. "He is just a boy. No one came for you. No one came for Andy. But there's still hope for Phoenix. He's just a kid ... a good kid.

She hesitated, uncertainty flashing in her eyes, "What then?" she asked. "When I have told you everything and they have marked me down as a traitor like Andy, what happens next? Will you come for me then? Will you risk your life to help me?" She glanced past Raven to Stephen. "Or will you dump me at the side of the road and leave me there?"

Raven held his hand out towards her, the sleeve of his shirt rising to reveal scars and tattoos. "I won't let them hurt you."

She snorted, but her eyes shone suddenly with something close to hope. She bit her lip. "You can't promise that."

"No, but I can promise you my loyalty." He took a step and closed the distance between them.

"Trust me," he said, holding his hand out to her. "Help us."

Anika shuffled from one foot to the other. Stephen half expected her to tell them both where they could go, but she raised her gaze to Raven's and swallowed.

"I won't let them hurt you," he repeated softly.

She stared at him for a long moment then reached for his hand.

Chapter Twenty-Two

The coldness of the icy water was a shock to Cade's nervous system. Every muscle in his body went rigid as he sank into its freezing depths. The cloth sack over his head was plastered to his face, covering his mouth and nose and rendering him blind. He barely managed to suck in a breath before the water swallowed him whole in less than a second.

His instinct and reflexes kicking in, he held onto the last, small breath that he had taken, fighting the sense of panic that surged to the surface. It wasn't that he was afraid to die, but dying meant that Gemma and his child were left unprotected, that he couldn't go back and save them.

Straining against his bonds, he struggled not to expel the last precious breath deep down in his lungs. He kicked at the water desperately, finding only empty space. There was no bottom, no ground beneath his feet so that he could launch himself back up. He kicked hard, but the surface seemed to never come. With the ferocity of a man who refused to accept this as his fate, he kicked hard. He wasn't ready to die yet. No fucking way. His lungs burnt in his chest from the effort of trying to hold in his breath as he fought to cling onto his life.

His *wolf* floundered, weak and poisoned and weighed down by the remnants of the silver. Barely able to lift its head, it fought desperately to come to the aid of its master.

Cade kicked and thrashed, his body twisting and fighting his bonds as the seconds ticked by, and with them, the need for oxygen grew. *Fuck*. He wasn't going to die this way. Life thundered through his veins as he strained against the rope that held his hands firmly in place behind his back.

He wouldn't give up.

Not today.

He called to his *wolf*, demanded that he come to him. This wasn't how they were going to end. Patterson was not going to win. Images of Gemma flashed through his mind. That was all that kept him going. He couldn't die—he had to get to his mate. He had to save her and his unborn child. Cade pulled at the cords around his wrists again. The *Humans* had entwined silver in the threads and they burnt his flesh each time he pulled. He gritted his teeth, unable to expel the pain from his body by shouting out, much as he needed to.

This wasn't going to be the end. Fuck the *Humans* and all their shit. His legs never ceasing their kicking, he focused on breaking the surface. The water couldn't be that deep, he thought. He kicked and twisted and pushed, and just when he thought he couldn't hold on any longer, his head broke the surface with a rush of cold air.

He tried to suck in air, but the bag over his head clung to his skin, creating a watertight vacuum around his head that he couldn't breathe through. With great difficulty, he made himself tread water and stay afloat while his mind bordered on some kind of panic.

He couldn't breathe.

He cleared his mind and kept his legs moving. Feeling he was about to pass out from the lack of oxygen, he opened his mouth for air. The momentary loss of focus on his legs caused his weight to pull him down again. He hastily thrust his head back to keep his face out of the water, but water sloshed over him and splashed into his mouth. He swallowed it down, forcing himself not to choke on it. Calm … he needed to calm. That was the only way.

His *wolf* was pushing for release, and Cade called to him. He couldn't shift fully—it would rip them both apart because his arms were tied behind his back. It would rip the *wolf's* chest in two. But he called the *wolf* in, the comfort of fur under his skin a welcome feeling. His bones began to move and Cade breathed in slowly, sucking air in as best he could through the wet cloth and then pausing when the water splashed over his face. His legs ached from the effort of treading water, his body begging him to stop and let go. But there was no way.

The bones in his hands moved and reformed as he focused all his energy on shifting only specific parts of his body. He knew once his shift began, he wasn't going to be able to stop it, but maybe he could control it and not kill himself and his *wolf* all in one go. His hands morphed into paws. *Wait … wait …* he pleaded with his wolf. His paws were slimmer than his hands when they were fully shifted, and he pulled, ignoring the pain of the silver as it tore at him. His paw slid out of the rope and he pulled his arms around front. They were stiff and ached, his shoulders in agony from being stuck in one position.

He had to move fast now … the *wolf* was there, ready. He clawed and scratched at the fabric covering his face to free himself, catching the naked skin underneath. Gasping, he gulped in lungfuls of cool air when he had removed the barrier. The water engulfed him again for a moment before he resurfaced spluttering and coughing.

Cade fumbled with the leather belt of his jeans—the *wolf* was fighting to take over. He slashed through it with his claws, gritting his teeth as he sliced through skin at the same time. Blood pooled around him in the water, the sight spurring his *wolf* on. His bones twisted and reshaped until man turned into *wolf*—whole, breathing and alive.

Near the edge of the water stood a building which, despite clearly being a new construction, very much resembled a castle from old. He paddled to the side of the edifice, his movements quiet and his senses keen. The water at the side was deep, and Cade knew that it ran to the lakes—they were way up in the hills. Trash bobbed on the water's surface, waste *Humans* threw out, not caring about the devastation they wreaked on nature. They polluted all that was beautiful, destroyed all that nature created.

Cade swam to the wall and then around it to where metal rungs fixed into the brickwork of the building served as steps. They led up to a high wall, where Cade could make out a gap to climb through. They were made for man, not *wolf*, and especially not for one so exhausted and weak from being poisoned with silver. Paddling with his hind legs, he tried to give himself the momentum to wrap his front paw around the first rung, but he missed, sending him under the cold water again.

He swore and tried once more to lunge for the rusty metal. When his paw slipped again, he realised this was not going to work. He needed fingers and hands. Backing away, he glided through the rubbish and against the current until he came to an embankment. But unlike a shore, the water didn't get shallower when he reached the edge. This lake had been purposely altered—deep troughs had been dug out and then filled with water.

With single-minded determination, Cade made his way to the edge and dug his claws into the mud and earth. The flow of the water pushed his body sideways, making him curl his claws in a desperate attempt to hold on. His body twisted at a strange angle, his shoulder dangerously close to popping out from the warped contortion. He swallowed down the excruciating pain and held on, focusing on his objective. She was in there— Gemma, his baby, and now Phoenix.

He had scented him there. His whole fucking life was in that building and they needed him to save them. He bared his teeth, upper lip curled back with a growl. With a mighty push, he rose and dug his other paw into the earth and pulled against the current.

He pulled himself up and lay on the mud panting for a moment. The silver was still coursing through his veins and the rope remained tied around one paw, but he was too exhausted to shake it off just now. He was too exhausted to move, but he had to.

Come on …. he scolded himself. *Come on.* He had to get up. He had to keep fighting. These fucking *Humans* weren't going to take everything from him. He would die before that happened. If he had to kill them all, then that's what he would do.

He closed his eyes and visualised the energy around him coming into his body and pushing him on. He searched for the man in his mind, ready to take over and let the *wolf* rest. The shift began and he exhaled heavily. In a matter of minutes, he lay panting, naked and cold on the ground. His limbs ached in ways he couldn't describe, and his flesh stung from where the silver had touched him. His skin was red raw and his stomach was marred with claw marks from where he had slashed at his belt. His face stung and he knew that he had clawed there, too.

It didn't matter. They would heal.

Cade stared at the water—there was no chance of getting his clothes back now. They were long gone, carried away by the current somewhere. Around him, the walls to the building burrowed into the earth, but there was nothing on them that he could reach—no low windows, no doors. The closest opening had to be at least twenty feet up, and there was no way he was getting to that. To one side, the ground had been dug away and it led to an opening that resembled a barn over the water—a boating shed, perhaps? Cade stumbled to his feet, stiff, tired legs making walking an ordeal. Every step was murder, but the thought of Gemma kept him moving.

He reached where the ground dipped. The water had eaten away at it, creating some kind of fissure in the earth that ran to the inside of the boat shed. This must be where they came in, but there was no water there now, just damp and dark, muddy sand. Cade slid down to it, his bare feet sinking into the mud. He leaned to the side, hands out. Even the earth that created the walls was soft and wet.

He kept moving, trudging towards the shed. Every time he pulled his feet up out of the mud, the ground tried to suck him in with each movement. He pulled himself to the shed, almost crawling, bits of stone and wood scratching against his naked skin. The earth was so wet that in places, he'd sink into the mud and sand to his knees.

There was a platform in the shed, high up from where he stood, and posts for them to tie boats to. There was one small boat, the kind that was used for fishing. It lay on its side on the dry earth devoid of water. Cade pulled himself around it and climbed inside. A box at the back held plastic trousers and a hooded jacket. They were almost three sizes too big for him—made for a greedy self-gratifying *Human*—but he pulled them on anyway. They were cold against his skin, clinging to his flesh. There were no shoes or boots, though. He pulled the chord at the elastic waistband to hold the pants in place. It was as he was fastening the pants that he saw her under the platform, where the supports had been wedged into the mud. A girl—a very young girl.

Instinct told Cade that this was just another like the girl Stephen had found in the river. She looked to be about ten years old … if that. Her dark hair was matted and tangled with sand and seaweed. Anger surged in him as he stared at her lifeless form. The glassy dead eyes that stared back at him would never see life again, never laugh and fill with joy. Leaving her there felt wrong, going against everything inside him. "I'm sorry," he whispered quietly.

He climbed out of the boat and didn't look at her again as he made his way to the ladder that led up to the platform.

The boat shed didn't have any doors to the main building. On the other side, however, stood big double doors that were large enough to drive cars through, but the space where a car would have parked was empty. There was a small door beside that, but the light between the slats told Cade that they just led to the outside. It was the only way to go, though.

As he got closer to it, he heard movement on the other side. Cade cursed silently. The boating shed had nowhere to hide. He crept to the wall next to the door and pressed himself against it, listening. There were no voices, no other sounds, just the rustling sounds of someone moving. The handle turned slowly, and Cade prepared to leap.

The door opened and Cade launched himself onto whomever it was before they knew he was there.

Chapter Twenty-Three

Stephen braced himself as Cade dove for him. Instinct warned him that his friend's state of mind was tenuous in that moment, his *wolf* more present than the man. He didn't try to fight him—instead, he took the brunt of Cade's weight and landed hard on the ground. Cade's hand shot out and wrapped itself around Stephen's throat, a wildness shining brightly in his eyes.

"Cade …" he rasped, grabbing onto his wrist. "It's me."

There was a moment's incomprehension before the haze slowly lifted from Cade's gaze and a flicker of recognition flashed in its blue depths.

Cade blinked hard and stared at the man he was choking. "Shit." He snatched his hand away and quickly shot to his feet.

Coughing, Stephen sat up abruptly and sucked in deep breaths.

"Shit … are you okay?"

Stephen glanced up at him, his breathing still heavy, and eyed the nervous energy rolling off Cade in waves. "The question is, mate," he choked out, "are *you* okay?"

Cade's hands shook as he ran them through his short hair in such a characteristic fashion. Images of Gemma danced through his mind, pictures of her bound and helpless as those filthy *Humans* abused and tortured her making him go out of his mind.

An old, dilapidated mill stood a little distance away. The paint that had once been white was now streaked with orange where the frames had rusted over the years. Without another word to Stephen, he turned and started towards the mill. They had to be in there— they hadn't gone far when they had bagged his head, loaded him onto the trolley and then dumped him into the lake.

"There's no one in there," Stephen called out behind him, but Cade wasn't listening. He needed to get in there. His mate was in danger.

Stephen raced behind Cade as he sprinted to the mill. When he reached the old building, Stephen was next to him. He grabbed Cade's arm to stop him, but he jerked it free with a growl and yanked open the large wooden door. It cracked open on old hinges and swung out awkwardly.

Gemma's scent spilled out, tugging inside his chest and making his *wolf* go crazy. The stench of *Humans* twisted Cade's gut and his eyes turned *wolf* as he flew to the open door in the back. He tore down the stairs, his instincts leading the way.

Stephen was hot on his heels, muttering quiet curses the entire way. When they came to the empty cages sitting in the subterranean vault, it didn't take Stephen long to put two and two together. "Fuckers," he swore violently.

Cade stared into the cage that had held Gemma. Her shoe lay upturned in the corner, and droplets of blood speckled the floor. His *wolf* surged to the surface, insistent and demanding. Some *Human* had dared to hurt his mate. Cade struggled not to completely lose it.

Not a lot, he told himself. It's *not a lot. Nothing fatal.* But that didn't matter to his *wolf*. His mate was bleeding, she was pregnant, she was alone, and she was in the hands of monsters. He gripped the bars of the cage and inhaled deeply, trying to steady himself and think lucidly. But his heart thundered in his chest, his pulse racing and his *wolf* going wild, thwarting any kind of rational thought.

Even without searching the floors, Cade knew the whole building was empty. He could hear it … smell it. The main room held a wooden table and four chairs. Empty cans and crumpled crisp bags littered the table and floor. He grabbed the back of one of the chairs and swung it around, slamming it into the wall. It shattered into pieces, broken bits of wood clattering to the floor.

Stephen stood silhouetted in the doorway, staying back. Getting in the way or trying to talk reason to a *wolf* in this state was a dangerous thing to do.

"She's not here," Cade roared. "I need to fucking find her."

"We'll find her," Stephen said firmly, trying to evoke some calm into his friend. *Shit*, he was barely keeping it together himself as he stared at the blood splatters and Gemma's shoe on the floor. He stepped back as Cade turned and strode out of the mill.

"God damn it," Cade shouted as he reached the road outside the mill. He didn't even have a fucking clue where he was. How the hell was he going to get back to her? God knows what the

Humans were doing to her with every minute that passed.

"Cade." He heard Stephen's voice as if from a great distance, barely able to register the words. He couldn't think straight, let alone follow a conversation. "Cade, you need to listen to me."

But Cade was pacing, frantic, desperate, lost in his head. Stephen dared to reach out and put a hand on his shoulder. The *wolf* spun around with a roar, ready to take out anyone who stood in the way of getting to his mate and unborn cub. Stephen raised his hands in a sign of amity and stepped back, knowing not to push things.

Stephen's mouth moved, and Cade could hear the words, but his brain wasn't processing them.

Stephen ran an agitated hand through his hair, jaw tight, face stern. "Bloody hell, mate. I need you to try focus. We can't help Gemma if you're losing it."

Maybe it was the desperate tone in Stephen's voice, or the comprehension that he needed help to find Gemma, Cade wasn't sure, but his *wolf* responded. He grew still and fixed his attention on Stephen.

Realising Cade was partially listening now, and knowing he was balancing precariously on the edge, Stephen hastened to get some answers before his friend lost it again. "Where is Gemma?"

Cade suddenly caught sight of Raven behind Stephen, but it was the woman standing next to him that made his *wolf* go on guard. He didn't know her—she was a stranger—and something felt off about her. His eyes flickered from man to *wolf*, his lips curling back to bare his teeth in a growl. He heard Stephen utter an oath.

Making sure his movements were non-threatening, Raven slowly pulled the uneasy woman behind him, his gesture one of protectiveness. He kept his eyes on Cade, dominant *panther* to dominant *wolf*. He didn't break eye contact, maintaining his dominance by refusing to back down. The intimation that the woman was under his protection and in no way a danger managed to ease Cade's *wolf*, his eyes gradually shifting back to man again.

"Cade, where is Gemma?" Stephen repeated cautiously.

Cade shook his head as if to clear it. "I don't know." He glanced back at the mill before meeting Stephen's gaze again. "I don't know. They covered my head and threw me in the water. They were here ... in there ... I don't know where she is ..." His voice trailed off and his face contorted with pain and terror. "I need to fucking find her."

"Who has her, Cade?" Stephen tried to keep his voice calm, even though inside he was ready for murder. "Who was it? Was it Patterson?"

A glassy stare met his and Cade gave a brisk nod. He was holding on by a thread. It would take just one slip up, just one small thing, for his *wolf* to take over. He would not stop until he found her.

Cade breathed hard, focusing his mind on where he was. "We go to Patterson's place," he said. "See what we can find."

"He's not there," Stephen said. "We've just come from there."

"How did you find me? Why are you here?"

Stephen tensed. Cade's mind was already on the edge; he wasn't going to take much more. "We went to Patterson's place," Stephen said tentatively. *Fuck*. How the hell was he supposed to tell Cade that not only was Gemma missing, but they now had Phoenix, too? And it was his fault. "It was a trap. They fucking set us up."

Cade frowned. "Set you up? I don't understand."

Stephen took a deep breath and then exhaled heavily. "They wanted Phoenix."

Cade stared at him for a long moment, then his eyes darted from Stephen to Anika to Raven. "Where's Phoenix?"

Stephen hesitated, his gaze meeting Raven's before replying. "They took him."

Cade's frown deepened into a scowl. "What? What do you mean? Where's Phoenix?"

"Patterson has him, Cade. It's him they've wanted all along."

Cade was on Stephen lightning fast, gripping him by the shirt and sticking his face into his.

Stephen didn't try to move away. "You're lying. You're fucking lying. Where is he?"

It was Anika who stepped forward and spoke, though she made sure to keep close to Raven. "He's a half-breed," she called out.

His head whipped around to look at Anika, and Raven took a small step closer to her. Cade let go of Stephen and narrowed his eyes at her. "So what? He's clear of all that crap of the past. What does being a half-breed have to do with anything?" He paused and his eyes raked over her slim form. "And who the fuck are you anyway?"

"She's helping us," Raven said silkily.

Cade watched as she swallowed and took a cautious step closer to Raven. She was a nervous thing—young, blonde, tall like Stephen—but her voice didn't match what her body portrayed. Weakly, she said, "He has power. *Humans* that become *Other* are stronger, more powerful."

That was no secret. Everyone knew that. "And what does the power mean to the *Humans*?"

She glanced nervously at Stephen and then Raven before replying. "When half-breeds are just turned, they go through a transition. It's a time when all of their powers become big and uncontrollable. This is when they die. When Phoenix was first changed over, was there anything that was big inside him?"

Stephen's eyebrows drew together. "His hunger."

She nodded. "When my powers came to me, they were so big and strong I didn't know what I was doing with them. It was like holding electricity in my hands." She held her hands out, palms facing up, and little sparks crackled. "But also, when the turn happens, the mind is capturable."

"What do you mean?" Cade demanded.

"Like all the cells in the body change. This is what Doctor Marcus told me. He said that when all the cells are fighting, then the mind can be caught and controlled—it is vulnerable then. This is when half-breeds die. Their minds go so mad that it kills them, but if they can link to another, then they can learn control."

Cade and Phoenix were connected in mind. It's what Cade had done to get through to the boy and try save his life when he had found him two years ago. Had he simply been taking control or had he actually saved his life by doing that? "What does that have to do with Phoenix?"

Anika shuffled from one foot to the other, ill at ease.

"What does it mean?" Stephen pushed.

Her eyes glinted with deep-rooted contempt. "They want to test what the limit is. Shifters can heal well." She paused before adding, "Can you imagine if that were multiplied?"

"You have something that is hard to kill," Raven murmured.

"Yes. And if you can take control of the mind …"

"Fuck," said Stephen. "You have an unstoppable soldier." He turned to Cade. ""We're going to have to take this to Society. It's too big for us."

Society. Right now they might be worse than Patterson, Cade thought. If they confronted them about the baby, Gemma would be dead for sure. Trevor would leap up and write the execution warrant in blood if he had to. It would get him Malcolm's seat. It would get him everything he had ever wanted. He'd treat it like a god damn prize.

"I am not leaving without Gemma. Go to your father if you like. I'm looking for her myself," Cade said. He wasn't leaving without her. He was sure about that. He turned from Stephen with grim determination. He had no idea where he was going, but he trusted his *wolf*—trusted that he would find the two things that he lived for. He turned and walked away. They could bring Society, but he wasn't wasting another moment.

Stephen followed him and grabbed his arm. "Come on, man. Think about this logically. You can't charge in there and save her by yourself. They'll just kill you. They already tried."

"I'm not afraid of them," Cade ground out. "I'll fucking kill them all. That's my life in there—all of it. Phoenix, Gemma, the baby. It's all I have." He choked out the last word. Saying it out loud was much harder than just thinking it.

"Well, you should be afraid of them. I am," Stephen said. "They're fucking maniacs, and that's my sister in there and a kid. I get you. I really do. I want to go in there and rip their heads off and shit down their necks, but I can't, and not being able to do that goes against everything in me. But the thought of finding them like that girl by the river, it scares me shitless. I can't even bear the thought of it. We've one shot at this. We can't screw it up. They ran when they dumped you right?"

Cade nodded grimly.

"So we barge in there, wherever there is because we don't have a bloody clue, they'll kill her. We have to do this properly. Society is properly. They're bigger than us. If you go there now, you're just going to end up dead."

"I will get in," Cade growled. "They won't stop me."

Anika and Raven had come up to them, standing just behind Stephen. "No," she said. "You won't. They are well-prepared. They've been planning all of this for a long time. You and Gemma were just an early opportunity for them."

Cade took a step closer to her and Raven stepped forward. "How do you know all of this? How do you know their plans?"

"She worked for them," Stephen said slowly.

Cade's eyes widened in surprise then cold, hard fury crossed his features. He lunged for Anika, but this time Stephen blocked his path. "She worked for them?" he yelled at him, shoving at his chest. "You let her stand there, still alive, when she has been a part of all this?"

"They've been using her, betrayed her. She's the one who helped us find this place. She doesn't know where they have taken Gemma now," Stephen said. "This was the last place she knew. They dumped her ass."

"I don't believe it."

Anika stepped back to Raven's protective parameter.

"Fighting about this isn't going to help," Stephen said, pushing Cade back.

"She has answers." Cade roared. He pushed Stephen but he didn't budge. A god damn brick wall of muscle.

"Cade ..."

Cade pointed at Anika, his face twisted with deep hatred. "You are a traitor to your kind? Is that what you are? You fucking helped them to do this?" He strode over to Anika, and Raven automatically shoved her back behind him. He held up his hands in warning to Cade. How dare he? Cade thought. Did he not know that he was dealing with Society? "Get out of my way."

"It's not her fault," Raven said to him.

"Who the fuck are you? Are you with the *Humans,* too? All strays go and lay down with that filth?"

Stephen sided next to Cade, blocking him from Anika and Raven now. "Come on. Think about this."

"I am thinking about this. They have my mate. They have the boy I took in. They're my life, both of them, and the baby. The *Humans* have them and people like her," he pointed to Anika, "they helped to take them from me. I can't just stop and think about it. Thinking isn't going to get them back."

"We've got to take this to Society. It's the only way. This is bigger than us. Don't you think that if I thought charging in there and killing the lot of them would get us Gemma and Phoenix back, I wouldn't do it? Because I would. I'd be there now slashing my way through. But we can't. Those *Humans* are afraid and that makes them dangerous as well as stupid. You know this."

"They have Gemma."

"I know. Let's do this right and get her back." Cade's *wolf* growled in protest, but Stephen was right. He'd not let Gemma just die if he could go and get her. It just went against everything inside of Cade. They were just fucking *Humans*—he hated them all.

"She isn't going anywhere." Stephen said calmly. "And we are going to get her and Phoenix. We just need some back up."

"If she dies?" Cade gritted out. "What if we are too late?"

"She won't. The *Humans* are idiots, but Patterson has more sense about him than to kill them. You know that."

"He wants war," Raven said.

Stephen nodded. "Of course he does. But he wants war that he can win. He's not going to kill them because that would be suicide. We need Society."

Cade breathed hard and pushed down all the negative thoughts of what could happen—what might happen. "Okay," he finally grated. "Let's go to Society."

*   *   *

Malcolm was outside at the back of the house when they found him. He must have just come back from a run because he wore black trousers, shirt open, revealing a well-muscled torso. Even age hadn't stopped him from retaining his muscle. His eyes shone brightly, his *tiger* still awake in there. He pushed his glasses up onto his nose before addressing his visitors.

"Where's Mum?" Stephen asked.

Malcolm buttoned up his shirt. "She's out running with your sister," he said flatly. He raised his eyes to Stephen, not acknowledging the others who were with him. "They are out of earshot so whatever it is that you want to tell me, I suggest that you do it now." He reached for his tie and put it around his neck. "I judge by the expression on your face that you're not here merely to enquire about your mother's whereabouts."

Stephen tensed. This was what it was to be alpha—reading people, knowing things and protecting others. He wasn't sure so much that when he took over he would be able to do it quite so well. "Patterson," he said bluntly. "He's taken Gemma and Phoenix."

Malcolm paused with his tie half knotted. It wasn't often that Malcom showed any emotion. He had the perfect poker face, but it was there, fleeting, and Stephen had caught it.

"Patterson has my daughter?" Malcolm's voice was gruff as he asked Stephen. "He has taken her? Where?"

"We don't know," Cade said, coming forward. "He had us at Christchurch. But she's gone."

Malcolm frowned. "They had *you*, too?"

"Yes. He took us both, but they let me go."

"And you left her there?"

The insinuation in Malcolm's question pierced icily through Cade's chest, but right now that didn't matter. Nothing did except for getting Gemma back. A tick worked along the side of Malcolm's jaw, his eyes betraying the stoney façade he tried to portray. Even the great Malcolm Davies couldn't hide his anger and concern when it came to his children.

"We don't know where she is," Cade said.

Malcolm nodded and said nothing. He strode past them all and went to the house, letting them follow. The back door swung open with such force that it slammed into the concrete wall and vibrated. He marched all the way to the quiet room, the four of them trailed after him. He sat and listened to the whole story from Stephen—the planned meeting after they had both been to the other Societies. He told them about Gemma and Cade not turning up and then going to the hotel they had booked. He didn't mention taking Phoenix to see his father. Or the fact that they hadn't had two separate bedrooms at the hotel. Cade filled in his side, keeping with Stephen and only saying what they needed to, missing out anything that would land them in trouble.

When they were done, Anika added quietly, "They're taking them to Exile." All faces in the room shot in her direction.

"What for?" Malcolm asked.

"They have Phoenix. He's a half-breed. In Exile … they aren't restricted like here."

"They experimented on her, too," Raven added. He reached out and brushed the hair from her ear, sweeping it back so they could all see the faded tattoo there. "She was *Human*, too, at one point."

"Do you know where this place is?" Cade demanded. "Did you purposely keep this information from us again? Gave them time to get away."

"No," she said meekly. "I don't know where it is. I always got taken to places in the dark or asleep."

"And now they have let you go?" Malcolm asked. "Just like that?"

"I was six. They took me and made me *Other*." She swallowed hard and took a breath, clearly uncomfortable in the room. She explained to Malcom about Phoenix and how he would be more powerful. Malcom listened, his jaw tight and his eyes fierce. The air around them became charged with each new piece of information that was revealed. His hands balled into fists, but he stayed put, listening and nodding until she was done.

"What does my daughter have to do with all of this? She is pure."

"I don't really know." Her eyes darted around the table at every single hostile face. Only Raven seemed to hold a softer expression, but even he sat waiting for her to answer that one. "Maybe because she is pregnant?"

Malcolm straightened. "Gemma is pregnant?"

Stephen shot to his feet, silently cursing. "We can explain," he said quickly.

Malcolm's nostrils flared and his glare landed on Cade. "Do you realise what you have done?"

Chapter Twenty-Four

The man with the lopsided smile stood cautiously off to the side. If he could have smiled properly, his grin would have been huge, Phoenix thought to himself. All teeth and thin lips. Except when he did smile, only half of his face lifted properly, exposing one crooked yellow front tooth. His eyes shone with wild excitement at the discovery he had made in the car—he was positively bouncing from it. Elation radiated from him in such a way that it was intoxicating. He was a child who had just got what he had always wanted for Christmas.

He peered into the boot, his eyes roaming up and down Phoenix in glee. Another *Human* came to stand next to him, his glum face a stark contrast. Phoenix recognised him as one of the men from the car. Next to him, another *Human* stood pointing a gun at Phoenix. It was the guy with the jacket that eventually leaned in and grabbed Phoenix's arm.

The strong odour of urine in the car burnt the inside of Phoenix's nose, making him want to retch. Stephen had been right. *Humans* had a stench to them when they were afraid. It rolled off them, putrid and lingering. The *Human* in the jacket pushed Phoenix's sleeve up and plunged a needle into his arm before he could react, depositing whatever liquid was in there into his veins.

Warmth spread, like a fiery flame under his skin. He grabbed his arm, pressing tightly in a futile attempt to stop it.

The three *Humans* took a step back together and some kind of trolley was wheeled closer, rattling against the concrete floor. Phoenix closed his eyes, bringing Stephen's words to mind. *If you can smell fear, you can use it.* He'd drummed it into him like a mantra for these moments. A person, *Human* or *Other*, could hide facial expressions, they could cover their body language with forced effort, but there was no one that could ever mask the scent of fear. It just wasn't possible.

If the *Humans* had been *Other*, they might have been able to detect the scent of Phoenix's emotions. As it were, Phoenix had the advantage here.

Use it, he thought.

He pushed himself up slowly, swinging one leg out first. The *Humans* backed up as he climbed out and stepped down, throwing nervous glances at each other as they did so.

The space they were in looked like a large garage. There were no cars parked around and no white lines marking the floor giving directions, but there was a large shutter at the back with a barrier pole across the top, and a small doorway that was closed.

Phoenix moved again, slow, unhurried steps that had the *Humans* backing away. Maybe he could drive them all the way to the door and then make a run for it. He pushed his shoulders back, making his presence bigger than it was. Stephen had told him how to do it. No matter what, walk it tall. Don't hide. Don't back away and no one will have a clue that you're shitting yourself with every move. So that was what he did—shoulders back, chest out and jaw clenched as he kept his eyes on the *Humans*. All he had to do now was not screw this up and get himself killed.

If he got them in the right place, he could charge. "Stop." The *Human* pointed a shaky gun at him, then quickly swapped it to his other hand so that he could wipe his palm down his jeans. Would he even have the courage to shoot? It wasn't him who was pathetic, it was the *Humans*—Stephen had every aspect of it right. He almost felt ashamed that he had once been one of them—blind and idiotic, weak and afraid.

"You need to let me go," Phoenix said, throwing confidence into his voice and hoping he sounded more in control than he felt.

The *Human* with the lopsided smile raised his hands nervously. "Calm down," he gulped. "We don't mean you any harm."

Phoenix moved quickly, rushing at the *Human* with the gun, his eyes on the gap between them.

A gunshot ricocheted around the room and pain exploded in Phoenix's shoulder, the force of it flinging him backwards. He landed on the ground with a thud, his hands clutching at his shoulder as he went down. With a grunt, he rolled with it and was back on his feet as fast as he had gone down. Blood trickled down his arm, and his skin grew taut. He pushed back his collar to inspect the damage— the hole was small and growing smaller by the second. Something thick and black oozed out of it, running down his arm. It didn't even mingle with his blood, oil and water rejecting each other ... but it wasn't oil.

"Silver doesn't work on me," Phoenix smiled at them derisively. He really did feel strong and confident suddenly. What could these *Humans* actually do to him?

"You gave him silver?" the *Human* with the lopsided smile asked his friend incredulously. "Are you an idiot?"

"He's a shifter," the *Human* said in defence.

"He's a half-breed. Silver doesn't work on him, for fuck's sake."

"Maybe this will work."

Phoenix spun around in the direction of the female voice behind him. A tall, slim woman stood by a door, which probably led to the main building, with a disparaging smile on her face.

"Gemma ..." Phoenix shot forward and the woman took a cautious step back and shook her head at him.

"Not so fast, half-breed." She shoved Gemma forward, and Gemma almost tripped over her own feet. Her head hung down, but Phoenix could see her tired face. Dark circles ran around her eyes even though it had only been a day. "You wouldn't want anything to happen to your friend now, would you?" she purred sweetly, and Phoenix clenched his fists at his sides.

If Cade or Stephen saw what they had done ... He had to think like them ... act like them. He couldn't run now. They would never leave Gemma behind, and neither could he.

"You were at the car, too?" She had an odd scent to her, even from where she stood. Phoenix could smell it—coppery and rich. She was definitely *Other*.

"Did you think that poor idiot just had a haemorrhage by himself?"

Thoughts of Andy sneaked into Phoenix's mind. No, of course he didn't. He didn't want to think about Andy at all or what he had seen. The woman flicked her hand in a circular motion, and the *Human* with the gun buckled over, clutching at his stomach. He screamed as she twisted her hand mid-air, holding nothing, but even from where she stood, the *Human* was affected by it.

"Stop it, Janie," the other *Human* said.

The woman laughed as she brought her hand down again, and the *Human* started to cough and heave until he vomited onto the concrete floor in front of him. "Fucking nice one," he said eventually, spitting out the last of what he had brought up. "You forget your place."

She rolled her eyes. "It was just a tickle." She pushed the half-sleeping Gemma ahead of her and Phoenix wondered whether this Janie was the only thing keeping Gemma upright at that moment. Phoenix's *wolf* reeled in anger and frustration that he couldn't go to her and help her. Gemma murmured something and tried to twist out of Janie's grasp, but Janie dug her fingers in, making Gemma wince.

"Let her go," Phoenix demanded.

The *Human* with the jacket came around then. "No can do, I'm afraid. We have our orders."

"Where's Cade?" Gemma asked hoarsely. She lifted her eyes to look at Phoenix, and just the sight of her made Phoenix's chest tighten. She had a faded bruise on her face, but that didn't mean it wasn't recent. She was a shifter; it could have happened ten minutes ago.

"I don't know," Phoenix said gently.

"The *wolf* is dead," the *Human* with the gun said as he holstered his weapon.

"No," Gemma cried out. "I don't believe you."

"Believe it, honey," Janie said. "He's dead. Down with the fish now."

Gemma had her eyes on Phoenix again, and despondency tore through him. He shook his head and touched his fingers to his temples, hoping that she would understand. If Cade was dead, he would know it. He would probably be dead himself. That was what he had been told anyway—their bond was a two-way thing. If Cade died, he would die, too.

Gemma bit her lower lip and gave a slight nod.

She understood.

"You need to get onto the trolley," the lopsided-mouthed man said. "We have work to do, and we're on a tight schedule."

Phoenix frowned. "Why should I?"

Janie came closer, pushing Gemma as she did. "Because we said so." She held her hand over Gemma's abdomen, and Gemma grabbed it and tried to pull it away, but Janie reached around and grabbed Gemma's wrist. Gemma's eyes shifted, the pupils turning to ovals. "I don't think so," Janie said. She turned her attention to Phoenix, her features hard. "Get on the trolley."

Gemma shook her head. "Don't do it," she rasped. She forced each word through whatever pain it was the woman was inflicting on her, doubling over and gasping for air while she fought to get the woman's hand off her. Still, she pleaded with Phoenix. "Don't …"

Janie narrowed her eyes and Gemma cried out with fresh pain. "How long do you think her baby can withstand this?"

"Fuck off," Gemma cried through gritted teeth and pushed against the woman, flinging her arm back, elbow to the jaw. Janie's head snapped back, but she didn't let go—like a fucking leech.

"Trolley," she glared at Phoenix, anger clear in her eyes now.

"Run, Phoenix," Gemma shouted, but he couldn't do that—wouldn't do that. Stephen and Cade would never have left her. They'd have fought until Gemma was free. They'd sacrifice themselves for her without a second thought. He wasn't afraid. He wasn't like them and they would know it. With long strides, he walked towards Gemma and lopsided man hesitated, unsure what Phoenix's intentions were. Phoenix stopped in front of the trolley, paused and looked at Gemma.

"I have to. I'm sorry." He climbed onto it and she sobbed, reaching for him even with Janie holding her tightly. Phoenix tried to shut out the sounds, unable to bear the way they ripped his heart to pieces.

"Good choice," Janie said to him. She gripped Gemma's upper arm and dragged her over to a wheelchair by the wall. It had bindings all around and Gemma was thrust into it. Phoenix didn't need to guess that they would be silver, but Gemma sat there with her lips firm, refusing to show them the pain she was feeling.

The lopsided smiler came to Phoenix's side. "Glad you chose to join us," he said as he began to fasten the straps around Phoenix. The urge to jump up and smack the stupid man and knock the smile off his face was almost too great for Phoenix, but he restrained himself. It would do him and Gemma no good.

The straps that went around Phoenix weren't silver, but they were extra strong. When they had him secure, lopsided nodded to the *Human* with the gun and the trolley began to move.

Phoenix couldn't see where he was going. They had placed a strap across his head so that he couldn't move it. All he could see was the old, cracked ceiling above him, lines of black mould patched across it. Gemma was close to him; he could feel her. He listened to the sound of the heavy footsteps of the *Human* men. The lights changed suddenly, going from the dull lamps to large fluorescent lights that hummed above him. The trolley jerked to a stop when one of the *Humans* applied the brake.

Phoenix's only sense was his hearing. There was a rattle of chains that came from either side of him, and above him, a chain hung from the ceiling. It ran through a sort of hook—a pulley mechanism. The chain started to come down, slowly, until it touched his chest, its heaviness pressing into him and the coldness of it seeping through his top.

"We won't be a moment," Janie said to him. He thought that they were unstrapping him as the buckles on the belts clanged, but his arms didn't come free. If anything, they were pulled apart tighter.

"Lean him forward," a male voice that Phoenix didn't recognise said. The trolley began to rattle and jolt as machinery inside it began to work. Phoenix felt himself begin to rise and then he tipped forward. They had attached a hook to the strap around his throat, and it pulled tight as gravity began to win and he started to slide from the trolley. His arms began to rise on either side of him, not stopping until he was suspended upright, arms out, feet barely touching the ground.

The man who had spoken came forward. He was tall—taller than Stephen—and wore latex gloves. He wrapped a hand around the back of Phoenix's neck and pulled his head forward. Phoenix felt the tip of a vibrating needle against the hard bit behind his ear, and he clenched his teeth, bracing himself for the pain.

Dark Veil

The man held him in place and tattooed a number behind his ear.

Chapter Twenty-Five

Malcom sat in the large, leather chair at the end of the long table in the silent room, a formidable force to be reckoned with. Patterson was a fool, although 'fool' was perhaps too weak a description for him. How he even dared to dream that he would get away with this plan was beyond reasoning. He'd not be coming out of this alive, that was certain.

Malcolm clasped his hands together in front of him, elbows on the table, thumbs tucked under his chin. He was a man of fact, much like Cade. He dealt with reason and logic and a great amount of control that held no bounds. Even now, as he sat staring at the phone waiting for someone to pick it up on the other end, his rage stayed down, bubbling under the surface as his mind stayed fixed on the task at hand. Stephen had no idea how he did it. How he could sit there and not drive to the *Human's* place and rip their fucking doors off. Stephen wasn't sure if he admired or hated his father for it—this was Gemma they were talking about it. He seethed just thinking about it.

Cade fidgeted in his seat, eager for the phone to be answered on the other end. The room hummed with electricity–an electrical charge that stemmed from a *tiger*, *wolf* and *panther*, all of them hunkered down in the grass, lying in wait and ready to leap out.

Malcolm showed no anger, but it was there, almost palpable. No one in the room spoke as they watched the phone and waited. The phone beeped and, once again, the female voice on the other end answered and informed them that the call could not be taken at this time. It ended with a click and the dull dialling tone echoed around the room until Stephen couldn't stand it any longer.

He reached over to shut it off. "Leave it," his father commanded.

Stephen paused mid-reach and looked at him, a tick working along his jaw. Why were they not acting? What the hell did they still need all this diplomacy for? Patterson had fucking taken Gemma. "Call them again," he gritted out. Right now, he wasn't talking to the alpha of *Others*, he was talking to his father—his sister's life was in danger.

Anger flashed in Malcolm's eyes as they fixed on his son. He did not appreciate insubordination—less so from his son and future alpha. "I said leave it." Before Stephen could say more, he reached for the phone panel and hit the button to end the call, then hit star-1—Trevor.

Cade inched forward uncomfortably, but Malcolm raised a hand before he could even voice his concern of his father being brought into this. He shot Stephen a concerned look, but Stephen's expression reflected his own. If Trevor found out about the baby, they'd all be fucking killed—Gemma being number one, and Cade being last just so that Trevor could make sure he had learnt his lesson before losing his life. It would be a race between the two alphas to see who could get the execution order first. He frowned—but then why rescue Gemma? She was already being taken care of by the *Humans*.

As he always did, Trevor answered immediately. Cade was sure that his father sat on the damn phone.

"Call the board," Malcolm said, not offering any kind of greeting. "We need them here right away. Patterson has taken my daughter."

There was a brief pause before Trevor spoke. "Are you sure?"

"Yes," was Malcolm's curt response. He shot a glance in Cade's direction. "They had your son, too."

Another pause. "Had?"

"Cade is here. He is fine, but we need Society here. Now. Every minute that gets wasted is another minute Gemma doesn't have. Call the board." Malcolm hung up the call without waiting for a confirmation. Trevor would do it. He might be an asshole, but he was efficient. God knows he wouldn't want anyone to see him as incapable if Malcolm finally fell off his perch.

Stephen leaned over to this father. This was so fucked up, all of it. "If Trevor finds out about the baby …" He would have a fucking field day. He could get rid of Phoenix, get rid of Gemma, and dig his hooks into Cade and command him like a puppy for the rest of his life. This really was as Cade had said—it was his life, literally.

Malcolm's jaw clenched, the only indication he had heard him. With a muttered curse, Stephen leaned back in his chair and glared at him.

Sometimes he wished his father could forget to be an alpha for at least one fucking minute.

Cade could barely stay in his seat. They were just sitting here waiting for a damn meeting to be arranged while Gemma was left at the mercy of the *Humans*. His *wolf* urged him to get out there and look for her, but his rational side told him that getting organised the way Malcolm was trying to was probably the right course of action. It was still hard to just sit there and wait, though.

Stephen glanced over at him, knowing exactly how Cade was feeling. There was no question in his mind that when Gemma got back—because there was no *if* about that—she and Cade had to leave. So much as it would hurt him for them to go, so much as he needed them there, he couldn't see them killed for this.

"Trevor will not find out about the baby. No one will," Malcolm said sternly. He turned to Raven and Anika with a harsh expression on his face. "Do you understand the consequences for yourselves if you mention this to anyone?"

Dark Veil

Anika nodded in quick compliance, and Raven raised his hands. "It ain't none of my business," he said smoothly.

With a brusque nod, he turned back to Stephen. "You need to go and find Evie and your mother. Tell them what is going on before they walk in on a big meeting and panic. You can make our guests comfortable in the summer lounge. Get them something to eat and drink." Code for *Leave Cade and me alone*.

Stephen glanced at Cade as he got up with Raven and Anika, sure that his friend wasn't worried about whatever Malcolm wanted. His mind was too preoccupied with Gemma and Phoenix.

"Close the door behind you," Malcolm said.

When the three had gone and Malcolm and Cade were left alone, Malcolm rose from his seat and went to the bureau by the wall. He moved some papers around and exchanged one set of glasses for another before turning to face Cade again. His nostrils flared and he crossed his arms over his chest as he fixed Cade with a non-too-friendly glare. "Do I need to enquire who the father is, or have my assumptions served me correctly and you and my daughter have gone against not just Society law, but the laws pinned down by our Council and the Council before them?"

"We didn't plan for this to happen."

"But you didn't plan for it not to happen, either?"

In truth? No, they hadn't. They had never thought that it would be possible. "I am in love with your daughter," Cade refused to back down. Arguing about what they should have done and what they had done wasn't going to change a thing. It wouldn't make the pregnancy not exist. It wouldn't bring Gemma back. She was pregnant and they had fucked up, but Cade didn't regret a thing.

Gemma was his.

Malcolm nodded slowly. "You do realise that there can never be anything more serious between the two of you? This cannot be allowed to continue."

"More serious than a baby?"

"She can't keep it. You are not a foolish man, Cadence. If you were, I would not have allowed you to be working on the DSA or dealing with any Society affairs." Malcolm moved closer and leaned onto the back of the chair he had previously vacated. "What did you think could happen? You are already promised to a mate. Gemma has a place here."

"To produce heirs?" It was seditious, he knew it, but he really didn't care in that moment. Who was Malcolm to tell him that his baby couldn't exist?

Aware that Cade's *wolf* must be going wild—after all, this was his unborn cub they were talking about—Malcolm seemed to excuse his bout of rebelliousness. "Yes ... *tigers*, not *wolves*."

Cade stood, shoving his chair back so that it scraped along the floor. This wasn't out of disrespect for Malcolm; this was respect for himself. He was not submitting on this one. No fucking way. This was his child they were discussing, not some pet that he wanted to keep. It was his and Gemma's, and no Society or Council was going to tell them what to do about it. "What if Gemma wants the baby? Will you forcefully kill it?"

Malcolm sighed and stood upright again. "There are laws that we must abide by. We may not like them, but they are there, and they are what we follow when we choose Society. We …"

"I didn't choose Society," Cade ground out, cutting him off. "I didn't choose any of this. It was all chosen for me. Why should I stick to laws that I never agreed to being a part of?"

Malcolm inhaled slowly, his eyes on Cade as he did. His voice held no room for objection any longer. "This child cannot be born. You know this. There can be nothing between you and my daughter. You know this, too. The pregnancy will be terminated, and then you and Gemma will deal with one another only as Society needs. I cannot cast you out without raising questions. I do not wish for your father to seek an execution order for my …"

Cade leaned forward, hands on the desk. "So you can break the laws when it is your child? It is okay then? When your flesh and blood might be killed or your precious seat on the Council is at stake? If we are forced into an abortion, I will speak out."

A tic worked along Malcolm's jaw. "Then you will die."

"I don't fucking care about dying."

"But you do care about Gemma dying. You would not risk her life."

"I will not risk my child's life," Cade shot back just as the door to the meeting room burst open and Emily stormed in.

"Tell me it isn't true … what Stephen told me," she said. "Tell me …"

Stephen stood behind her. "I tried to tell her you were busy," he said before his father could unleash his anger at the intrusion.

Emily walked around the table to where Cade was standing, and Stephen came in fully and shut the door behind him, closing all four of them in the room. "I told Stephen that I don't care if you are busy when one of my children has been taken," she told him furiously. "I want in on it. The *Humans*? They have her?"

"We're dealing with it," Malcolm said grimly.

She narrowed her eyes and wagged her finger at him. "Don't you leave me in the dark on this one, Malcolm Davies. She is my daughter, too. I want to know where she is and who has her."

Malcolm gripped the back of his seat, the leather creaking under his grasp. "Patterson has her and Phoenix, too."

"She's pregnant," Cade added, and Malcolm's eyes darkened. He had crossed the line, but he didn't care. He knew that Emily would never allow for her grandchild to be aborted, no matter what Society ordered.

She gasped, putting her hand over her mouth, her pale green eyes widening. "Is this true?" She turned to Stephen, not Malcolm. "Gemma is pregnant?"

Stephen gave a curt nod.

Emily turned to Cade. "They have Phoenix, too," she said softly, not as a question. He had expected lots of things, but what he wasn't prepared for was Emily suddenly reaching up and wrapping her arms around him to pull him into an embrace that he hadn't realised he needed until that very moment. His heart ached as she held him.

It thudded in his chest, his emotions begging for release at the sudden onslaught of comfort. He wrapped his arms around her, closing his eyes for a moment and taking what he needed. When she let him go, she wiped her eyes and sniffled before turning back around to face her son and husband.

"I will start letting the others in," she said, and then she walked out of the room with her head held high.

The Society members arrived not long after. Trevor wasn't first, and that probably pissed him off to no end, Stephen supposed—although the man could be pissed off if his own shadow dared to walk in front of him.

Malcolm opened the meeting when there were five of them there—Angela, from the *foxes*, Trevor from the *wolves*, and Aaron his shadow and heir. The bears finally arrived, and Malcolm filled them in on the things that he did know, without the details of the baby. He told them about Phoenix and gave them the story that Stephen and Cade had fed to him.

Cade and Stephen hadn't given him the true events, but what did it matter? They had been staying in the hotel for the night when Gemma and Cade were taken. Phoenix was caught later when Stephen went looking for them. They didn't need to know about the tickets or the trip to Phoenix's father. None of that mattered. Before the meeting was done, the phone at the centre of the table rang and for one, long moment, they all just stared at it.

Malcolm hit accept and put the call on loudspeaker—Patterson's voice rang out. "Malcolm," he said in a purr of fake, sleazy delight. "I had a couple of missed calls from you it would seem. Is there something bothering the top cat?"

"I believe we have a problem," Malcolm said tersely.

"We do?"

Malcolm leaned in, palms down on the table. "It would seem that you may have seen fit to detain my daughter, and I was calling to enquire why that is and demand that she be returned home immediately."

The other Society members said nothing, listening intently. It was doubtful that Patterson would realise he was talking to a room full of *Others*. He gasped at Malcolm's accusation. "I have no idea what you're talking about," he said. "In fact, I think I am quite offended that you would insinuate ..."

"I am not bothered what you are. I have it on good authority that you took Cadence MacDonald, Gemma Davies, and now the boy. I am not calling you to ask about it. I am calling to tell you that you need to release them. Immediately."

Silence greeted him from the other end for a moment, then Patterson's stern voice was heard again. "I told you I have no idea what you're talking about. Now, if you don't mind, I have business to attend to."

The phone clicked and the line went dead.

Chapter Twenty-Six

One thing that Phoenix never imagined he would learn was the terrifying lessons about the *Humans* and all the badness they held inside of them. He had been one of them. He had lived with them. Yet now, he was at their mercy, their cruelty uninhibited. Vile and disgusting and dripping with greed, it was beyond belief. His father's words and teachings echoed in the back of his mind always. *Others* were monsters—unnatural creatures that shouldn't be allowed to exist. *Others* killed for fun and sport. *Others* wanted to turn the world for their own benefit and rid it of the *Humans*. It was lies, all of it, and it stared Phoenix in the face right now. How foolish he had been growing up, blind and gullible, taking everything in and never questioning it. If only his father could see this—maybe then he would see the truth of things.

Phoenix squinted and let his eyes roam the brightly-lit room—a room made by *Humans*, purpose-built and designed to hold *Others* prisoner.

Humans—such sick and disgusting creatures.

His head throbbed unbearably and his stomach churned. His eyes shone brightly against the dull room, a kaleidoscope of colour captured within them.

Patterson stood in front of him, or was it *Fucking* Patterson, as Stephen so often called him. It seemed to suit him more. Phoenix chuckled as the thought first entered his mind, causing him to flinch and regret the action immediately as the action rocked his brain in the confines of his skull and sent bolts of agony around every single nerve fibre, turning his laughing into an agonising growl. When the pain eased and he could open his eyes again, Phoenix focused his sights on Patterson—fucking Patterson—and breathed, short, shallow breaths to better control the pain. God damn them, he wouldn't give them the satisfaction of crying from it. He had even managed to grit his teeth through the pain in his shoulder where the stupid *Human* had shot him—with silver of all things. Did they really not know?

"Why are we here?" Gemma asked. She had been wheeled into the room and shoved into a cage. It was close enough to Phoenix that he could see every detail on her exhausted features, but far enough away that Patterson could stand between them with the reassurance that he was safely out of reach of either of them. Phoenix entertained the thought of kicking Patterson square in his smug, smiling face, slamming him back against Gemma's cage so she could hopefully rip his throat out. But the probability of that working out well for them was low. Chains held Phoenix's arms out to either side, and another pressed around his throat, keeping his head back and cutting off his own air supply if he tried to look down. Yeah, Stephen had it right—*fucking* Patterson.

The *Human* with the wonky smile stood at the side of the room working on one of the many computers that lined the long counter. He had drawn blood from Phoenix and gave the impression of being some kind of doctor. The machine spat out a printout to him and he yelped and squealed, his excitement rising with each new piece of information. "This is amazing," he exclaimed and hurriedly brought the papers to Patterson. He thrust them in front of his face, breathing rapidly. "Look at this ... just look. I have never seen anything like it. It's incredible."

Phoenix watched them curiously, wondering what the hell the guy was yapping about. After a moment, Patterson and the doctor lifted their eyes to stare at Phoenix. His mouth had transformed into a wide, lopsided smile even worse than the one he had displayed back at the car. All he needed was a white coat and a wiry hairstyle, and he would be set.

"So this is the half-breed," Patterson murmured, glancing at Phoenix before turning to the next sheet. Phoenix was sure that at any moment, the doctor was going to start bouncing on the spot. Patterson raised his eyes to him once more. "You're very special, do you know that?" he smiled. "It is such a shame that it took us so long to get you here." His smile broadened. "Not to worry, though. You're here now."

The doctor grabbed the papers from Patterson's hands, who earned himself a dangerous stare, but he didn't seem to notice. His excitement over his findings seemed to outweigh everything else. "Look at this one," he said animatedly, pointing at one of the pages from the back. "It's not like usual. The *Other* blood didn't take over the *Human* blood. It's like ... like ... they joined hands. This is even better than Anika."

"Let us go," Gemma suddenly shouted from her cage, but Patterson ignored her. She slammed her hand against the bars of her cage, making it rattle loudly. "Hey, Patterson. I'm talking to you."

Patterson tilted his head at her and smiled. "Patience, my dear."

"Fuck patience. What do you want with us?"

The *Human* in the leather jacket sat in a chair close to Gemma. While the doctor had been examining Phoenix's blood, he had kept smiling lewdly at Gemma until she had fixed him with a stare and explained to him exactly what she would do to his testicles if he even considered coming near her. He had laughed and told her he "liked 'em wild" until Patterson had told him to cut it out.

Patterson paid no more mind to Gemma, however, and turned his full attention back to Phoenix. "You have a very special gift I want. It can teach us so much."

"Aren't gifts meant to be just that? *Gifts*?" Phoenix replied.

Patterson laughed. "Oh, it will be. I promise."

Phoenix had no idea what the fuck he was talking about. His eyes glanced around the room, trying to look for any means of escape. There were two doors to this room—the one behind Phoenix where they had entered, and the one near Gemma's cage. It opened just at that moment, and as it did, Patterson's smile widened, lighting up his eyes.

Janie walked in … except she wasn't alone. A small hand held hers, that of a *Human* child. She looked frightened, her eyes darting around the room before she quickly, shyly, averted them to her shoes. She can't have been more than six or seven.

Gemma moved to the side of the cage closest to Janie and gripped the bars. "What are you doing with her?"

The young girl reminded Phoenix of a small fairy that belonged on the top of a birthday cake rather than here in this room—her dainty feet made next to no sound as she walked. Phoenix's stomach recoiled with images of what the *Human's* intent might be. He had no idea what Patterson was planning, but to go to all of this trouble, to set this all up and to dare to kidnap Gemma Davies …

There had to be worse things to come.

Ignoring both Gemma and Phoenix now, Patterson walked to the little girl and crouched in front of her, smiling a malicious smile. He raised a hand to her hair, and stroked it, but then his fingers sunk under the strands and twisted. She whimpered and reached up to stop him, but her small fingers could not pry his fingers away. He twisted her hair tighter, bringing a cry from her. "Beautiful, isn't she?" Patterson asked as he forced her head back for Gemma to see.

"Leave her alone," Gemma growled at him. "She's just a girl."

"Yes," he grinned and nodded before motioning to the *Human* outside her cage. "Unlock the gate."

Gemma stepped back in her cage and went to stand at the far side.

"Don't worry," Patterson said to the child, "you're quite safe in there." He pulled her by her hair, dragging her along and she started to sob, tears streaking down her dirty face. She pulled at his large hand, where his fingers twisted in her hair and kicked out at him with bare feet as she shrieked, but he ignored her, making her small legs work quickly.

When he got to Gemma's gate, he grinned at her. "A gift for you," he said, and then he launched the child into the cage. She stumbled, tripping over her small feet. Gemma lunged for her, trying to catch her before she slammed into the concrete floor, but the girl scrambled away and threw herself into the corner farthest from Gemma. "Your progeny," he laughed.

"My progeny?" Gemma padded over to Patterson, barefooted, as they closed the gate, shutting the child in with Gemma. "Do you think that I am going to turn her? I do not bite *Humans*."

Patterson's smug smile told Gemma that that was exactly what he wanted. "She is yours to create. Just a little bite. It doesn't matter to me where as long as you don't kill her. Wouldn't want you giving in to those hunger pangs at the wrong moment."

"I'm not biting her," Gemma said, setting her jaw in a determined line. "I'll sit here and fucking starve if I have to."

"Oh, there is no need for that." He sauntered over to Phoenix, sure of himself. Positioning himself behind him, like he had with the girl, he reached up and twisted his fingers in Phoenix's hair. Phoenix wasn't a child, though, and it didn't hurt the same for him. His head was yanked back, exposing his throat, the chains that held him in place rattling from the movement. Patterson held his hand out to one of the *Humans,* who placed a small knife in it. "What about now?" he asked and pressed the blade to Phoenix's throat.

"You're not going to kill him," Gemma said. "You've gone to too much trouble to get him here."

Patterson leaned forward, glaring at Gemma over Phoenix's shoulder. He pressed the blade against Phoenix's Adam's apple. Patterson's breath was thick and hot against Phoenix's face, his every word dripping with poison. Patterson wasn't like the others, Phoenix realised. He didn't smell like fear. No ... it was something else, something worse.

Patterson was power-hungry.

He laughed at Gemma. "No, you're right there. I won't kill him. But you know something we have discovered with this half-breed business?" He paused as if waiting for her to answer. "It's that they have this amazing resilience to death. I mean, we have shot young Phoenix here ..." He used the tip of the knife to point at the wound in Phoenix's shoulder that was nothing more than a dark bruised lump now. It was hard to tell that he had been shot. "His body even rejected the silver. I know you all heal fast, but thirty minutes?" He raised his eyebrows at Gemma. "Bite the child."

The girl huddled in the corner sobbing, her legs raised, face pressing into her knees. Phoenix pulled against his chains, and Patterson pressed the knife against his throat again, harder this time.

Gemma shook her head. "I'm not going to bite her."

"Very well," Patterson said, lowering his hand until it was in line with Phoenix's sternum. He angled the knife slowly, taking pleasure in what he was doing. Phoenix tensed as the tip of the knife pierced his skin.

"Don't," Gemma called out.

"You will bite her," Patterson said silkily. "Should we see just how much Phoenix can heal from?" He dragged the knife down Phoenix's chest, slicing through his skin. Phoenix clenched his jaw as his flesh parted in a hot trail. He pulled hard against his binds, but the one around his neck cut off his airway.

Gemma slammed her hands onto the bars, grabbing them tightly and then shaking them with enough power that Phoenix thought they might actually come away, even though they were embedded into the concrete floor. "Stop it."

Patterson brought the knife all the way down to Phoenix's navel. He pressed it in and Phoenix rocked against the chains, trying to loosen them from around his throat, but Patterson shoved him hard from behind and stepped back. Blood ran down Phoenix's chest and stomach. He breathed hard, panting, and grabbed the chains that held him. With his head back, he let out a howl. The wound on his chest visibly healed, stitching itself together. "Do you see how fast he can heal?" Patterson asked in admiration. Before anyone could answer, Patterson swung around, knife out and slashed across Phoenix's stomach. Phoenix yelled, his skin glistening with perspiration. Blood dripped down to the waist of Phoenix's jeans, soaking in. In a matter of seconds, the wound slowly started to close again.

Patterson cocked his head at Gemma. "Still no?"

"Fuck you," she spat, tears brimming in her eyes.

"As you wish." He moved around again so that he could stand behind Phoenix once more. His face held enough evil intent that Gemma wished the fucking devil would come back to claim him. But perhaps even hell didn't want the *Humans*. They were vile, disgusting, vicious creatures, and she swore that she would see every last one of them dead by the time she got out of here.

Phoenix's pain-filled eyes met hers, his fists clenched tightly. Patterson wrapped his arms around Phoenix and held the blade over the flesh just above his navel. Ever so slowly, he pushed it in and Phoenix gritted his teeth as pain tore through him. His eyes stayed firmly fixed on Gemma, drawing strength from her as Patterson continued to push the blade in and peel his skin away.

Phoenix held his scream in for as long as possible while Gemma sobbed and yelled for him to stop. His *wolf* seethed inside, but he couldn't come out, not like this, not with his arms bound all the way up. He had never felt pain like this before—it was rich, thick, lava running under his flesh.

"Stop it," Gemma screamed. "Please, stop it."

"The girl," Patterson said calmly, unfazed.

"She's just a child …" Gemma wailed.

Patterson pulled the knife out of the wound and brought it to the other side.

Phoenix sagged.

"Matching set." His eyes shone like that of a madman's. "Last chance."

With a sob, Gemma turned towards the girl.

Chapter Twenty-Seven

Perspiration ran down Phoenix's flushed face, beading on his skin. His eyes glistened with the pain that racked his body. Gemma stared at him with respect. Not once had he cried nor begged for them to stop. He had gritted his teeth, clenched his jaw and taken every god damn thing that they had done. The *Humans* were pathetic—their victims a small child, a sixteen-year-old boy and a pregnant woman.

Gemma's heart pounded so loudly that it echoed in her ears. There was blood everywhere. It ran down Phoenix's side, staining his jeans red, and pooled beneath him on the floor. He slipped a couple of times as his bare feet slid with the slick blood. For each cut the *Humans* made, the previous one healed with incredible speed. Phoenix healed in a way that she had never seen before. He put back his head and gritted his teeth as the last cut miraculously stitched itself together again.

Patterson pulled out a white handkerchief from his pocket—he was vain enough that it probably had his name embroidered on it. He wiped it along the blooded knife, staining it. Maybe it did have his name. It would be fitting, for sure, to be stained with his deeds. Hatred bubbled in Gemma's chest and she rested a hand on her abdomen. Why bring a child into this world? So tarnished and cruel and filled with endless suffering.

Gemma was well aware of the small girl's presence in the corner of the cage. She was small and tiny—a little bird that hadn't been fed in a while. Yet, the meaning of her being there was far from small. Where had they got her from? Every scent in the room flooded Gemma's senses, but the scent of urine—however disgusting—from where the little girl sat pulled at something inside of her. Maybe it was her motherly instincts kicking in. Maybe it was the humanity she had—yet the *Humans* didn't. Ironic that.

The ground had darkened where the little girl crouched. Gemma's heart broke—to be so afraid that she would soil herself.

"I'm not going to wait all day," Patterson said as he handed the knife over to the doctor. "He heals fast."

The doctor grinned crookedly. "It's wonderful, isn't it?" He approached Phoenix and touched a delicate finger to the last wound. There wasn't much of it left now—a raised bump, some scarring—but that faded as every second passed. "He heals faster than any shifter I have seen."

Janie sat in the corner of the room, next to the end of the counter where the computers stood. They hummed with life as they processed samples that the doctor had loaded into them, codes running down the screen like green rain. She crossed her long legs, a look of bored disinterest upon her perfectly formed face. "His mind is locked tight as shit," she said, picking at one of the bracelets on her wrists. "I can't get into it."

"You're not strong enough?" mocked the doctor.

Janie raised her eyebrows and pinned him with a glare. "No. Someone has already locked minds with him." She jumped down from the stool, landing on her feet. Her hips swayed gracefully from side to side as she walked towards the men.

She was taller than Phoenix, and she smiled sweetly at him as she approached. Long delicate fingers slid across his chest as she slid behind him and rested with her hand holding his neck, her fingers splayed across his jaw.

Gemma's *tiger* rumbled from within the depths of her soul, her protectiveness over Phoenix pushing to the forefront. "Someone has already linked themselves to his mind," she whispered against his ear, "but maybe we can break it." Janie's eyes locked onto Patterson and she grinned, abruptly stopping with the seductress act. "The girl will be easy—open and ready. Like Anika was, but better."

Janie placed her hands on Phoenix's shoulders, her gaze firmly fixed on Gemma as she slid her hands along Phoenix's bare arms until she mirrored him with her arms out. She wrapped her fingers around the chains that held him in place and mumbled inaudible words. The chains clinked as they began to move. Phoenix's face contorted with pain and an irrepressible cry left his lips, echoing around the room. The muscles in his arms tensed as he threw his head back, letting out a pain-filled growl. The chains pulled tighter, spreading his arms wider.

"Stop it. He's done nothing to you," Gemma cried out, tears running down her face.

His fingers stretched and wrapped around the chains, pulling himself so tightly that he almost brought himself up off the ground. Holding his breath, he ground his teeth so hard that the muscles in his neck bulged from the strain. Gemma could only stare at him in horror. She would never get these images from her mind for as long as she lived, and she would never look at *Humans* again with any kind of compassion. They had none, so nor would she. Nothing would ever wipe away the sight of the agony in the depths of Phoenix's eyes as Janie mumbled more words, and the flesh at the centre of Phoenix's chest began to spilt open, sizzling as it did, the sound loud in the room—loud enough that even the little girl covered her ears and cried from it.

"Bite the child," Patterson said, his expression hard. Gone was the look of delight he had held before. His mask had fallen away and in its place was the face of something evil.

Gemma gripped the bars, her expression as hard as his. "She's a fucking child, you asshole."

Phoenix cried out again, louder this time. Janie had both of her hands on his chest and she clawed them down his flesh, leaving four lines on either side. His skin came apart, zipping open, exposing dark red flesh underneath. Blood oozed from the wounds, dripping down his sides to his jeans and to the ground. He breathed hard, panting with every breath. His stomach tensed. Everything was so red, so much blood. Gemma's own breath caught in her throat from the sight of it. How could they?

"Bite the child."

Janie raised her hands and placed them dramatically against Phoenix's shoulders before dragging them down his back. She didn't watch as she did it—she watched Gemma instead. Her eyes locked on her as she performed her magic. Phoenix arched his back as much as he could manage, his cry piercing through Gemma. She couldn't watch. She couldn't stand to hear it a moment longer. She covered her ears, her insides twisting from the agonising sound. It pressed in on her, making her breathless and her mind chaotic. Her *tiger* rose, scenting the blood, the coppery aroma calling to her protective senses. She craved with a need to go to Phoenix and the child in the corner. A need to protect them both and eliminate the threat.

"Bite the child and this can all stop," Patterson said as he came closer to the cage.

Gemma shook her head, her words lost now as she wept. Patterson sighed and went back to Phoenix. Janie moved out of his way as Patterson reached up and wrapped hands around Phoenix's damp blond hair and tilted his head forward. Phoenix's eyes were open, but only slightly. He was somewhere close to going unconscious. "Wake up, half-breed," Patterson said, slapping his cheek repeatedly to rouse him. Phoenix jumped and inhaled sharply through his nose, his eyes opening wildly. Patterson moved to the side so that Gemma could get a good view of Phoenix. "Look into his eyes," he said to Gemma. "Do you think he has had enough yet? You can make it stop if you want to."

"Don't," Phoenix said to her weakly. He coughed, sending his body into spasms and forcing more blood to ooze from the wounds that marred his body. They hadn't fully healed yet.

"Maybe we should do it again?" Janie said as she positioned her hand over Phoenix's chest, pushing her nails in, deeper this time and then she slowly dragging them down. Phoenix was unable to hold his cries in any longer. They came like swords in Gemma's mind, sending her into some kind of madness. She charged at them, letting her *tiger* take the lead for a moment. Powerful and strong, the *tiger* would never back down—not when there were young in need. She'd fucking kill them all before they managed to do more. Gemma launched herself at the bars, grasping at the air as she reached through the gap, claws extending from her fingertips. "Stop it," she growled, her teeth elongating in a half shift.

"If you want it to stop, stop being such a Society whore and bite the girl. This can all stop, Gemma. You just have to want it to."

Gemma spun around and strode to the girl without giving herself time to think. She picked her up in one swift movement, surprised at how light and delicate she felt. The slightest hold might snap her fragile *Human* bones. She fought desperately to get herself free from Gemma's grasp, but she was no match for a grown woman–a shifter no less.

"What if I kill the girl? What will you do then?" Gemma growled.

Patterson leaned closer, a smirk on his face. "You're not going to kill the girl. We both know that. You're Society. That makes you soft, pampered. Now, bite the girl."

She wasn't soft or pampered. Did Patterson really believe that? Was that the image Society gave out, that they were weak? Maybe it was time to show them differently. To show the *Humans* just what they were capable of.

Phoenix shook his head at Gemma, his eyes bright, bluer than usual, his *wolf* present. If they pushed the *wolf*, he would have no choice but to come out and protect himself. Gemma stared at him, his skin no longer visible under all the blood and cuts. Even where they were healing, his skin was horribly marked with shades of red.

Cade wouldn't bite the girl.

Stephen wouldn't bite the girl.

Would they?

Would they watch Phoenix suffer? The girl in her arms had stopped fighting and she looked up at Gemma with wide, terrified eyes. They had the same innocence that was still visible in Phoenix's eyes. Fucking *Humans*. How much more could Phoenix take before the innocence got replaced by that haunted look? She grabbed the girl's arm and raised it to her mouth, the girl's resistance nothing to Gemma. Her skin smelt baby powder sweet.

Gemma's canines came down fully in her mouth and her eyes shifted. The bones in her nose pressed against her skin, fighting to move and to change. Gemma welcomed the dull ache in her jaw as the bones shifted. She breathed hard, her heart beating wildly. Tears welled in her eyes, not just for Phoenix and herself, but for the girl whose life she was about to destroy. She choked down her sob. "I'm sorry," she whispered, to the girl, to Cade and Stephen and Phoenix for letting them all down and not being as strong as she knew they would be in this situation. They would never relent to the *Humans*. They'd die first.

The girl screamed in Gemma's embrace as her teeth pierced her delicate flesh. The bones were so fragile that it would take nothing for her to bite down and break the arm away. She had to restrain herself. When she was done and the taste of blood trickled into her mouth, she pulled the girl's arm free and licked across the wound, sealing it with saliva. She let the girl go, putting the unconscious girl down gently. It was done now.

But there was no stopping the shift, either. It had come this far, and it had to be finished. Frantically, Gemma pulled at her blouse and then at the vest she wore under it. She raced to take her clothes off, not caring as the *Humans* stared at her naked form. She roared with such ferocity that it seemed to shake the very walls of the place.

Patterson grinned, relishing in his victory as Gemma completed her shift and a *tiger* remained in her place. "Very good," he breathed delightedly. He nodded at Janie and the doctor handed her the knife that Patterson had used earlier. Gemma ran at the gate, roaring at them, paws slashing for them to stop. "You know, Phoenix healing so fast ... makes you wonder just what he can survive, doesn't it?"

Janie grinned at Gemma as she took the knife and plunged it into Phoenix's gut all the way to the hilt. He cried out as she twisted it, the sound lancing through Gemma and sending her *tiger* into a frenzy. Blood filled Phoenix's lungs and his cry became a gurgling sound. Janie pulled the knife out and, as she did, the *Human* with the jacket pressed a button on the wall and the chains dropped straight away, leaving Phoenix to crumple to a heap on the ground, landing in his own blood. Masses of it, from every wound.

The *Human* with the gun aimed it at Gemma's head. "Back off."

Gemma snarled at him and he pulled back the trigger. Janie came around and unlocked the gate so that the jacket *Human* could drag Phoenix in. He was out of it, his eyes rolled back in his head. They threw his limp form into the cage and quickly locked it up again.

"We'll be back soon," Patterson said. "Maybe your little progeny will need a snack."

Chapter Twenty-Eight

The door closed with a bang behind Cade as he stormed out of the meeting room. How could they all just sit around talking when Gemma and Phoenix were still somewhere out there in the hands of the *Humans*? Every second that passed was another second they did not have. *God damn it*.

Horrific images of what they could be doing to Gemma and Phoenix slammed through his mind in dreadful chaos. He pressed the heel of his palm to his pounding heart to dull the ache there. *Fuck*, he couldn't think like this. He couldn't breathe— everything clawed at his skin. His *wolf* demanded to be released so that he could find Gemma and Phoenix.

Cade stalked through the kitchen to the back door and yanked the door handle. He swore under his breath when it wouldn't open and tugged at it again, letting out a strangled growl of frustration when he realised the latch was still down. He heaved the heavy door open and hauled himself outside to breathe and think away from them all. Having to hide his feelings for Gemma from the rest of Society was inconceivably difficult to do when he was going out of his mind with worry. Yet, revealing any deeper feelings for Gemma Davies could mean punishment or death—and being locked up or dead would mean not being able to save Gemma. His father's scrutinising stare, as if he knew Cade was hiding something, and just waiting for him to fuck it all up, was just as disconcerting.

He braced his hands against the stone wall to the Davies' porch and only turned at the sound of approaching footsteps. He pushed himself up and pulled himself together. It would do no good to show his weakness and fall off the edge and into the waiting pool of snapping alligators all out for blood.

"I need to find her, Stephen," he said desperately when his friend stopped in front of him. "I need to find her and bring her back. I can't …" Cade ran his hands through his hair, roaring in anger. "I can't fucking do this. I can't bear it another minute."

His senses were overwhelmed with the scent of her in the house, his *wolf* clawing at him, frantic to go and find his mate before he descended into some kind of madness. For once, Stephen said nothing—no witty remarks, no sarcasm, his expression as worried as Cade's. The minutes ticked by, slow and agonising. His skin felt raw now, the sands of time having ground it down to almost the bone. "Give me your car keys," he demanded, holding his hand out to Stephen.

"For what?"

"I'm going back to the mill." He stepped towards the back door again, pushing Stephen backwards. "Give me the keys. I need to go and look for her."

"We'll all go," Stephen said, jaw set.

"All? They aren't going to look for her. They sit inside on their backsides talking. That isn't looking." Cade's voice pitched with urgency as he spoke.

Stephen got it. He really did. He wanted to find Gemma and Phoenix and those *Humans* as much as Cade did … but they had to calm down.

"We'll find her."

They both turned to the sound of soft footsteps on the kitchen tiles behind them.

Emily.

Her eyes were red, and it was obvious she had been crying. That was the thing with Emily, maybe what Cade admired about her the most—every ounce of her oozed housewife, but anyone who knew her saw that she was more than that. She was mother to the alpha's cubs. You didn't birth children like Stephen and raise him to become soft. Far from it. But Cade didn't think about that as she came out to him. Today, she looked like a mother whose child was missing. She wrapped her arms arounds his neck once more, and he returned her embrace, burying his face in her hair as his arms encircled her slender waist, taking a selfish moment of comfort and relishing in the scent that was so similar to Gemma's.

"I want to go back to the mill," he said gently. "It's the only lead we have and we can search it properly. Who knows what we missed."

She kissed his cheek before whispering, "You find my baby girl."

He nodded solemnly and slowly released her. With determination hardening his features, he turned back to Stephen. "We need to go back."

The kitchen began to fill with sound as the meeting was adjourned and the Society members started to file out. Fury bubbled in Cade's chest as he watched them. How could they act so complacent, chatting and leisurely strolling out of the room, when his life was hanging in the balance like this? If anything happened to Gemma or Phoenix, he didn't even know what he would do.

"Cade thinks you should all start at the mill." Stephen's expression was hard as he stared at his father, who had come out onto the porch. Like Cade, he did not agree with sitting around and having meetings when his little sister's life was at stake.

"We might have missed something," Cade added.

"Not doing your job properly?" Trevor asked with derision, appearing from behind Malcolm.

Emily's hand squeezed his a little tighter, and Cade was thankful for that moment of contact and touch, but it wasn't enough to calm the rage of his *wolf* who just wanted to find his mate. Nothing would stand between him and Gemma, not even his alpha.

"We will all go to the mill," Malcolm said and turned to Trevor. "You and Aaron come as well. We can use your noses." He glanced at Angela. "You too. The rest of you can search the area. We will not stop until we have found my daughter." He turned to Stephen. "You get the witch and the *panther*. They come, too."

Twenty minutes later—and it was a long fucking twenty minutes, too—they were at the mill and in the basement. Everything was gone. If Cade hadn't been there himself, if Gemma's scent wasn't alive in the air, he would have thought that he had got the location wrong. He breathed in deeply, taking in Gemma's unique scent, his *wolf* roaring inside of him. If he closed his eyes, she was right there next to him.

"They had stuff set up here—computers, a workbench." He gritted his teeth. "They had silver."

Malcolm's jaw clenched, but he said nothing.

Cade pointed to the second cage. "Gemma was in there. I was in this one."

The cages were down below in what looked like a basement. It was below water level, which explained why it was so damp and humid. The water on the outside created perfect soundproofing for any noise from the inside. The place reeked of *Humans*—every surface, every crevice, their stench thick in the air, infesting the place.

Cade tried to engage his DSA brain so that it would disconnect long enough from Gemma and Phoenix to actually find them—it didn't work. The teachings of Harvey echoed in his mind and he found his focus, but as soon as his guard dropped, an image of Gemma resurfaced and he would lose himself again. The others were searching the rooms above. The mill had three floors, but they were mostly filled with dusty boxes and piles of junk, old machinery for the mill, and an old rotten wooden table. The remnants of the chair Cade had smashed were where he had left them. Malcolm stood in the doorway taking in everything. When Stephen came down the cracked stone steps with papers in his hand, he turned to face him.

"I found these."

Malcolm pulled his glasses from his top pocket, flicked them open and pushed them onto his face before taking the papers to read. They were double bound and wound tight—clean, freshly printed, the white paper a stark contrast to the dilapidated building. "Purchase papers?"

Stephen nodded. "Found them in the room upstairs. There are loads of boxes up there. *Norton* shit."

Malcolm peered over the top of his glasses. "Norton?"

"Yep. Found them at Patterson's house, too. Empty, though, except for those papers."

Cade itched to look at them, but Malcolm gripped them tightly, the paper crinkling in his grasp as he exited the mill and went outside to where the others were searching the grounds. "You knew this place?" he asked Anika, who was standing with Raven and Angela. "You were here when my daughter was?"

Anika looked up at the mill. "No, I've never been here before. They made me stay at the house. But I knew it was here. They bought it about a month ago."

"No," Malcolm said. "*You* bought it a month ago."

Anika's eyes widened with shock and her back stiffened. "What?" She reached for the papers, but Malcolm pulled them back. "No, I didn't. I …"

"It's fine." Stephen took the papers from his father. "This has been set up." He flicked to the page with her name on it and showed her without giving it to her. "Do you still believe that they sent you out because they believed you could get rid of me?" At her despondent look, he continued, "They sent you out so that I would end you—deal with their problem and have you cop for all of this."

She shook her head, her long blonde hair shimmering in the sun as she did, making her seem younger and more fragile than she was. "They wouldn't."

"Wouldn't they?" Cade took the papers from Stephen and inspected them himself, then looked up at Anika with barely-contained anger. "Where are they now?" He waved the papers at her. "This is what happens with *Humans*. You work for them and they fuck you over and take what they want."

Mason Sabre

"I'm sorry," she murmured. "I didn't mean
..."

Cade stepped forward, but Stephen slapped
a hand against his chest, and Raven pulled Anika
next to him. "This isn't helping," he said to Cade. "I
want her back as much as you do, but you've got to
get your shit under control. There is nothing here ...
and your father is around. You need to make sure
he doesn't realise anything. He's not a stupid man.
You losing it will make him suspicious, and it won't
be long before he connects the pieces."

"I don't fucking care," Cade spat just as
Trevor came from around the boat house with a tall,
magnificent *wolf* behind him—Aaron. Thick, black
fur that matched his hair colour covered him, eyes
as blue as Cade's staring back at them.

"What don't you care about?" he enquired
with raised eyebrows.

Cade clamped his jaw shut and stared at him
with hatred.

"He's just a half-breed," Trevor drawled.
"You really did get attached, didn't you?"

Not bothering to respond to his jibe, Cade turned to Stephen. "Anika must know something, even if she doesn't know she does." He turned to his father. "Did you find the girl in the boat house? With your fully pure pet there? There's a dead girl just under the jetty."

Trevor's face flushed with anger.

"Have you tried to contact Phoenix?" Malcolm cut off the argument that was about to start.

"There is nothing there when I try," Cade ground out, his frustration at not being able to connect with the boy overwhelming.

Trevor gave a smug laugh. "You mean, like he might be dead?"

Cade lunged, and Stephen jumped in front of him, holding him back. Malcolm took a step between them and fixed Trevor with a hard look. "I'm trying to find my daughter, MacDonald, not start rows."

Cade leaned around Stephen. "You'd like that, wouldn't you?" He pointed at his father. "If

Phoenix is dead, then you can shove your fucking deal with the Castle's up your arse."

Trevor's face darkened once more, the union between the two families something he had sought for years.

"Come on," Stephen urged, pushing against Cade's chest and walking him backwards. "You two can fight your shit later, but right now, we need to find Gemma and Phoenix. He pushed Cade into the mill and away from everyone. "Try again. Try to reach Phoenix."

"I've tried," he gritted out. "Do you think I didn't think about that?"

"Try again," Stephen insisted. "What harm can it do?"

Cade didn't want to try again. He wanted to go back outside and smash his father's arrogant face in. He wanted someone to pay for all of this, and Patterson wasn't there, so Trevor would have to do.

"Try," Stephen urged.

"Fuck." Cade took a calming breath before muttering, "Fine." He closed his eyes with a curse, taking himself to the white room where they met in their minds—a safe place, neutral.

He was there …

Cade's heart leapt at the sight and he fought not to let his eyes snap open and break the link. "Phoenix," he called in his mind, walking and then running to him. "Phoenix." He sank down to his knees next to the *wolf*, but there was no response from the young *wolf*. Cade slid his hand under the *wolf's* snout and tilted his head back. The fur was sticky and wet, and when Cade brought his hand away, it was red.

Blood.

The sight of it fuelled Cade's anger even more. "Phoenix, answer me."

Blood pooled beneath the *wolf*, staining the white room crimson. Cade stumbled back, his mind losing it. His eyes snapped opened, severing the link between them.

Phoenix hadn't been breathing.

Chapter Twenty-Nine

The stench of blood was so thick in the air that Gemma drank it in with every breath that she took. Phoenix's head rested in her lap, the warmth of it comforting her as she stroked his hair, pushing it away from his face. Maybe it was more soothing for her than it was for him. She avoided his thick red wounds, her hand hovering just above them. She tore a piece of fabric from her blouse and tried to mop up the blood, touching only where she wouldn't hurt him more than the healing was already doing.

As each wound knitted together from the inside out, blood spurted out occasionally and ran down his side, pooling beneath them both. The sight of it tore Gemma up inside, and she had to stop to catch her breath. Phoenix slowly reached a hand up for hers, gasping through the pain of the action. Gemma laced her fingers through his and pressed her cheek against his cool hand.

"I'm right here," she whispered to him. God, he smelt so much like Cade now. Her heart hurt from the absence of him, a longing deep within her chest. She pressed her mouth to Phoenix's knuckles and breathed him in deeply. He was a mix of Cade and his maker, a scent that made him unique, a beacon that called to her *tiger* and begged her to come home. God, she would if she could.

She leaned back against the bars, pressing hard against the cold metal. The minutes ground her down. Patterson and his buddies had vanished somewhere—not that she cared. She wished they would all just drop dead.

She let her eyes close and held Phoenix's hand. He coughed, wincing from the effort, and Gemma leaned forward again. More blood oozed from his wound, but it was less this time. He healed so amazingly fast, but the pain was evident on his features. Gemma let go of his hand and cupped his face, looking down at him, her face upside down to his. "I'm right here," she reassured him again. His chest was marred with so many wounds that it was hard to decide where one ended and the next one started, the flesh underneath swollen and red.

The small girl had regained consciousness and sat trembling in the corner of the cage, her body turned away from them. Gemma glanced at her once or twice—she couldn't help it. Defiance pulsed through Gemma's veins as she refused to go over to her to comfort her. To comfort her would give the *Humans* what they wanted—it would make her lay claim to the child and that she was, in fact, her progeny. Gemma wanted nothing to do with it, even if it meant leaving a child to die in the corner …

The thought crashed into her mind several times. That was what she was doing, wasn't it? Leaving a six-year-old to die in the corner.

But she couldn't be part of this.

Suddenly aware of the life inside her, Gemma bit down on her lip. What if this had been her child? What if someone sat by and let it die in the corner of some damp and rotten cage like this. Phoenix's breathing slowed—he was resting again, the pain alleviated somewhat. She smoothed his hair back once more and eased herself from under him, trying not to wake him.

After a moment's hesitation, she slowly crawled along the floor towards the girl, stopping a couple of feet from the child. The girl's clothes were wet with perspiration and she was shivering, yet Gemma knew it wasn't from cold. Even from this distance, she could feel the heat emanating from her.

"What's your name," she said softly, trying not to startle her.

The girl peered at Gemma over her shoulder. Angry, accusing eyes stared at Gemma. How did she make the child understand that she had had no choice—but then what did it matter? The girl's life was changed now, forever. She would be *Other* … if she made it that far.

"I'm sorry," Gemma whispered, not that it made much difference. The girl might one day remember those words, maybe realise why Gemma had had to do it. Maybe she would die like most half-breeds—many didn't make it past the first hour.

The room they were in was completely empty. The computer in the corner was off—even the weird-looking doctor had vanished. Was this why? To see if the girl would make it through the first hour? Were they such cowards that they didn't want to witness the result of what they had caused? A small, red blinking light in the corner caught her eye. She frowned and looked closer—cameras, in every corner of the room. She resisted the urge to give them the finger.

She turned her attention back to the girl. "My name is Gemma," she said, "and this is my friend, Phoenix. He is very hurt."

The girl said nothing, just stared at Gemma. Did she even understand? She was probably a stray. Maybe she hadn't been taught to talk. Gemma bowed her head, the weight of everything so heavy in her mind. Just another minute, she told the girl in her head. Survive the next minute, and then the one after that. She sat back, her legs in front of her and sighed. The girl didn't seem inclined to come to her, but at least Gemma could say she had tried.

"Sage." Gemma's head snapped up. It was said faintly, but she had heard it.

"Sage? That's your name?"

The girl turned and leaned with her back to the wall, her mouth set in a straight line. She had tiny dimples in her little cheeks, making her look angelic. In the next minute, her eyes began to change, shimmering with emerald fire, flames dancing inside her eyes.

It was mesmerising.

She cradled her arm where Gemma had bitten her, the wound not having healed a bit—just like when Phoenix had been bitten. It was still bleeding, blood trickling out from under her small hand.

"Can I look at that?" Gemma asked, pointing to her arm. Sage stared at her for a long moment then gave a small nod of her head. Gemma smiled at her and slowly shuffled along the dusty floor towards her. She gently took hold of Sage's arm and used the cleanest corner of fabric she could find on her top to clean it. The girl was so dirty—she really was a stray, she realised. She had dark lines under her eyes, shadows that she was too young to have, and bones jutted out under the shape of her clothes. Did the *Humans* just go and pick these kids up off the streets?

Sage began to shake again, shivers wracking her small delicate frame. Her head fell back suddenly, smacking painfully against one of the bars. Gemma lunged for her and scooped her up in her arms.

"Sshhhh," she soothed. Sage's eyes rolled back into their sockets, leaving only whites to stare up at Gemma. She held her to her chest, rocking her, finding some strange kind of comfort as she held her there. Was this how Cade had felt with Phoenix? Was this why he would seemingly do anything for him? But then it wasn't Cade who had made Phoenix, was it? Maybe this would be how he'd feel with his own child.

The shuddering began to ease until Sage stilled. Her eyes were closed and Gemma rested her face against the child's chest, stifling the desperate sob in her throat. If she made it out of here, if she saw Cade again, she'd do anything to keep him and their baby. Was this punishment for thinking of killing their child? Was it karma whipping her like a bitch for almost breaking his heart? Lord knows she deserved it. She deserved every ounce of this. The craving inside her, the urge to have Cade with her, her very soul ached for him, but all she felt was the vast emptiness.

He was missing.

Sage suddenly jolted in Gemma's arms, her arms shooting up and her legs going rigid as the mixings of the blood struck like lightning through her small body. The first shift ... Sage's face twisted, seeming deformed as the bones in her nose moved and changed. Her cheekbones rose higher in her face, pushing her eye sockets up.

"Sage?" When the girl opened her eyes, they were slits of green and gold, so very *tiger*. Gemma's own *tiger* rose to the surface, feeling the pull of the young cub next to her. Gemma pushed her back down—not now, not another shift so soon. Cade had done this with Phoenix. He'd helped him through his shifts … but that had created a bond. Gemma didn't want to bond with this child. Despite it all, she closed her eyes and tried to find the small *tiger* in her mind, searching for her in the darkness. But all she found were the remnants of her memories, her longings, her own thoughts, and her *tiger* sitting there waiting for her.

Then it was there, just in the back corner of her mind—a frightened child hiding.

Gemma lay down in the cage next to Sage so that their heads were together and her hand rested against the girl's chest. Her chest rose violently, her back arching, limbs flailing. When Sage relaxed again, Gemma soothed her, hushed her.

And then the shift began for real. First, her face, and then it ran through her body in waves, like someone had wiped down and replaced a small girl with a *tiger*.

"Shit." Gemma had forgotten the girl's clothes. They would rip, but the problem was they would hurt, strangulating her. Gemma bolted upright and frantically pulled at them to get them off the girl, but Sage's arms and legs thrashed in every direction, making it difficult. "Hold on, I've got you."

Sage fought as Gemma struggled to get her clothes off. They stank to high heaven, a mixture of dirt and sweat and urine. It would probably be a blessing if these clothes got torn. They needed incinerating. Gemma threw them to the side and slid back as Sage finished her transformation. A *tiger* cub lay on its side, panting. Frightened eyes stared up at Gemma. Body mass didn't change when they shifted—they didn't become bigger because of what they were. The cub was the same size as Sage had been, somewhere bigger than a tiny cub, but not big enough yet.

She let out a slight whimper. "Shhhh," Gemma soothed her. "I'm here." She ran delicate fingers through the small *tiger's* soft fur.

"She did it," Phoenix said. He hadn't moved, but he had turned his head to the side and was smiling weakly at Gemma and the cub.

"She did," Gemma smiled back.

"That's the worst one," he said. "Feels like your bones are going to snap in half. It's what made my mum …."

"You made it, too," Gemma said, cutting him off. She didn't mean to, but maybe the topic of his mother was best left for another time.

Phoenix nodded. He understood.

The small cub tried to stand, four paws going in all different directions. Gemma helped her, holding her sides and letting her lean into her. "Like you're crawling," she encouraged her.

Sage put one paw in front of the other, but she got them mixed up and Gemma caught her as she toppled to the side. It would take some time, she guessed, for her to be able to walk on four paws. For Gemma, it was just as natural as walking on two.

The door at the top of the stairs opened and Patterson emerged with his smarmy smile. He was like a fucking snake sliding out of a basket. Gemma glared at him.

"She survived," he said gleefully.

"Not thanks to you."

"I had every faith in you," he said. "But now it seems your father is a little annoyed at you staying with me."

Gemma held the cub to her. "Good, then let me go and be sure to please him."

Patterson smiled. The other *Humans* and the witch, Janie the betrayer, were all with him. They'd all been waiting to see if the girl made it. Gemma had news for them—she still had a long way to go.

When Patterson was standing in front of the gate, one of the men came to stand next to him. He had a large pet carrier, the kind one might transport a large dog in. "I want the girl."

Gemma narrowed her eyes at him. "You can't have her."

The other *Human* came to the side of the cage and aimed a gun through the bars at Gemma.

"We're going to open the gate," Patterson said. "And then you're going to let Jason here come in and take the girl. If you don't …" The *Human* next to the cage cocked the barrel on the gun with a click.

"She needs to be with me. She has to learn things. I have to …"

"Oh, don't worry, you will be. But first, we need the girl."

"I can feel her mind," Janie said breathlessly as if she had just felt the most pleasurable thing going. "It's there."

"You can take it?"

Janie nodded gleefully. "Yes." She inhaled deeply.

Shit. She was bonding with the girl. Gemma should have done it. She lifted the cub to her, but Sage fussed in her arms, paws flailing, claws out. She nicked Gemma's arm and she flinched.

"Give us the girl." The man opened the gate, every move slow and cautious, petrified. He put the cage down on the floor and opened the door on it before taking a step in.

"Give me the girl," he repeated. The *Human* with the gun leaned in, gun almost touching Gemma. Her heart pounded. She had let this girl down already, and now she was going to do it again.

"She needs my help."

"The girl ..." Patterson commanded. Gemma held her tighter, her reluctance evident. But could she sacrifice her life, her baby's life, for this girl? Sage would likely die anyway. What did it matter? Gemma reluctantly let go of the girl and slid backwards in the cage. Sage looked up with bright eyes and went to pad over to her, but the man scooped her up, wrapping his arms under her belly before shoving her into the cage and shutting the gate on it. Once he was safely out of the cage, Patterson nodded to the man with the gun. "Shoot her, but watch what you're doing. I want her incapacitated, not dead."

The *Human* grinned as Patterson turned away, raising the gun to Gemma's head. Gemma reacted without thinking, leaping for him.

A loud bang sent her ears ringing and something punched into her side.

She fell back, stunned.

When she tried to get up, she found that her limbs were lead. She touched her fingers to her side, and they came away with blood.

She'd been shot.

The *Human* raised the gun again.

Chapter Thirty

"We take the half-breed, too." Patterson's voice reverberated in Phoenix's ears as he lay there with his eyes open, still struggling to move and breathe. His eyes were on Gemma, who lay crumpled on the ground near him, blinking heavily as the silver the *Human* had shot her with invaded her body. He wanted to reach out to her, but his limbs were leaden, refusing to function.

"She's not going to give you any trouble." The doctor's scent gave away his fear even as he uttered those words. He crouched down and pressed a hand to Gemma's throat. "You should be able to move her now, too." The doctor peered down at her and ran a hand through her hair the way a lover might do.

Fury burned inside Phoenix. Something protective rose up in his own *wolf* at the sight of another man touching her.

She was Cade's.

The *Humans* came prepared—they brought in stretchers like the one they had strapped Phoenix to earlier. As soon as they had loaded him onto his, the doctor began to poke and prod at the wounds on his chest, making Phoenix wince and grit his teeth. "It truly is amazing how fast he heals," he murmured to Patterson, "but you could have killed him."

"But I didn't."

The doctor shook his head in disapproval before spreading his fingers along Phoenix's chest to inspect the burning claw marks Janie had caused. "I'd give him an hour and you won't know anything had happened to him."

"An hour?"

The doctor nodded. "When I said that these half-breeds have such power, I meant it." He leaned over Phoenix and pulled a penlight out of his top pocket. He pushed Phoenix's eyelids open and shone the bright light into his pupils, sending shards of pain shooting through Phoenix's head. "It's amazing." The doctor pulled the chest strap across him gently, preparing to tie him to the stretcher. The *Human* next to him shoved him out of the way, however, and pulled tight.

Phoenix bit down on his tongue and swallowed his scream.

"It'll fuse with his skin," the doctor protested.

The *Human* shrugged, unperturbed. "He'll heal from that, too." They lifted Gemma next, placing her on her own stretcher. Her straps were different—silver—and wrapped around her ankles and wrists, as well as her throat. But she was out cold now, her face grey and mottled from the silver surging through her body. Phoenix's *wolf* desperately needed her touch, craved it, the same way it did sometimes when Cade was around. This need inside was the oddest of things. Sometimes, if Cade was gone for a while because of work, Phoenix could hardly focus on anything, like part of him was missing. His *wolf* would stir in the background, waiting. Stephen and Gemma seemed to calm the *wolf*, the four of them seeming to share some unique link he wouldn't ever be able to explain. When he was with them, he was home.

Phoenix let his eyes close. Wherever they were going, whatever it was that these *Humans* had planned, he couldn't fight them while his chest was torn open. He let his mind wander to the white room, the one where he met Cade. Except Cade wasn't there. The empty room reminded him of a secure, sterile room of a psychiatric ward—nothing to do, nothing to hurt himself with.

Something yellow and orange and small suddenly flashed in the corner.

Phoenix's heart lurched.

Sage.

His eyes shot open, half-afraid the *Humans* knew what he had just seen. The silent fog in his mind fell away and he found himself still on the stretcher in the back of a van, Gemma strapped down beside him. His skin prickled with the familiar itch, but it wasn't that time yet. He had shifted with Stephen, so there was no reason for his change to demand in this way—yet he couldn't deny it. It ran up his back and between his shoulder blades.

He turned his head as much as he could and spotted the witch sitting on a seat at the end of his stretcher. The man with the gun was sitting across from her, and between them was the small black cage that held the girl. She lay perfectly still, back to girl now. Phoenix couldn't see her properly, but there was no orange fur—all he saw was pale flesh.

He closed his eyes again and called out to her in his mind. "Sage. Sage, can you hear me?"

The white room shifted, tilted like some kind of haunted house with the mirrors that make a person seem too tall or too fat. The girl was strong in his mind—it was her who was tilting the room, he realised in shock. He wore jeans and a shirt, but his feet were bare as he padded lightly in her direction. "Sage?" he whispered again, gently so as not to scare her away.

Her *tiger*—so small, so tiny—sat huddled but alert in the corner. Phoenix lowered himself to his knees, his wounds non-existent in his mind.

"I won't hurt you," he promised. "My name is Phoenix. You know me from outside?"

The *tiger's* head lowered to the ground, tucking her tail slinking between her legs, caught between fear and the need to protect herself. She watched him with large, green eyes as he slid closer. She stayed vigilant but didn't move away, though.

His eyes fluttered open, his body alive with the itch. It had spread to his legs and arms and now ran through every part of him.

Realisation struck hard.

This wasn't him, this was her—he had found her hunger. He forced his eyes closed again, keeping them tightly shut. The cub hissed at him and let off a warning growl, but he reached a hand out to her anyway. Dominance, that was what Stephen always said. No matter how scared you are, no matter how much you want to run the fuck away, don't. You stand there and burn in the fire if you have to, but never back down.

His hand inched closer and the cub backed up slowly, its fur sticking up and its hiss growing louder. Phoenix stared her right in the eye. "Come out," he urged.

An almost audible snap echoed in his ears as their minds made some kind of connection. Had the *Humans* heard it? His heart pounded loudly in his chest. Yet, when he opened his eyes, the van was moving and everyone was quiet. The witch stared out of the back window and the man sat staring lasciviously at Gemma, gun resting in his lap. But the girl was awake—Phoenix could feel her presence. Had they just bonded? Was that what it was?

Mason Sabre

His skin burned with the itch, but he forced
his mind to ignore it. The girl slammed into the side
of the cage suddenly, making the witch and the
Human jump.

"What the fuck," the man said, springing up
from his seat.

Phoenix pulled against the binds that held
him down. Stupid *Humans* actually thought this
could hold him down. The fabric around him ripped
as he thrust every last bit of strength he had into his
arms, causing the bind around them to snap. In one
swift move, he reached down to the cage door and
quickly pulled the catch.

The witch and the *Human* stood as best they
could, but Sage lunged from the small cage,
madness in her eyes. The hunger had her, vast and
deep, the way it had got Phoenix the day when he
had killed that boy and protected himself. He called
to her *tiger*, and Sage leapt onto Phoenix, curling up
in a very feminine pose. Though she was still girl,
the hiss that came from her was inhuman.

Phoenix held her in the white room and
fuelled everything that was inside her, pushed her.
"Go, Sage. Go." He gritted his teeth in real life as

well as in his mind, giving her every ounce of strength and hunger that he had inside him. She leapt from his lap, and something banged. Phoenix knew that the *Human* had shot at her.

Idiot.

The silver would do nothing.

Phoenix hastily pulled at the strap across his chest, snapping it. A scream echoed in the back of the van, the sound bone-chilling. Something thick and wet landed beside him—the lifeless body of the *Human*, his face half bitten off.

The witch had gripped Sage around her waist, fighting to keep her away. But her hands were somewhere in transition and she slashed deformed paws at the witch. She slipped from Janie's grasp and Janie twisted her hand in a fluid motion, muttering incantations. But Sage was too fast. She was on Janie in a heartbeat.

Janie held her back, making it hard for her to cast a spell when she was using her hands to defend herself. Sage was just six—her paws didn't go far. Blood dripped from her mouth and down her chest, her hair matted with it. Phoenix leaned over to Gemma and unsnapped the silver binds that held her in place. Where they touched her flesh, her skin was red and sticky—it had been burnt away.

The van swerved suddenly. They were going fast, probably on the motorway. Phoenix crawled over the *Human* to Sage and wrapped his arms around her middle, pulling her to him. The witch scrambled back to the door of the van, her eyes fixed on Sage as she continued to chant.

"Shhhhh," he soothed her, calming her. She hissed in his arms, her cub-like roar echoing in the confines of the van. Janie lifted her hands to cast.

"Don't," Phoenix warned her. "Or I'll drop her right on you. You get them to stop this van."

Janie laughed, an evil sound. "No."

"Get them to stop it."

The witch continued to smile as she chanted. Phoenix stood up, and his head hit the top of the van. He held Sage to him tightly, clinging to her, and then he raised his foot and smacked it into the double doors at the back of the van. They swung open with a thump.

"Get out," he growled.

She lifted her eyebrows mockingly. "Why don't you rather?"

The trolley that had held Phoenix lurched suddenly, smashing into the side of the witch with force. She reached out to latch onto something, but the trolley hit her again and she fell. Phoenix didn't look away as she hit the tarmac and bounced and rolled, leaving a trail of blood on the fast-moving ground of the motorway as it sped away from them.

The trolley followed and Gemma lurched. She fell forward, weak, and Phoenix rushed to her, Sage still in his arms, and caught her before she went out, too. He took them all to the floor of the van and held them both tightly in his arms.

"Thank you," she whispered against him, clutching at him.

The van swerved to the side, pulling onto the hard shoulder, and Phoenix wasted no time dragging Gemma out before the front doors opened and the van pulled to a total stop. The Doctor, the other *Human* and Patterson all came running around the back.

Gemma picked the gun up and aimed it straight at an unpleasantly surprised Patterson, who quickly jumped behind the doctor.

"Silver might not kill you," she said hoarsely, "but it's still a bullet."

Chapter Thirty-One

The room was dark, save for the light that spilt out from the small lamp in the corner on the dresser. Gemma tried to roll onto her back but winced as pain lanced through her entire body. The dull ache in her stomach filled her with fear and she froze.

Her baby.

Her hand shot to her flat abdomen, trepidation pervading her every cell. A lump rose in her throat, and she whispered a silent prayer. It *had* to be okay ... She didn't even want to think about it not being.

The life was still in there—she could sense it. Warm and comforting, it filled her with peace.

Would it be a boy or a girl? *Tiger* or *wolf*? Would it look like her or Cade? Whose eyes would it have? Whose hair? The questions raced through her mind, leaving her a little giddy and breathless.

So many things.

Did all mothers-to-be have thoughts like this? Going over and over all the could-bes and would-bes, and everything in between that might go wrong. Did they spend their time dreaming of the life that slowly grew inside?

When she was awake, it was all she could think about. Even if her mind drifted to something else, it would snap right back again to all the hopes and the promises. The hard part was in sleep, where her fears grew and monstrous images crawled into her dreams—things that she didn't want to see. Could just imagining them make them happen? What kind of mother was she that she could imagine such horrible things happening to her unborn child? In her dreams, she saw deformities, a sick baby who died in her arms. She saw a lifeless child, heard her own screams, but no one ever stopped to help her. Her mind constantly flitted between this place of limbo and these horrific dreams.

She let out an audible breath and something moved. She tensed—someone else was in the room with her. A familiar musky scent filled her senses and her heart skipped a beat.

Cade.

He was there.

Worried she might be dreaming, she whispered tentatively, "Cade?"

The bed shifted and dipped. "I'm right here." Her breath hitched, his deep, quiet voice a balm to her frayed nerves. She reached for him, suddenly desperate for his touch, her calmness nothing but a fleeting memory as a craving roused deep inside. "I'm right here," he reassured her gently, catching her hand in his and lacing his fingers through hers. He brought his face close to hers, so close that she could feel his breath against her face—a mixture of coffee and whiskey. The scent ignited her need even more, a part of her calling to him, starving. Her fingers tightened around his and a small sob tore from her—she thought she'd never see him again, never touch him or smell him. She tugged at his hand, trying to pull him down and he immediately leaned in close, bracing a hand above her head.

"I'm here, Gem." She lifted her arm so that she could wrap it around the back of his neck, but pain speared through her, red and hot. It burnt with a fury and she whimpered, the torn muscles from where she had been shot still not fully healed. "Don't try to move." But she couldn't help it. He was so close, but she wanted closer. She pulled herself up, an overwhelming need to feel him against her. She wanted to be in his arms. She wanted every part of him. Her *tiger* had awoken and she was demanding and determined. She didn't care about the pain—all she cared about was Cade. She called to his *wolf*, called to her mate.

Her mate …

No one else's. Not the Castle woman's. Not anyone's. He was hers. Gemma turned her head and their mouths met in a tender kiss. Warm lips pressed against hers, kissing her so deeply that her mind threatened to fall away and lose itself.

"Cade," she breathed.

He leaned into her, the stubble along his jaw grazing her cheek as he buried his face in her shoulder. His breath was warm against her bare skin and he clung to her with a need that matched her own.

"I didn't think I would ever see you again," she sobbed after a long moment. "I thought they would kill us. I …"

"It's okay," he soothed her, a muscle working in his jaw. "It's all over … you're here with me now. I'm never letting you go." His voice was laced with a vehemence that promised retribution.

"They shot me … with silver." She pulled back so that she could look at him without letting him go. "The baby …"

Cade reached up and brushed a stray hair back from her face, tucking it behind her ear. "The baby is okay." His hand trailed around and gently cupped her face.

She wanted to believe that. She really did. She turned her face into his palm and breathed him in deep.

"Do you promise?" she asked, her eyes searching his desperately, looking for any hint of a lie, and hoping to find none.

His hand slide down her body, his touch electrifying as it travelled down her bare skin. All she wore was her underwear and every nerve in her body came to life from his touch alone. He stopped when he reached her abdomen, warmth seeping into her skin as his large hand spread over the smooth expanse if skin. God, how she had missed his touch.

"I promise," he said. "You've been asleep a few days, you know? The doctor says that the baby is absolutely fine."

"How can he be sure?"

"Because he is a doctor," he said, a small smile dancing at the corners of his mouth. When that answer didn't seem to satisfy her, he added, "They did tests. Something about the hormones and the bloods. I promise the baby is okay."

She nodded weakly. Cade wouldn't lie to her. This was his child, too. "How is Phoenix?" The sudden memory of everything that had happened suddenly crashed into her mind.

"He's fine," Cade assured her. "He's healed. He healed pretty fast."

"He saved my life," she whispered. "And the girl's."

"Sage."

Gemma nodded and bit down on her lip. She'd taken that little girl's life away, perhaps taken her away from her family, her race. She would be wanted by no one now, and it was all her fault. "I had to …"

Cade touched a finger to Gemma's lips. "Phoenix told us. It's okay."

"I took her life away. Is she okay? Did she … make it?"

"She's with your mum. It's early days still. But she's giving her some of that gunk she gives to Phoenix."

"But long term?" Gemma wasn't so sure she wanted to know. It had been a fight to keep Phoenix, one that was still very much ongoing. How would Trevor take to a second half-breed in his Society? But he was a fool. She had seen the things that Phoenix was capable of. He had strength that they only dreamt about.

"I don't know," Cade said. "No one has talked about it yet." Maybe that wasn't so bad, Gemma thought to herself. At least it wasn't that she was being thrown out.

"What happened to Patterson? It's all such a blur." Every time she tried to bring the *Humans* to mind, all she saw was the witch and the way she had rolled onto the tarmac, streaking it with blood. That part had imprinted itself in her mind and refused to let her see anything else.

"He's at his house." Underlying anger edged his words.

"What?" She shot up, then groaned at the jolt of pain.

Cade pushed her back down gently. "Shh, take it easy."

"How? After what he did, how can he be at home?"

Cade clenched his jaw. "DSA verses the *Humans*," he said pejoratively. "Stephen met a witch at Patterson's house—Anika. Bastard had her name on everything."

"Everything? But it wasn't her ..."

Cade nodded grimly. "Fucking asshole pinned the shit on her and the other witch. Claimed they were in cahoots."

When Cade frowned and looked away, she touched his arm gently. "What is it?"

"Anika ..." he said quietly. "She's like Sage. They took her when she was little and raped her mind. They took her, bred her and set her the hell up all so they could gain control. That's all this shit is."

Of course it was. That was the only reason *Humans* hated *Others*, because quite frankly, they couldn't control them—not if it ever came down to it. Not if *Others* ever got truly pissed and went against them. The *Humans* would be wiped out.

"Phoenix told you why they wanted him?"

"A controllable army. The poor witch stands no chance against the *Humans*."

"Where is she?"

"House arrest. Apparently, she lives with some *Human* ... a Marcus." He lowered his voice. "If she is found guilty, they'll execute her."

Gemma stared at him for a long minute, a million thoughts zooming through her mind. "We've got to leave this place, haven't we?"

He nodded solemnly. "Yeah, we do." He reached down to pick up a white envelope from the floor and place it on Gemma's lap—it bulged from whatever was in there.

A light tapping on the door made Cade squeeze her hand before leaning down to place a kiss on her forehead. "Your father has been worried, like everyone else. He has been waiting to see you." Her heart pounded in her ears at the sudden empty space Cade left as he stood up to open the door. She stuffed the envelope under the sheet as Malcolm walked in.

"I heard you were awake," he said. Heard her awake? How much had he heard? He turned to Cade. "Can we have a few moments? I think Stephen needs a hand with something out back."

Cade glanced back at Gemma, a fiercely protective expression on his face. "I'll just be outside."

When Cade was gone and her father was sure that he was far enough away, he sat down on the end of Gemma's bed. It had been years since he had done that. She hardly remembered when it was or if it had even happened at all. The father she had had long ago was not the father she had now. He had hardened with the years as their leader, becoming more alpha with every moment that passed, but right in that moment, as he sat at the end of her bed, he looked like the man she remembered.

"I know about the baby."

Gemma's eyes widened. "I …"

He raised his hand to silence her. "Your mum knows, too. No one else."

She tensed herself, ready for what was coming next. If he mentioned execution order and Cade, she was out of there. Alpha or father, it wouldn't matter.

"I have to make hard decisions sometimes," he sighed, turning his head to look at her. "Some of them people don't like. Sometimes people don't understand them, but I do them always with the good of my people in mind. Not just the *tigers*, but for all *Others*—for all of Society."

Gemma nodded but said nothing, waiting with dread for what was next.

"Mixing breeds is against the rules that we have set down, and as alpha and Council and

Society leader, it is my job to enforce those rules, no matter who is on the receiving end. It is not my place to discriminate."

Gemma swallowed, her fingers gripping the bedsheets.

Malcom leaned forward and clasped his hands together. Normally, he was so hard to read, but tonight, his face was almost animated with emotion. "However," he said, "I am also a father." His eyes met hers. "I swore that I would protect my children always. Sometimes my roles clash, and it leaves me not knowing what to do."

"What will you decide?" she asked cautiously.

Gemma wasn't sure what she had expected, but Malcom twisting around from where he sat, and wrapping his arms around her to pull her close, was the last thing that she imagined. For a long moment, he just held her.

When he finally let her go, he stood up and straightened his suit—and with it, his expression. "Your mother wants to see you, as well."

Gemma nodded, but said nothing as Malcolm left the room. The door closed behind him with a soft click and Gemma thumbed the envelope Cade had left her. She bit down on her lip as she turned it over and unstuck the seal.

Inside were papers—three of them.

She opened them up and gasped.

Their tickets to Exile.

The End

Mason Sabre

Street Team.

Alicia Reitz Huckleby
Amy Cortez Rangel
Andrea Whittle
Angela Peters
Becky Rios
Carolann Evans
Carolyn Mueller
Cathy Dionne
Colette Trainor
Cyn Thia
Danielle Wittenberg Fulton
Diana Murphey
Jan Kinder
Jan Wade
Jenny McKinney Shepherd
Karine Russell
Kirha Rodriguez formerly-McMillan
Kirsty Adams
Krystal Waters
Lauren Stryker
Lilli Collier
Lori Van Buren
Mary Lena Strataface
Melissa Jackson Morris
Misty Chapman
Nichole Watson
Nina Stevenson
Roxie Phelps
Stella Martin
Terrie Meerschaert
Tina Eastridge Henry
Vanessa Renee Place
Wendy Tucker Wignall
Yvette Grimes

Thank you so much for reading. Please feel free to drop me an email or visit me on Facebook. While every attempt was made to ensure that this book was free from error, mistakes happen. If you happen to have spotted anything, please drop me a message and let me know so that I can correct it.

Mason

masonsabre2@gmail.com

https://www.facebook.com/msabre3

Printed in Great Britain
by Amazon

80423616R00253